"A tale of tension and psychological suspense from one of our major authors."
—*The Mystery Review*

"Pronzini's gripping tale is liable to linger for a long time in the minds of dedicated fans of thrillers."
—*State Journal* (Lansing, Michigan)

"From its suspenseful beginning to its jaw-dropping conclusion, this taut thriller is a fascinating read."
—*Library Journal*

"*Nothing But the Night* may be the psychological thriller of the year. . . . Pronzini brilliantly reveals the inner souls of his two male protagonists as their pasts converge in the night."
—*The Midwest Book Review*

"Bill Pronzini is a consummate pro who gives life to both hunter and prey."
—*The Washington Times*

"The characters are superb, complex yet appealing. Pronzini pulls readers' strings like the expert he is."
—*Publishers Weekly*

NOTHING BUT THE NIGHT

NOTHING BUT THE NIGHT

Bill Pronzini

WALKER & COMPANY

New York

First published in the United States of America in 1999 by
Walker Publishing Company, Inc.;
first paperback edition published in 2000

Published simultaneously in Canada by Fitzhenry and Whiteside,
Markham, Ontario L3R 4T8

Library of Congress Cataloging-in-Publication Data
Pronzini, Bill.
Nothing but the night/Bill Pronzini.
p. cm.
ISBN 0-8027-3330-1 (hc)
I. Title.
PS3566.R67N68   1999
813′ .54—dc21   98-43720
CIP
ISBN 0-8027-7582-9 (paperback)

Series design by Mauna Eichner

Printed in Canada
2 4 6 8 10 9 7 5 3 1

For Suzette Lalime and

Lawrence Davidson

A first anniversary present

And with thanks to Michael Seidman for his usual astute editorial advice; to Jackie Lee and Melissa Ward for supplying research material; and to Marcia for helping to make Cam Gallagher a much better person.

Oh never fear, man, nought's to dread

Look not left nor right:

In all the endless road you tread

There's nothing but the night.

—A. E. Housman

PART 1

Discovery

Warm Indian-summer night.

Kind of night he'd always liked, best kind for long drives. Window rolled down. Breeze cool against the side of his face. Engine humming, tires whispering a sort of bluesy accompaniment to the golden oldies playing on the radio. Highway and night both clear, sharp in every detail, lights from passing cars and trucks like distant spokes of fire in the dark. Good feeling strong in him. Hope, determination. Wasn't just driving from somewhere to nowhere, picking through straws in the world's biggest haystack; he felt close to the needle, getting closer all the time. Keep hunting, keep the faith. Keep reminding himself everything ended sooner or later and what he was really doing was going home one mile at a time, one day at a time, the long way around.

Home. Annalisa.

"Earth Angel" on the radio now. Annalisa.

Tires whispering fast and sweet, like her breath in his ear. Annalisa . . . Annalisa . . . Annalisa . . .

He saw her face like he sometimes did, right there on the windshield glass. Skin smooth and white as the inside of a shell, eyes a cool green like deep water, hair soft and yellow like corn silk. A surge of feeling went through him, so sudden, so hot, it was like fire. He gripped the wheel tight, clenched his teeth and jaw, until it eased and he felt cool again.

God, he missed her! Times like this, love and hurt and need flaring up all at once, he wanted to take the quickest route back to Denver. Just see her again for a few minutes, touch her face and hair, hold her hand. Look into her eyes and tell her everything would be all right, he'd make it all right. More than once he'd started for home, only to shift routes again before he'd done more than a couple of hours' driving. Other times he'd stopped at pay phones, called Mom and Pop Foster to find out how she was. Never called the hospital, they'd just say she was too sick to take calls, have visitors. Better to just write her regular like he did, call Mom and Pop now and then. Better to keep moving, keep hunting.

Hard, though. Real hard sometimes. Writing his letters, three or four a month, and knowing it might be a long time before she'd be able to read them. But he had to do it. When she got better, she'd want to know all the places he'd been, the kinds of jobs he'd worked, that he'd never given up even for a minute. So he kept writing and sending the letters to Mom and Pop for safekeeping. Each envelope marked Personal and Private, even though they'd promised they wouldn't open them and he knew they'd keep their promise. Good people, the Fosters. How could Annalisa's folks be anything else?

Truck stop coming up. He saw the neon sign ahead, scatter of big rigs in the floodlit lot. Getting low on gas, better fill the tank. Gnaw of hunger in his belly, too. He hadn't eaten anything but a bag of M&Ms, his last bag, since the early dinner in Eureka.

He took the next freeway exit, came back on the frontage road. Gas first—and when he'd paid for it, he had a little over two hundred left in his wallet. About time to stop somewhere again and work for a while. Start looking tomorrow, maybe, depending on where tonight led him. By the weekend, latest.

Café was like a thousand others he'd eaten and worked in: crowded, noisy, too hot in spite of the ceiling fans, heavy with the smells of fried food and sweaty bodies. Truckers, mostly, at the counter and in the booths. Same breed as him. Long haul, short haul, big rigs and small— he'd driven them all, back in Denver and on the road since he'd left. Night riders, too, a lot of them, used to driving the dark highways, comfortable with it, even craving it. He'd get back into steady trucking when he finally went home. His old job at Miller Freight Lines. Sam Miller understood why he'd quit, would make a place for him when he came back.

He found an empty stool at the counter. Harried waitress got around to him, he ordered coffee and the breakfast special—eggs, sausage, hotcakes—and then showed her the sketch. She glanced at it, at him again. Shook her head and moved off.

Guy sitting on his left was big and bearded, tattoos on his arms and a Giants cap pushed back off his forehead. Nick caught the guy's eye, said, "How you doing?" and made a little road talk before he showed him the sketch. "Ever see this man?" he asked. "Anywhere, anytime?"

Giants fan squinted; plucked the square of laminated plastic from Nick's fingers, and squinted some more. "Not too clear."

"Clear enough. Good likeness."

"You draw it?"

"No. Artist." Police artist, but he never said that.

"Looks pretty old."

"Just worn."

"That why you had it sealed in plastic?"

"That's why. Familiar to you?"

"Can't say he is. Friend of yours?"

"No."

"Relative?"

"No. Guy I'm trying to find."

"How come? He owe you money?"

Nick shook his head, tucked the sketch into his shirt pocket.

"So how come you're looking for him?" Giants fan asked.

Answer was on his tongue, as hot and bitter as the coffee the waitress had set in front of him. He had to tighten his lips, turn his head away to keep the words from slipping out. He'd never said them to anyone, not even Annalisa. Only one he'd ever say them to was the son of a bitch in the sketch.

arm Indian-summer night.

And here sits Cameron Gallagher, he thought, master of the manor, lord of all he surveys. Object of envy on this fine end-of-October night: successful businessman, happily married to the same woman for thirteen years, two smart and pretty daughters, few debts, enough money to afford playthings like the brand-new custom Skagit cruiser, Paloma Wine Systems such a thriving concern he'd had to hire three new employees this year, for a total now of twenty-two. Sitting here in the tree-shaded privacy of his half-acre backyard behind his $400,000 luxury home, gin and tonic in hand (Bombay gin, nothing but the best), wife by his side, kids happily tossing a glow-in-the-dark Frisbee on the lawn. Oh yes, old Cam Gallagher had it all. Realized the American dream at the tender age of thirty-five.

That was the general consensus, no doubt. The ones who knew differently were the ones who mattered: Hallie, at least some of the time. And Caitlin—or maybe she bought the trappings and the image, too. And himself. The truth was why he had three gin and tonic tonics inside him, the fourth in his hand, and a fifth on his mind. Why he suffered recurring nightmares, bouts of depression, and headaches occasionally so severe they brought on short-term blackouts. Why he'd spent a quarter of a century in the offices of child psychologists, psychoanalysts, and specialists in neurasthenic and manic-depressive disorders. Why he sometimes felt—as he felt tonight—that if he wasn't very, very careful, someday he would come apart at the seams.

The truth was Rose Adams Gallagher. Paul Gallagher, too, but the old man had been only a supporting player, not the lead actor in this long-running drama, even though he'd been the one who had turned it from cheap soap opera into high tragedy. Good old Ma. The prettiest girl in Los Alegres—somebody'd written that next to her photo in her high school yearbook. Not so pretty, though, when he'd been growing up. Not so full of sugar and spice and everything nice. And not pretty at all that last terrible night at the river house—

Don't go there, Gallagher. Better stay the hell away from there if you want to sleep tonight.

He wondered if he were feeling sorry for himself. Self-pity wasn't one of his flaws, usually; he disliked Cam Gallagher far more than he pitied him. No, it was his family he felt sorry for. Hallie most of all. The girls were young, resilient, and they had been protected from birth; never been told about his past, and wouldn't be until they were adults. The one vow he'd made and been able, for the most part, to keep was that his children would not grow up in the kind of household he and Caitlin had been subjected to in their early years. Still, kids were sensitive, and they couldn't help but intuit his problems, feel some of their effects. They deserved a better father than he could ever be.

Hallie deserved a far better husband. How she'd managed to stand in the firing line of his hang-ups and neuroses over the past thirteen years and remain supportive, upbeat, hopeful, was beyond him. Not a saint but a rock. Babied him when he needed it, kicked his sorry butt when he needed it, played all the right roles at the right time in the right way, or at least tried to—friend, lover, confidante. She was the glue holding him together. As long as he had Hallie and his kids, he felt he might be able to hang in for the long haul. Win his private Armageddon, in Dr. Beloit's cute little phrase.

But it had taken its toll on her. She wasn't as high-spirited or easygoing as she'd once been, or as happy as she should be. There was premature gray in her ash-blond hair that she covered with a rinse, premature age lines in her fine-boned face. And she had developed an alcohol dependency of her own that only a strong effort of will (he knew this without them ever having discussed it) prevented from getting out of hand.

He hated what he'd done to her. Had fought to keep it from happening, to control the dark side of himself, and failed as often as he succeeded. His worst brooding fear was that someday he'd drive her past the point of no return; that she'd leave him, take Leah and Shannon with her, and then he'd have nothing, then his demons really would destroy him.

He glanced at her beside him. At ease tonight, as she should always be, smiling her quirky little smile as she watched the girls at their game. Still as slim and sexy as the day they'd met at the Paloma Valley Wine Festival. Still the most attractive woman he'd ever set eyes on. The ache that built inside him as he looked at her was love and desire and compassion and guilt and sadness and something close to prayer, even though he was not a particularly religious man.

Hallie felt his gaze, turned her head to give him a quizzical look. "What?"

"Nothing. Just looking at you."

"Wondering what you see in me?"

"On the contrary. Thinking how much I love you."

"Well, that's nice." Then she said, "Ah."

"What does 'ah' mean?"

"I can read your mind." Her smile had become teasing, but her gaze was tender. She liked hearing him say he loved her; it was reassuring to her, too. "Must be the gin."

"I haven't had that much. Besides, you're the one who gets horny on gin."

"Shh, not so loud. Me and Dorothy Parker."

"Who?"

"You remember. 'I cannot drink martinis / Only one or two at the most. / After three I'm under the table / After four I'm under mine host.'"

He laughed. But he was serious when he said, "I do love you, Hallie. You know that."

"Of course I know it." She ran the tips of her fingers across the tendons in his wrist.

Leah let out a squeal from the lawn, the indignant kind that meant sibling conflict. "Mom! Shannon's trying to hurt me!"

"Am not." From the oldest. Twelve going on twenty.

"Are too. You threw it too hard. Look at my knee, it's bleeding."

"It's not bleeding, you big baby."

"It is. Dork! You made it bleed."

"I'd better referee this," Hallie said. "It's past their bedtime anyway."

He nodded and watched her move away across the flagstones. Watched the tight roll and sway of her hips, then finished the last third of his drink at a swallow. He lifted himself out of the patio chair, went into the house to make the fifth gin and tonic even though he didn't really want it.

Peace had been restored when he came back outside; now the girls were united in their usual nightly complaint against bed. Hallie said, "No more arguments," and shooed them inside. "I'm coming in in fifteen minutes. You'd better be in bed with the lights off, both of you."

That was all it took. She seldom had any trouble reining them in, getting them to obey her. The opposite was true when he was the parent in charge. Always an ongoing hassle; they ran roughshod over him every time. Too soft, too permissive, too eager to be a good dad. Once it had been a small bone of contention between Hallie and him, though she knew as well as he did where it came from. Now she didn't argue about it, just used her own firm hand when the situation called for it.

She glanced at his full glass as she sat down beside him. Didn't say anything, but he could tell from her expression that she wished he wouldn't drink anymore tonight. Irritation moved through him; he had to struggle to keep his mouth shut, not to become confrontational for no reason. Verbal abuse was as wounding as physical abuse—he knew that well enough. He'd never lifted a hand against Hallie, but too often he'd lifted his goddamn tongue.

God, he thought, I don't want to hurt her anymore. Then why can't I stop doing it? Why do I keep finding new ways, new excuses?

Hallie said, "What're you thinking?"

"Thinking? Why?"

"Big frown there. Something bothering you?"

"No."

"Sure? You've been on the quiet side tonight."

"Minor problem at PWS that keeps nagging at me."

"Do you want to talk about it?"

"Not tonight. It's not important."

Liar. The problem wasn't minor, and if he let it, it could become damned important. But Hallie couldn't help him with this one. She was the last person he could talk to about this one.

He sipped his drink. The gin was suddenly sour in his mouth. He set the glass down, pushed it away.

"Why don't we go to bed?" he said.

"It's only nine o'clock."

"Bed," he said, and waggled his eyebrows at her.

"Aha, I knew it. *Bed*." She rumpled her thick hair with both hands, lifting the strands slowly and letting them fall—a gesture he'd always found sensual, that she knew he found sensual. "Well, gee, I don't know—"

"Not enough gin, Dorothy?"

"More than enough, mine host. Okay, let's go and tuck the girls in, and then you can have your way with me."

He let her go first, again watching the play of her hips beneath the white shorts. He wanted her as much as ever; the stirring in his loins proved it. Wanted her, loved her, needed her. Nothing had changed. Thirteen faithful years, a couple of close calls but the specter of Rose had been better than a dozen cold showers, and now all of a sudden, this very minute—

Images of Jenna Bailey in his mind.

Lust for Jenna Bailey in his heart.

And a part of him—the dark, perverse part—yearning to be on his way to make love to Jenna Bailey instead of his wife.

B ack in the car and driving again.

Only place where he felt safe and secure, completely in control. Been that way for him since Pa had first let him drive the old Ford pickup off the farm when he was, what, fourteen? Twenty years of wheels good and bad since then. 'Fifty-six Chevy Impala with a dumped front end and mag rims and a shimmy so bad above sixty he'd never dared open her up. 'Eighty-two Ford Taurus, real piece of crap, but that'd been his last year in the army and he'd been short on money. 'Sixty-five Pontiac GTO, candy-apple red, four-banger engine, sweet-and-mean driving machine. Half a dozen more recent models, all Detroit products except the '94 Mazda wrapped around him now like a metal-and-leather co-coon. He didn't like the Mazda much, but when the Plymouth died on him a while back—four months? six?—the Mazda was all he'd been able to afford. Not a bad choice, really. Good gas mileage, upward of thirty mpg on the highway, and he'd never had any trouble with it, knock wood.

He'd been a night rider from the first, too. That was what they called people like him, people who functioned better in darkness than daylight, in and out of their cars. People who preferred their own company, the tight confines of their cars or trucks, to open rooms, open spaces. He'd read an article about it once. Guy he knew called him a night rider, he'd never heard the term, so he'd gone to the library and looked it up. Some psychologist quoted in the article said night riders used their vehicles the way others used books or movies or hobbies, as ways of escape from the tensions and pressures of everyday living. Said that by insulating themselves in their cars they created an illusion of invulnerability that for short periods allowed them to hold their personal problems at bay, exercise the same control over their lives and destinies as they had over their modes of transportation. Psychologist's exact words. Nick remembered them even after all these years.

Made sense to him, gist of it anyhow. Night riding made him feel he was capable of doing things that seemed out of reach in the daylight. And it'd saved him from cracking up after what happened to Annalisa, kept him going since.

One thing that hadn't been in the article was the sheer pleasure you got from night riding. Even made him hot sometimes, on warm, sweet-smelling nights, like that first time he'd made love with Annalisa. Major highways, two-laners, backcountry roads, unpaved mountain tracks—didn't matter which kind, only that he was part of a missile like a huge lighted cock splitting the night, holding it apart as if it were two black thighs, penetrating it, taking it for his own.

First date he'd had with Annalisa, he'd tried to explain some of that to her. Not the cock part, the way night riding made him feel. Two months free of Fort Huachuca's motor pool, back in Denver with a brand-new job at Miller Freight Lines, met her when he stopped in at Pop Foster's grocery store and finally talked her into going out with him, two of them in his car heading up to Boulder to this club he knew about—and she put her head back and laughed when he told her about night riding. Hadn't bothered him. God, no. Hearing her laugh like that, with her head back and her throat so long and white, that was when he knew for sure he was in love with her. That very second.

So he'd said all right, I'll prove it to you. And he had. Started that night, and before long she wasn't only convinced, she was a night rider herself. Some of the rides they'd taken together . . . man! Before and after they were married. Just one of the things he loved about her. Not only her becoming a night rider like him, her being willing to try new things, accept him for what he was and join right in, no complaints or hassles or attempts to change him.

Annalisa, Annalisa . . . tires murmuring her name again in the light-spattered dark. Tears in his eyes all of a sudden. All the memories, and wanting to be with her so much he could hardly stand the loneliness.

Someday it'll be the way it used to be, he thought, and said the one word, "Someday," out loud. New nights, thousands of new nights, Nick and Annalisa rushing through the darkness together, safe and secure in the one place where nobody nobody nobody could ever hurt them again.

I n the darkness of their bedroom, Hallie's arms and legs wrapped tightly around him, her breath hot and moist in his ear, she whispered, "Cam, oh . . . jockey . . . jockey . . ."

He felt the muscles in his back stiffen. It was the only thing, with slight variations, that she ever said to him while they were making love. She uttered sounds, little moans and purrs, and he could always tell when she had an orgasm by the long, low, sighing hum that came from her throat. But she was not a bed talker. No urgings, no endearments, no love or sex words of any kind. She never even said his name except as part of that damn jockey reference.

> Man was a jockey,
> He taught me how to ride,
> Said good down the middle,
> Better easin' round the side.

An old blues refrain, she'd told him once, long ago. A product of her college days at Long Beach State, like the Dorothy Parker verse she'd quoted earlier, except that this one hadn't been learned in either a classroom or polite company. It sounded African American to him, its roots in Storyville or Chicago's South Side jazz clubs, but she'd said no, she'd never had a black lover. It didn't matter to him, one way or the other, any more than it mattered that she hadn't been a virgin the first time they slept together. How many women of twenty-one were inexperienced in the mid-eighties, after all? The first time she sang the little blues refrain to him, at some now-forgotten point between their first sexual encounter and their marriage a few months later, he'd found it funny. So she'd sung it again, off and on when they were in bed, and somehow, somewhere during the past thirteen years, it had evolved into a shorthand signal whenever he was too excited or too distracted or too tired to pay proper attention to her needs and his pacing. Slow down, Cam, don't be in such a hurry. Make it last, make it good for both of us. But she'd never say those words, just come right out and tell him to slow down, make it last. She'd never say, Don't go so fast, honey. She'd never say, Quit humping like Brer Rabbit. All she'd ever say was—

"Jockey . . . jockey, Cam . . ."

Tonight the words were like a worm wriggling through his pleasure, spoiling it by degrees. They made him feel as though he wasn't a husband or a lover but somebody who was providing an impersonal service, like a TV repairman or a carpet cleaner or a plumber hired to flush out the pipes. The Cameron Gallagher Stud Service. Good enough down the middle, but the poor dolt still had to be coaxed into easin' round the side.

Well, the hell with that tonight. He increased rather than slowed his rhythm, climaxed almost immediately, and heard, instead of the long, low, sighing hum, a disappointed little whimper of protest. Bad Cam. Bad jockey that couldn't learn how to ride.

Usually he remained joined with her for a while afterward, to rest and cuddle, but not this time; he lifted away from her, flopped over on his back. She didn't try to hold him. Didn't have anything to say, either. Waiting for him to apologize for his bad ride. How many jockeys at Bay Meadows or Tanforan issued apologies? How many plumbers said they were sorry for one of their bad screws?

He lay staring into the darkness. And as his breathing gentled, so did his thoughts—and he began to feel ashamed of himself. Selfish and petty. It wasn't Hallie's fault. Stupid, cruel to blame her. The jockey thing, all the rest of what he'd been thinking, just an excuse to go ahead and do what the nasty, perverse part of him wanted to do—have an affair with Jenna Bailey.

He moved close to her again, touched her hand, and whispered, "I'm sorry, baby. I don't know what's the matter with me tonight."

"It's all right," she said, but her tone said she was hurt. She had a right to be hurt. Another wound, another empty apology. "Let's not talk, okay? Let's just go to sleep."

She put on her nightgown, rolled away to the far side of the bed. And he lay there, wide awake, trying to shut down the furious swirl of his thoughts. It was as if there was a cancer growing inside him, a genetic cancer of the soul. Rose's Blight. Old Ma Melanoma. He'd been trying to deny it for twenty-five years, one of his last pathetic conceits, and all the while it had been metastasizing until now he could see it for exactly what it was. You can't deny what you can look straight in its pestilent eye.

Cameron Gallagher was his mother's son. Or would be if he went to bed with Jenna Bailey.

Terminally.

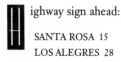ighway sign ahead:

SANTA ROSA 15
LOS ALEGRES 28

Names were vaguely familiar. Been here before? Probably. Wasn't much of California he hadn't covered, except for the northern and eastern mountain areas where not too many people lived. He'd get to them, too, sooner or later.

Late now. Or early. Four A.M, give or take a few minutes. He knew that because of the way the darkness looked. Gotten so he could judge the subtle differences in the night sky—positions of moon and stars on clear nights, but he could read cloudy nights just as well. Never been off by more than half an hour. Another good thing about being a night rider.

Santa Rosa, Los Alegres—towns somewhere north of San Francisco. Not too far, fifty or sixty miles. Keep on going into the city, it'd be first light by the time he found a place to sleep, Golden Gate Park or out along the beach. He remembered Frisco, all right. Not a good place for daylight sleeping in your car. Cops were liable to hassle you. Or kids, homeless people, junkies, street punks. Besides, he'd given the city a pretty thorough canvass the last time. Job he'd had just before he went there, driving for a supply outfit near Sacramento, paid well, and he'd had enough cash to rent a room for a week in a South of Market fleabag. Hadn't bought him a thing. Half the people he showed the sketch to wouldn't even look at it. Big cities were all like that, even Denver. Seemed like nobody wanted to help, nobody cared—they all had too many troubles of their own.

He couldn't remember anything about Santa Rosa or Los Alegres, so maybe he'd missed them. So many towns . . . you just couldn't cover them all or keep track of them all. Easier in the beginning, when it'd just been the Denver area and then the rest of Colorado. But the farther he traveled, the more he went back to recanvass territory he'd gone over before, the harder it got. Hard to remember, even, all the towns he'd covered the last time through Colorado. Sometimes it seemed he'd been in most of the cities and towns and wide spots west of the Rockies, but he knew that couldn't be right. Half, maybe, and maybe a lot less than half. So many had the same name or ones that sounded the same—how could anybody keep them all straight in his head?

Getting tired. Better put an end to this ride pretty soon. Motels along the highway here—Motel 8 up there on the right—but he couldn't afford to waste any of the cash he had left on a motel. Homeless shelter or rescue mission or a few hours in the car, and he'd pretty much given up on shelters and missions for overnight stays. Took time to find one, usually the beds were all full, and anyway he didn't like the atmosphere. Despair and hopelessness hung and crawled in every one. He wasn't homeless, that was the thing. Not the way the others in those places were. Didn't have a steady job or the apartment in Aurora anymore, but he did have Mom and Pop Foster's house to stay in when he went home. And Annalisa to go home to. Options and a future—hardly anybody in the shelters and missions had either one.

Exit coming up. Find a park or country road or shopping center with a spread-out parking lot, some quiet place where he could hole up for a few hours without being hassled. Then he'd see what tomorrow, a new day, had in store for him.

He flipped on his turn signal, swung into the far lane and then the exit lane. Not thinking anymore by then. Just driving and looking for a place to sleep.

am's first incoming call at the office Thursday morning was from Jenna.

Strictly business, he warned himself when he heard her voice. Keep it that way even if she doesn't. He said, "Good morning, Jenna. How're things at Fenwood Creek?"

"Just fine. You sound a little flat this morning, Cam. Anything wrong?"

"Not a thing," he lied. "I'm still trying to jump-start the day."

"You mean the drive over from Los Alegres doesn't do it for you?"

"Most days. What can I do for you?"

"Any number of things," she said. The dual meaning was plain enough and no doubt intentional; she had never made any secret of her attraction to him or her availability. No pretense, no b.s.—that was Jenna. He let the comment pass, waiting, and at length she said, "Right now I'll settle for an update on our BATF federal label approvals."

"We should have them by now. I'll check with Maureen."

"I can hold, or do you want to call back?"

"Better let me call you back."

"I'll be here. Don't take too long."

He cradled the receiver, went out and down the hall to Maureen Stannard's office. Maureen, fifty, quiet and efficient, was both a friend and his good right hand. She'd been the first person he hired when he started Paloma Wine Systems eight years ago. Now she supervised most of the company's compliance services, domestic and foreign, for three dozen of the Paloma, Napa, and Alexander Valleys' wineries—business licensing, label registration, price posting, sales solicitor permits, federal label approvals, vintage and price changes. Her supervision allowed him to concentrate on the marketing and distributing end.

The BATF approval for Fenwood Creek's new labels was just in; Maureen said a copy would go out to Jenna later today. Then, "Why didn't she call me about it? Or did you and the lady have something else to discuss?"

"That was all she wanted."

"No other kind of approval?"

"I don't . . . what does that mean?"

"Do I really have to explain it to you?"

"No, but you can explain why you don't like Jenna."

"The same reason I don't like mountain lions."

"Is that what you think she is? Predatory?"

"Give her half a chance," Maureen said, "she'll eat you alive and purr like hell afterward."

"Come on, she's not like that."

"Isn't she?"

"No. Anyway, I don't intend to let her get close enough to find out."

Maureen gave him a slantwise look over the top of her glasses. "I hope not," she said.

He went to the men's room to take a couple of Advil, then returned to his desk and sat staring out through the window at the vineyards stretching away behind the office and warehouse buildings. *Is it that obvious?* he thought. *Horns sprouting already?* Three drop-in visits from Jenna this month, the lunch last week, half a dozen phone calls—it had the look and feel of a budding affair, all right, especially to someone as perceptive as Maureen. But Maureen knew him well enough to know that he loved his wife, didn't have a roving eye, and didn't play around—that he hadn't succumbed yet. Reacting to vibes from Jenna, misinterpreting them as predatory, and warning him off.

Still, he wondered if Maureen knew something about Fenwood Creek's product manager that he didn't know. Rumor, gossip . . . she lived in the Paloma Valley, was hooked in to the upper echelons of local society. But for that matter, so was he, by the nature of the business. Wine was the valley's lifeblood, and he was privy to just about everything that went on in or was connected with the industry, whether he wanted to be or not. He'd heard nothing particularly negative about Jenna in the three years she'd been here. Sure, she liked men and was reputed to have had several affairs, including one with Toby Charbonneau, heir apparent to the Charbonneau Cellars combine and "a hard-on lugging a man around with it," as a Charbonneau sales rep had once characterized him. Cam played golf with Toby once a month; if there had been anything predatory about her, Toby would've related it. He was anything but reticent about the good and bad points of his conquests.

The hell with it, Cam thought. The problem here isn't Maureen's, or even Jenna's. It's mine.

He wondered if he ought to make an appointment to see Beloit again. Dr. Randolph Beloit, M.D., Paloma County's preeminent psychoanalyst. It had been seven months since his last session, and before that his visits had been sporadic for nearly a year. Too many demands on his time—that was the official excuse. But the fact was, the good doctor rubbed him the wrong way. Aloof, supercilious, secure in his own importance. Beloit had helped him for a while, but there was only so much insight and direction a shrink could provide. Point of diminishing returns. Now, though, he might be a worthwhile option again. Who else but Beloit could he talk to about Jenna?

What he really wanted to do was to get away. From work, from temptation, from everybody and everything except Hallie. Just the two of them on a two- or three-week cruise on the *Hallie Too*. The twenty-seven-foot Skagit Orca XLC he'd bought new in April was specifically designed for the rugged waters of the Pacific; the shakedown cruise he and Hallie and the girls had taken to San Diego in June had been one of the best times he'd ever had. He'd always enjoyed boating; it had been Uncle Frank's favorite pastime, so he'd grown up around small boats, owned two himself before the *Hallie Too*. But they'd been runabouts, and he'd never gone farther in them than San Francisco Bay. Ocean cruising was a whole new exciting world. There was something about being out at sea, alone except for the people he loved, no pressures or outside influences, that opened him up and cleaned him out and filled him back up with peace and well-being. Nightmare and memory hadn't bothered him out there. Rose and his other demons were landlocked.

But a cruise now was out of the question. Wrong time of year for ocean travel in a small boat, especially with the weather an iffy proposition these days; and one of the busiest times for PWS, with the fall harvest just over and announcements and promotion for new releases, increased sales and distribution for the upcoming holiday season. Hallie was committed to her volunteer work at the senior center, too. And they could neither take Leah and Shannon out of school nor turn them over to somebody else for a lengthy supervision; Aunt Ida was too old and crotchety and unreliable, and asking the Edmondses or any of their other friends was too much of an imposition. He'd have to be content, as long as the weather cooperated, with weekend day trips down to the Bay and out through the Gate. Any extended cruising would have to wait until next spring at the earliest, and probably until well into the summer if El Niño produced another long, wet winter as was being predicted.

Winter. He'd always hated it, even before the night of January 4, 1974. Dark, wet, cold. Bleak days and long nights. His mood swings and bouts of depression were always worse during the winter months.

Abruptly he swiveled away from the window. Winter was still on his mind when he picked up the phone and called Fenwood Creek.

Jenna's voice purred in his ear. He relayed word of the BATF approval. Then he said, "Anything else I can do for you, Jenna?" He didn't realize the suggestiveness of the phrasing until after the words were out. Or maybe the perverse part of him had done it deliberately.

"As a matter of fact, there is. Buy me a drink."

"I can't today. I have a lunch."

"I wasn't thinking of lunch. After work."

"I don't know, Jenna—"

"Say five-fifteen. Meet me in the square, by the duck pond, and we'll go to Santucci's or the Hotel Paloma."

He hesitated. Thinking: You don't want to do this. Just say no.

"All right," he said. "Five-fifteen in the square."

arly in the morning Nick drove into Santa Rosa. First place he hunted up was a cheap Laundromat. All his clothes were dirty, he was starting to smell himself; time to get cleaned up, whether he went job hunting today or not. People shied away from you on the street when you looked and smelled like a bum. And nobody'd give you a job.

He washed and dried everything he owned, one load. A woman who came in told him there was a rescue mission on Fourth Street and how to get there. He didn't like standing around, waiting in line with a bunch of poor buggers who stank worse than he did, all that hopelessness and despair, but he needed a place to shower and shave. Missions were good for that. Decent meal, too.

He got inside finally. Sat through the usual religious stuff, not even listening to it. Once he'd believed in God, but not anymore. If there was a God and He was somebody who'd let Annalisa be hurt the way she'd been, suffer so much, Nick didn't want anything to do with Him.

Shower, shave, breakfast, and he was out of there before eleven. Section nearby of antique shops and restaurants, so he tried that first. Then he went downtown, different part of Fourth Street. Then out to a big junior college campus. Then across town until he came to a mall called the Montgomery Village Shopping Center. Stores, eating places, bus stops, service stations; pedestrians, salesclerks, newspaper vendors, drivers waiting at stoplights. Holding the plastic-encased sketch up at eye level, saying, "You know this man? You ever see him anywhere?"

Same thing he always got. Head shakes, blank stares, dozen different versions of no. Now and then a sneer or muttered curse. People walking away from him, some of them in a hurry, a few with a quick glance back as if they were afraid he might start chasing them. Like he was some kind of crazy person. Made him feel frustrated and alone, like always. As alone as if he were standing on top of the Continental Divide instead of on a crowded street or mall.

He knew what it was made them act that way. Fear. Fear of him, what he might do or know. Fear of the unknown face in the sketch. Sometimes it gave him a funny sense of power, like he really did know something they didn't—kind of feeling those religious nuts who went around handing out leaflets and yelling about the end of the world must have. Like Nick Hendryx was different from everybody else, stronger, smarter, somebody who could do things they couldn't.

Mostly, though, the way they acted left him with the urge to shout, "Hey, don't run away from me. I don't want anything from you except a little help, a little understanding." But he never said anything like that. He'd never begged in his life, and he never would. Not even to find the man in the sketch.

Midafternoon. A young fat guy out at Montgomery Village looked at the sketch, and something changed in his eyes. "You know him?" Nick said, but the fat guy shook his head and started away. Nick went after him, grabbed his arm. "You know him," he said, not a question this time, and the fat guy said, "No, I thought for a second I did, but I don't." Nick said, "Please don't lie to me, it's real important," and the guy said, "I'm not lying, I don't know him, leave me alone," and pulled his arm away and got into a car and drove off fast. Nick would've chased him, but the Mazda was parked too far away. All he could do was watch the direction the fat guy took—and wonder.

Soon as he got to the Mazda, he left Montgomery Village and went in the same direction. Big intersection, no sign of the fat guy's car. Which way? Then he saw a sign with a name on it, Paloma, and an arrow pointing south. He turned that way because the light was green and he had to go somewhere.

Road took him down a long, narrow valley bordered by wooded hills, packed with vineyards and wineries and fancy homes. He didn't pay much attention to it beyond that. He'd liked places like this, green, quiet places, when he was with Annalisa, but they had nothing to do with the life he was living now. He kept thinking about the fat guy, wondering if he'd recognized the face in the sketch.

Paloma turned out to be an old California mission town clogged with tourists, even on a weekday afternoon. In the middle of town was a big tree-shaded square, surrounded by a mission and a fort and a bunch of expensive-looking shops. Nick found a parking spot for the Mazda, went out walking and showing the sketch.

Same blank here. No signs of recognition or of the fat guy. Even so, he had a good feeling about this town. Nothing to get excited about, not yet, but a feeling with hope in it. Spend the night somewhere close by, come back in the morning, and if the feeling was still good, start job hunting. Too late in the day for that now.

After a while he got tired of walking around and around the square and went into it and sat down on a bench opposite a pond with floating ducks and a stone bridge across it. A steady stream of pedestrians came along the connecting paths, and whenever somebody passed his bench, he got up and flashed the sketch.

Sun went down, and it got a little chilly. Time to start moving again. Find someplace to eat and then someplace to sleep out in the country. He was thinking that when the woman came along one of the paths. Tall brunette about thirty, nice looking. She stopped at the near end of the bridge and stood there as if she was waiting for somebody—kept glancing at her watch. Nick pushed off the bench again, taking his time because his legs were stiff and his back muscles tight. Somebody else to show the sketch to.

Then he saw the man. Cutting across from one of the other paths to join the brunette. Guy wasn't there, then he was, and then Nick was seeing his face—clear and straight on, from a distance of five or six feet.

It was like being kicked in the groin. He pulled up short, felt his eyes pop with a sudden bulging pressure. Thought he'd made a sound, grunt or gasp, but neither of them looked his way. He backed off a couple of steps, stood staring as the brunette linked her arm through the guy's and the two of them moved off across the bridge.

Nick couldn't get his breath. Blood-pound in his ears was like the ocean during a storm, a wild roaring that was hate and excitement and thankfulness and a dozen other feelings all wrapped up together.

Him. Man in the sketch, the face he lived with every day, that haunted his sleep, that he'd been hunting for so long. No doubt of it, no mistake. Bastard who'd hurt Annalisa—right here, not fifteen feet away.

It was him!

"Cam, do you know that man standing at the bar?"

It took a few seconds for the question to register. Jenna had leaned close across the little table, close enough so he could smell the spiciness of her perfume and the gin on her breath; had laid her hand over his, long fingers gently squeezing. Her touch, her scent, were sensory stimuli that acted as a verbal delay. When the meaning of her question got through, Cam stiffened and looked up and away from her, shifting his body and guiltily withdrawing his hand.

"What man?"

"The thin one in the corduroy jacket. He keeps looking over here. Staring is more like it."

The bar at the Hotel Paloma was softly lit and crowded; Cam had to squint and eye-roam to pick out the man Jenna had indicated. Not looking their way now, just standing at the far end of the bar. Alone, apart, a mug of draft beer in one hand. Then the head moved, the eyes shifted, and he was staring right at them. Cam felt a small twinge of anxiety. Unwarranted, because he'd never seen the man before and there was nothing threatening about him, despite the intensity of his stare. Wiry rather than thin. Thirty-something, dark-haired, clean-shaven, wearing faded trousers and a workman's shirt with an old cord jacket. Just a guy having an after-work beer.

"No," he said, "I don't know him."

"Neither do I. He doesn't belong in here."

"Why not? You mean the way he's dressed?"

"He looks like a day laborer."

"Come on."

"Or a refugee from a homeless shelter."

Her attitude nettled him. "Don't be an elitist, Jenna. So what if he's blue-collar? He has a right to drink where he pleases, same as we do."

"Why here? Draft beer is three dollars a glass."

"Jenna, what difference does it make?"

"I don't like to be stared at."

"Why should it bother you? You're a woman men stare at."

"Not that way. Besides, it's mostly you he's interested in."

"Me?"

"Watch him when he looks again. Follow his eyes."

She was right. The eyes were fixed on him next time—he was sure of it. It shouldn't have bothered him, but it did. Someone who knew him, knew he was married and that Jenna wasn't his wife?

"You see?"

"It doesn't mean anything," he said.

"Why don't you go ask him what he wants."

"You're not serious?"

"I'll do it, if you'd rather."

"And make a scene? What's the sense in—"

"He knows we're talking about him," Jenna said.

"What?"

"Look at his body language."

The man had turned aside, was standing stiff-backed with the mug at chest level. Cam had the impression of a person poised on the edge of either flight or decision. Jerkily, the stranger lifted his mug, took a quick sip, moved to the bar and set it down—it was still half full—and pushed his way through the crowd. He didn't glance their way again before he disappeared through the lobby entrance.

Jenna said, "Well, that's a relief. As long as we don't find him hanging around outside when we leave."

Cam said nothing. He drank the last of his martini, letting the gin bite on the back of his tongue before he swallowed.

"Weirdos," she said moodily. "Everywhere you go these days. Half of them ought to be in prison. The other half ought to be exterminated."

The casual malice in the words shocked him. "You can't mean that."

"Can't I? We'd all be better off."

"Christ, Jenna. Just do away with masses of people who don't conform to some arbitrary norm?"

"Of course not. I mean the real weirdos, the dangerous misfits."

"Criminals? Mental cases?"

"Anyone who commits a violent act—murder, rape, assault—no matter what the reason. Zero tolerance. It'd eliminate stalking and spousal abuse, among other problems."

She was smiling, making light of it now, but there was nothing amusing in the concept. Besides, she was serious enough; the passion was there beneath the smile and the bantering tone.

He said, "It's a crazy idea. Look what happened the last time something like that was done."

"I don't know what you mean. Last time?"

"Germany, Austria, Poland. Six million Jews died because Hitler considered them dangerous misfits."

"That's not the same thing."

"It's exactly the same thing."

"No, it isn't. What the Nazis did had a racial and religious basis. I'm not advocating genocide, for heaven's sake."

"What would you call destroying masses of people simply because they're different?"

"Not different, destructive. Menaces to society. Sick, evil, worthless individuals. I call getting rid of them a benefit to the common good. The only sensible way to preserve life and liberty for the rest of us."

"The 'normal' ones."

"The productive, nonviolent ones."

"Where do you draw the line, Jenna?"

"Between them and us? I just told you—"

"I meant the line between sick and healthy, evil and good, productive and nonproductive."

"I'll tell you where *I* draw it. Anyone who tries to hurt me, anyone for any damn reason, doesn't deserve to go on living. Give me the chance, and I'd make sure he didn't."

"That sounds pretty bloodthirsty."

"Does it? I'm not kidding, Cam."

"You'd take someone's life for a small offense?"

"If it was intentional, if he hurt me—yes."

"No extenuating circumstances?"

"None. Zero tolerance."

He shook his head. He'd had no idea she harbored such hard-core fascist ideas. "I just don't agree."

"Well, maybe that's because you've never been hurt. You know the definition of a liberal, Cam, somebody who's never been mugged."

"I've been hurt," he said.

"Attacked, physically assaulted by a weirdo?"

"No, but—"

"No buts is right, my handsome friend. Until it's happened to you, you'll never understand what it's like and your point of view doesn't carry much weight."

"Meaning it has happened to you?"

"That's right. And no, I don't want to talk about it." She put her hand on his again; her touch seemed cooler now, almost cold. "Let's get off this subject, shall we? Have another round and discuss more pleasant topics. What were we talking about before? Fenwood's new cabernet franc, wasn't it? Or had I gotten around to inviting you to dinner?"

"Dinner?"

"I guess I hadn't. Saturday night at my place."

"What's the occasion?"

"Don't you know?"

"No. Who else is coming?"

She laughed. Her nails, long and plum colored, stroked the backs of his fingers. "Don't be naive. Just the two of us, naturally."

He didn't say anything. Out in the open now, like something bright and alluring laid on the table between them. All he had to do was pick it up.

But he didn't. If the invitation had come before the little episode with the staring stranger, before the conversation about dangerous misfits and the new and less than appealing side of Jenna it had revealed, the temptation would have been hard to resist. Now . . . no. There was nothing like a dose of harsh reality to keep your libido in check.

He said, "I think I'd better pass."

Her violet eyes showed disappointment. In him, he thought, as well as in his answer. "Can't get away?"

"Other plans," he lied.

"Sunday, then? Next weekend?"

"I . . . don't think so, Jenna."

"No? I'm very good, you know."

"Good?"

"In the kitchen, among other places."

Euphemisms. Game playing. It had the reverse effect of what she'd intended; it turned him off completely. "I'm sure you are," he said.

"But you're not interested in a demonstration."

He smiled and shrugged. The smile felt stiff on his mouth.

"So be it," she said, but her words had an edge now. "Shall we have that second drink?"

"Not for me. It's after six, and I should be on my way. But I'll buy you another if you want to stay—"

"No point in that. I don't like to drink alone, and I'm not in the mood to be picked up tonight." She gathered her coat and purse. "Walk me to my car?"

"Sure."

Outside, Jenna paused to glance both ways along the sidewalk, across the street at the shadowed square. He found himself doing the same. Both of them looking for the man in the corduroy jacket, as if he'd actually be lurking somewhere waiting to pounce on them. Silly on his part, but perhaps not so silly on hers. He wondered again what it was in her past that had made her so wary of strangers, built such a virulent hatred of "dangerous misfits."

She took his arm as they quartered across to the square, followed one of the lighted paths through its center. At her Lexus, waiting while she unlocked the door, he felt pretty good about the way he'd handled her overture, at not weakening to it. Now if he could just—

Jenna turned without warning, leaned her body close to his, slid her arms around his neck, and kissed him. A hard, passionate kiss, letting her tongue flick between his lips. It surprised, dismayed, excited him, as she must have intended it to, and shattered his self-congratulation the way heat shatters glass.

"The invitation is still open," she said. "Call me after you've thought it over. Or I'll call you."

uy who'd hurt Annalisa lived in Los Alegres, in the next long narrow valley west of Paloma. Thirteen miles of two-lane road winding through low foothills, flat farmland. Following him was easy as waiting in the dark Mazda for him and the brunette to leave the hotel bar. Guy's car was a silver BMW with a personalized license plate: WINEMAN. And there was plenty of traffic on the road and in Los Alegres.

Town was bigger than Paloma but not as big as Santa Rosa. Had a river slicing through it, an old-fashioned downtown, a west-side residential district that stretched up into another set of low hills. That was where Wineman lived, on one of the hillside lots. Crooked street, sprawly house with a gated driveway, shade trees in front. Couple of acres of prime real estate. Rich bugger. Seeing that made Nick hate him all the more.

He drove up to where the street—Ridgeway Terrace—dead-ended, turned around, and rolled by the property again. BMW was in his garage now. Front door of the house was open, and a blond woman and a little girl were standing on the lighted porch, waiting for Wineman.

Yeah, that figured. Wife and daughter. Nick had had a feeling the brunette Wineman'd been drinking with wasn't his wife. Something about the way the two of them were sitting in the bar, their—what was it, body language? Something about the woman herself. Classy, but with an edge like shined-up steel. Big shot like Wineman could afford the best of everything, including a piece on the side. Get away with everything he did, son of a bitch like that.

Until now.

Nick let the Mazda drift to the curb a short way downhill, at the edge of Wineman's property where there weren't any streetlamps. No cars on the street, nobody on the sidewalk when he got out and walked back uphill, taking his time, just a guy out for an evening stroll. One of the gate pillars had a number on it: 74. No nameplate. Wineman. Bastard's name or what he did for a living?

He walked on past the driveway. Wineman was on the porch now, one arm around the blond's waist, the other around the kid, three of them turning in to the house. Door shut behind them as Nick reached the second pillar.

No nameplate on that one, either, but just inside, at the edge of the drive, a mailbox on an iron pole with what looked to be printing on the side of the box. He couldn't make out the words from the sidewalk.

Front windows of the house were all curtained or draped, nobody peering out. Street was still empty. He moved in fast, bent to squint at the printing on the box. Came back out and kept walking, uphill a short distance, then back on the other side to the Mazda.

The Gallaghers.

Okay. Guy's name was Gallagher. Wineman must be what he was, what he did for a living. Drove a new silver BMW, lived at 74 Ridgeway Terrace in Los Alegres with a wife and at least one kid, had some sort of big-salary job in the wine business over in Paloma, had a classy brunette girlfriend who drove a white Lexus. Enough for tonight. He'd know more, maybe a lot more, by this time tomorrow.

T he attic. Hiding in the attic.

Cold, damp, dark. Smells of mold and mildew, rain and dust and mouse turds. Sound of the rain outside, beating on the roof, wind-flung against the dormer windows. He hears it dripping, a leak somewhere inside one of the walls. Drip. Drip. Drip. He doesn't dare shut his eyes because then it won't be rain he'll see and hear dripping, it'll be something else wet, glistening. Something bright red.

Blood.

Downstairs, on the bed. Blood.

Downstairs, on the bedroom floor. Blood.

He lies curled on the old bare mattress, his knees drawn tight against his chest, his eyes wide open and full of the dark. Shivers rack his body. He has never been so cold. Or so scared. Or so alone.

Drip. Drip.

Dad. Daddy.

Help me.

He can't move. He wants desperately to be somewhere else, somewhere warm and safe and far away from here. But he can't make himself get up. Afraid, so cold, and all he can do is lie there shaking with his eyes wide open, listening to the rain blood rain drip drip drip inside the wall, on the bed downstairs, on the bedroom floor downstairs.

The rain slackens and then stops. Not the dripping, just the rain and the boom of the wind. He hears something else outside, another car turning in off the road. Light splashes over the window, making it into a dead, staring eye. He trembles, and a sound comes out like the one his puppy made when it got run over on his fifth birthday and he rushed out and found it all broken and covered with wet, glistening red in the street. "Happy birthday, Cameron, your damn mutt just got squashed out front." Ma's voice echoing inside his head.

Drip.

Door slamming downstairs.

Oh God, is it Fatso? Is he back?

Footsteps.

A voice, calling something he can't understand. Fatso's voice?

Scared, so scared, and I have to go real bad and I can't get up, I can't move. Please God don't let me wet myself. "Pissed your bed again, you little shit." Please God don't let me wet myself!

The voice yelling again, and this time he hears it clearly.

"Cameron! Where are you, son?"

Not Fatso. Stranger's voice.

Somebody worse than Fatso?

More footsteps, somebody else yelling. Another stranger. Two strangers in the house now.

Go away. No, help me. No, go away.

Daddy, don't be dead. Mama—

Drip.

Dust and mouse turds and red rain.

Footsteps louder, closer. On the attic stairs.

Have to go so bad I can't hold it much longer.

Thump. Drip. Thump.

Creak of the door opening.

Beam of light stabbing through the dark. Poking at him like a sharp thing.

"Boy? You in here, Cameron?"

Warm wet flowing under him. No! But he can't help it, he couldn't hold it anymore, it isn't his fault! All he can do is lie there peeing on himself while the sharp light stabs closer and the red rain drips and the stranger's voice calls his name. And when the light slices into his eyes his mouth opens and the scream comes out—

CAM JERKED AWAKE with the scream in his ears, a shrill tremolo that was a hammering pressure against the drums. As always, the first thing he did was to feel the crotch of his pajamas, the sheet under him. Dry. He hadn't actually lost control of his bladder during one of the nightmares since the first year or so. But the fear was still part of him, mixed together with the other fears of boy and man.

"Oh, Cam," Hallie said, "it's been so long I was beginning to hope—" She broke off as he lay back down, limp against the wadded pillows. Moved closer and slid an arm across his chest, held him until his breathing slowed. Then she asked, "Which one was it?"

"One in the attic."

"It must've been . . . intense."

"No worse than any of the others."

"You were making noises."

He winced. "What kind of noises?"

"Moans. Hurt sounds."

His mouth was hot and dry; he sipped water from the bedside glass. "I'm sorry I woke you."

"Honey, I don't care about that. I care about you."

"I'm all right."

"Are you? Really?"

No, he thought. At length he said, "Maybe I ought to start seeing Beloit again."

"If you think it's a good idea."

"I don't know. It might be."

"With winter coming. Yes."

"Winter," he said.

"It might be a good idea to talk to Caitlin again, too."

"Waste of time. She's not going to change her mind, you know that as well as I do."

"She needs money, doesn't she?"

"She always needs money. It hasn't made any difference in the past."

"Well, what about some sort of cash incentive? In addition to her share of the sale, I mean. Payable immediately. We can afford it."

"I tried that once, remember?"

"Years ago. Maybe now that the house is vacant again and there's no rent money coming in—"

"She won't take a dime from me, Hallie. And she won't agree to sell the damn house, not even if she and Teddy are starving. Besides, even if by some miracle I could talk her into it, I'm not convinced it'd make much difference, any difference, in her life or mine."

"But it might. Didn't Dr. Beloit indicate it might?"

"He's not God," Cam said.

"I'm not God, either, but I believe it will. Get the river house out of your life, and the nightmares and the rest of it will stop. If you could only make Caitlin understand—"

"Caitlin doesn't care about my problems. She has enough of her own, and hers happen to be bound up in *not* getting rid of the river house."

"Cam—"

He said bitterly, "A couple of head cases, Cat and me. Rose must be laughing up a storm in her little corner of hell."

"Your mother didn't hate you and your sister."

"The hell she didn't."

"Aunt Ida—"

"Aunt Ida doesn't know everything. Rose resented Cat and me, treated us like dirt when nobody else was around, flaunted her affairs in front of us, and if that's not hatred it amounts to the same thing."

"And you can't stop hating her in return. Until you do, you won't have any peace. How many times have we had this discussion? How many times have you had it with Dr. Beloit and the others?"

"All right," he said.

"I'm sorry, I didn't mean to snap at you—"

"It's all right."

"Will you please try to talk to Caitlin?"

"If it's what you want."

"What I want is what's best for you. I can't stand the thought of losing you."

Her words touched him, pushed aside the bitterness. He turned to her, nuzzled the warmth and softness of her breast. "You're not going to lose me. We're not going to lose each other."

"We could if you can't find some way to resolve what happened twenty-five years ago. I'll lose you, because sooner or later you'll end up losing yourself."

She was right—of course she was right. He folded her into his arms, held her tightly. Loving her, hating himself, he said, "I'll call Beloit's office first thing in the morning. And talk to Caitlin as soon as she'll let me."

aloma Wine Systems. That was the place Gallagher worked. Led Nick straight to it from Los Alegres on Friday morning.

Good-size outfit on Blackwell Road, semirural section on the eastern edge of Paloma. One Quonset-type building, like a small airplane hangar, that looked like it'd been there a long time; one newer L-shaped building made of cinder block, part warehouse and part office wing. Property enclosed by a tall Cyclone fence, night-lights on poles that were more for show than real security. Trucking outfit on one side, some kind of animal shelter on the other. Mixed-bag area, mostly industrial. In all maybe a dozen businesses stretching for about a mile along one side of the road, open farmland on the other.

So what did Gallagher do there? Honcho of some kind—BMW, fancy home, suit and tie he wore said that. But what kind?

Nick drove next door to the shelter. Animal Lifeline, seemed to be a sort of halfway house for strays waiting for adoption. Type of place Annalisa'd like. That big old orange tom of her folks', curled up and died with his head in his food dish—Annalisa'd cried for days over that poor cat. She had a soft heart. He wished he'd let her have a kitten like she'd wanted after they were married. Allergic to cat fur, sneezed his head off when he was around one too long, but still he should've let her have a kitten. Sneezing and a snotty nose were a small price to pay to make someone you loved happy. He'd get her a cat when she was well, first thing. Orange tom like the one that'd died . . . Rufus, that was his name. Hell of a name for a cat, Rufus. But if she wanted to call it Rufus II or Rufus Junior, that was all right with him.

Animal Lifeline was two buildings, tin-roofed shelter in back and a cottagelike one nearest the road that had a sign on it saying Thrift Shop. Elderly woman was opening up the shop as Nick pulled in and parked. She'd gone inside and was behind the counter when he walked in.

He smiled at her. "Morning, ma'am. Nice morning, isn't it."

Got him a smile and a "Yes, it is" in return. You could almost always put people on your side, get what you needed out of them, with a polite and sunny approach. He'd learned that long ago, even before he met Annalisa. Not that he had to fake it much. He was naturally friendly, liked most people, enjoyed their company. Or had before Gallagher came along and tore up his life along with Annalisa's.

He browsed through the shop for a few minutes—patience was something else he'd learned how to use. Picked out a couple of paperback books, took them to the old woman at the counter, paid her fifty cents. While she was ringing up the sale he said, "That big place next door, Paloma Wine Systems. What kind of business is that?"

"Oh, PWS represents several wineries in the area. Sales, distribution, compliance services."

"What's that, compliance services?"

"Oh, you know, business licensing and that sort of thing."

"Looks like a pretty successful operation."

" Largest in the valley," she said. "Mr. Gallagher is a good businessman."

"He the owner? Mr. Gallagher?"

"Yes, that's right."

"Been at it a long time?"

"Seven or eight years."

"Lot of people working for him?"

"More than twenty, yes."

"I bet he's one of those workaholics."

"Oh, not so much as you might think."

"What's his first name?"

"Everyone calls him Cam."

"Cam. Short for camera?"

She laughed. "No, Cameron. You seem very curious about him, I must say."

"Well, I thought I'd talk to him about a job. If he's hiring. You happen to know?"

"I'm afraid I don't. You're looking for work, then?"

"I sure am. Had some bad luck lately and I . . . well, I'm trying to get back on my feet."

Woman said, "Oh, I'm sorry," as if she meant it. "What sort of work do you do?"

"Any kind, long as it's honest. Wouldn't happen to need somebody here at the shelter, by any chance?"

"No. We're mostly volunteers here."

"Know of any place around town that's hiring? In case Mr. Gallagher isn't?"

Sad shake of her head. Nice old lady, somebody's mother, probably somebody's grandmother. Reminded him of Mom Foster, except Mom wasn't this old. Never knew his own mom. Died when he was two. Freak accident, slipped on some grease and hit her head on the kitchen stove, old man came in from plowing and found her dead. Poor Pa. Must've felt the same way, finding her like that, that Nick'd felt when they came and told him about Annalisa.

"Well, I'll find a job somewhere," he said. "All you have to do is keep looking and something'll turn up."

Woman said, "That's the spirit. It's too bad more folks don't have your attitude, young man. There'd be far less homelessness and welfare cheating. Far less crime, too."

"You're right about that, ma'am."

"Well, good luck and God bless. I'm sure things will work out for you, as you hope they will."

"I'm sure of it, too," Nick said. "Just as sure as I can be."

D r. Beloit couldn't see him for nearly a week. "If it's an emergency, Mr. Gallagher," the receptionist said, "perhaps the doctor could find a few minutes. . . ." No, it wasn't an emergency. He'd felt like saying, I can keep my pants zipped until Thursday, I'm not that far gone. But of course he didn't.

None of this was funny. Not the slightest bit funny.

He wished he had more faith in Beloit, in the whole psychiatric process. He'd been able to open up to Beloit and the others before him, but only to a point—revealing some of the more painfully intimate details about himself, his childhood, his mother, yet withholding others. The night he'd walked in on Rose and Fatso, both of them naked, her legs wrapped around him and her heels beating on his hairy jiggling ass— and the wet dream he'd had about it later. Some of the things he'd seen and heard on Rose and Paul's last night on earth. And other, later incidents, such as the time a few years ago when he'd been away on business and suffered a blackout migraine and woke up in his motel room with blood on his shirt and hands. Just a nosebleed, but God, he'd been frightened. Blood always disturbed him; seeing it, even talking about it, made him physically ill. He'd never confided any of these things to anyone, even Hallie, and they wouldn't dislodge for professional scrutiny no matter how hard he tried.

Beloit's manner didn't particularly inspire confidence, either. He was too smug, too glib. He used words to fill up time the way pharmacists used pills and powders to fill up containers. It wasn't so much that he liked the sound of his own voice (though he probably did), or even that he considered his comments to be profound. (Though he surely seemed to when he said things like "Nightmares, according to ancient Indian superstition, are the result of the soul leaving the body, visiting the nether regions, and returning with visual imprints of the terrible acts it witnessed there. A modern interpretation of that superstition may be helpful in understanding the insidious nature of your nightmares, Mr. Gallagher.") It was as if his main concern, aside from dispensing aid and comfort to the troubled, was in making sure each session was crammed to the brim to avoid complaint. He charged $100 an hour, but the sessions were only forty-five minutes long; you paid for the extra fifteen minutes as a kind of surcharge, so Beloit could clean his professional palette before the next poor bastard hobbled in, like a gourmet priming his taste buds between courses. He didn't want you to realize it and feel cheated.

Could Beloit help him with the Jenna problem? He didn't need to know what to do about his compulsion; he'd had enough psychoanalysis to figure that out for himself. Negate the power of it by using common sense to maintain self-control. Force his conscious mind to lock into other channels—work, hobbies, domestic activities. Keep reminding himself of how much he loved Hallie and didn't want to hurt her anymore, how it would be if he lost her and the girls. Things he was already doing. What he needed from Beloit was insight into *why* he was so strongly tempted. Understand that, and he could make the obsession go away. Or at least he'd have an easier time controlling it. Knowledge was strength. One of Beloit's dictums. So maybe the good doctor could help. It was worth at least one session to find out.

Next Thursday. Six days. He'd have to take pains to avoid Jenna until he saw Beloit. Then, when he saw her again and she forced the issue, as he was sure she would, his defenses would be stronger. The way they were now, he was afraid they wouldn't hold up under a direct assault.

inding a job wasn't much of a problem. Man could always work if he wanted to. Some of the guys he'd run into in the shelters and missions kept pissing and moaning about being out of work. He had no sympathy for anybody like that. Being homeless, sure, that was something else. But you could be homeless and still earn a living, even if it was a lousy living. People he respected were willing to take any job they could get, get along on minimum wage if it was the best they could manage. Bottom line was to work, don't be choosy.

Best jobs for him were night driving jobs. Short-haul trucking for gypsy freighters and small supply outfits that didn't care much about references or union cards—they were the cream. But they didn't come along very often. Kind he'd held most often was pizza deliveryman. Every town, no matter how small, had a pizzeria, and they were always looking for drivers.

When he couldn't get a driving job, there was other night work: busboy, dishwasher, janitor for one of the services that specialized in cleaning offices and stores after they closed. Plenty of day jobs, too, driving and nondriving. Deliveryman, handyman's helper, trash hauler, pickup driver for Goodwill and the Sally Ann; farmhand, day laborer, fast-food worker, supermarket stockboy. He'd done all of those and others he couldn't even remember. Honest work for honest pay, every job he'd held in his life.

First thing he did when he left Animal Lifeline was buy a Paloma paper. Two possibilities in the help-wanted listings, but one turned out to be already filled and he didn't get the other. He walked around town looking for window signs in eating places and shops, checking a bulletin board in a supermarket. Nothing. So then he drove back over to Los Alegres, figuring bigger town, more opportunities.

Three large thrift stores on the main drag. Second one he tried, a Goodwill, had a Help Wanted sign in the front window. Two jobs open, stockboy and pickup driver. All he had to do to get the driving job was tell the store manager he'd done that kind of work before, show his commercial driver's license, fill out a form. Five days a week, eight to four. Little better than minimum wage, but that was all right for now. Manager told him he could start Monday morning, they didn't do pickups on Saturday.

After he left the Goodwill he drove around for a while, until he spotted a run-down auto court on the south end of town near the freeway. Part hotsheet motel, part long-term transient housing, from the look of it. Twelve units, little white stucco boxes in a three-quarter square around a courtyard, nothing growing in the courtyard except cars. Units rented by day, week, or month, and they had a vacancy. He took it, handing over a hundred and a quarter for one week.

His unit was one of those in back, one room and bath. Beat-up furniture, board-hard bed, waterstained wallpaper, cheap portable TV, no phone. Bed wasn't too bad, the TV worked all right, and the bath had a chipped tub in it.

He took the two framed photographs out of his suitcase, always the first thing he did when he took a room someplace. Head-and-shoulders color portrait of Annalisa, smiling, her corn-silk hair brushed out long over her shoulders. And their wedding photo, two of them all slicked up, smiling and happy, getting ready to cut the pink-and-white cake. He set the photos on the nightstand, the one of Annalisa alone closest to the bed and turned so he could look right at it when he was lying down.

He hadn't had a bath in so long he couldn't remember the last time. Showers but not a real soak. He ran hot water into the tub, as much as he could get from the tap, shucked out of his clothes, and lowered himself into the steamy water. Man! Washed all over, twice, then lay back with the water up to his chin and his eyes shut, thinking about Annalisa and Gallagher. He didn't even care when he couldn't coax any more hot out of the pipes and the bathwater turned cold.

He felt good. Hadn't felt this good in a long, long time.

aturday morning, a little before nine, Cam drove to Sebastopol to see Caitlin. Reluctantly. He'd called first, to make sure she'd be home, and the conversation had been brief and unenthusiastic on her part. At least she hadn't told him not to come. The way things were between Cat and him, a lukewarm reception was the best he could hope for.

It was fourteen miles from Los Alegres to Sebastopol, a mile or so more than his one-way, five-days-a-week commute to Paloma, but he seldom made the trip. He'd been there three times in the past year, twice on business—one of the local apple processors had branched out into winemaking—and once on a Sunday outing with Hallie and the girls; he hadn't stopped to see Caitlin on any of those occasions, hadn't been to her home in . . . what? Three years? At least that. Nor had she come down to Los Alegres to see him in at least that long, despite repeated invitations—not since Gus walked out on her. The only times he'd seen Cat in recent memory had been on neutral restaurant territory, a couple of quick lunches and one family dinner in Occidental that'd been a chore for all of them, Teddy acting out, Caitlin drinking too much of the cheap wine she preferred, Leah and Shannon cranky and uncomfortable because neither of them cared for their aunt. Shannon had said later, "Aunt Cat looks like a witch," and even though he'd scolded her for the comment, he'd thought privately that she was right. Caitlin, his once sweet-faced little sister—a broomstick refugee from Oz.

Dealing with her had become too painful. Rose's other legacy: They didn't even have each other for comfort. He loved Caitlin, he thought that down deep she still loved him, but there was no connection left between them. They couldn't agree on anything, much less the causes and events of the night of January 4, 1974. Familiar strangers was what they'd become. No, worse than that. Tolerant enemies.

Her house was beginning to fit the witch image, too. Once it had been an attractive five-room bungalow, but years of neglect had turned it into an eyesore with broken shutters, peeling paint, a yard choked with weeds and unmowed grass. The rest of the neighborhood, one of the small town's older residential sections, was the domain of determinedly civic-minded, lower-middle-class families: All the other houses and yards along the block were well maintained. Caitlin couldn't be popular with her neighbors—not that it would bother her. A woman who didn't give a damn about herself would hardly care about others' opinions of her.

Cam went up onto the creaky porch. The morning was warmish, tag end of the spell of Indian summer weather. (Perfect day for cruising. If it was like this tomorrow he'd take the *Hallie Too* down to San Pablo Bay, maybe San Francisco Bay.) The door stood open—welcome mat for flies, since there was no screen door. From somewhere at the rear he could hear the blaring percussion and obscene lyrics of bad gangsta rap. Little Teddy, all grown up too fast.

He tried ringing the bell, but if it made any sound inside, he couldn't hear it above the noise of the music. Probably broken, like so many other things here. Like Caitlin herself. He walked in, calling her name.

Pretty soon she came out of the kitchen, wiping her hands on a dish towel. He was in the middle of the living room by then, looking around at a clutter of newspapers and dirty wine and beer glasses and unemptied ashtrays and strewn articles of clothing. And taking note that more than half the butts in the trays were unfiltered, a grease-stained uniform shirt was draped over the arm of a recliner, and a pair of equally greasy work shoes had been tossed on the floor nearby. The name Hal was stitched over the shirt pocket.

Caitlin stopped a few feet away, making no move to embrace him. As a little girl she'd been a toucher, a hugger, but not anymore. Not with him, anyway. Whenever he put his arms around her after that night she'd gone rigid, and finally he'd given up on contact of any kind. She didn't like to be touched, she'd told him, but it was obvious from one ex-husband and a long parade of lovers that she didn't mind or at least tolerated being touched by other men. She had an almost pathological fear of being alone, yet the turnover rate in her relationships indicated dissatisfaction on her lovers' part as well as on hers. She didn't seem to take pleasure in anything, to be able to express her feelings or to let anyone else's feelings reach her.

As damaged as he was, he'd still managed to build a decent life for himself, to form a lasting relationship with one person, and to make most of the right choices, while Caitlin, who hadn't seen the horror he had, who should have had fewer scars and an easier time adjusting, had made all the wrong choices and completely screwed up her life. The irony in that was as bitter as gall.

"Finished, bro?"

" . . . What?"

"Examining me and how I live."

"I wasn't—"

"Sure you were. Both look like hell, right?"

He managed to restrain a wince as he looked at her. Right. Slat-thin except for the potbelly she was growing. Brown hair unwashed and uncombed, skin sallow and splotchy without makeup. Faded Levi's raggedly cut off to expose bony knees, Grateful Dead T-shirt showing the sag of unbound breasts. Thirty-three years old. His little sister.

Her eyes snapped at him. Saying plainly, *I don't need your goddamn pity.*

He cleared his throat. "New man in your life?" he asked, gesturing toward the greasy shirt.

"Hal Ullman. He's a mechanic."

"Serious?"

"He thinks it could be."

"How long have you been living together?"

"Two months. He's— *Damn that music!*"

They'd been talking in loud voices, to compete with the thud-and-pound of the gangsta rap, and now Teddy had raised the volume even higher. Caitlin stalked out of the room, and after a few seconds Cam could hear her screaming at her son. There was a defiant answering shout, then another shriek from Caitlin: "Turn that fucking thing off or I'll break it with a hammer, I swear to God!" The music sheered off abruptly. The sudden silence seemed to tremble with afterechoes.

Caitlin came back and flopped onto the raggedy sofa. "He drives me crazy sometimes with that rap crap." She lit a Marlboro, waved it vaguely at the other furniture. "Sit down, Cameron. You look uncomfortable standing there."

He started to sit in the recliner, changed his mind because of Hal's shirt, and put himself in a chair that matched the sofa in upholstery, stains, and frays. He watched her make sucking noises on her cigarette and said automatically, "You smoke too much."

"My lungs. You come here to lecture me or what?"

"No. Just to talk."

"Uh-huh. About the river house, I suppose."

"It's empty again, Cat."

"I know that. Don't you think I know that?"

"It's liable to stay that way all winter. Longer, if the river floods again this year."

"I know that too. Tell me something I don't know."

"How are you going to—"

He shut off the rest of the question because his nephew came stomping into the room, a boom box the size of a microwave under one skinny arm. Pimples and a ten-hair mustache. Baggy basketball shorts, tank top, Nike basketball shoes. Spiked hair with purple streaks, an earring in each ear and another hanging from a nostril. Gangsta look, complete with gangsta scowl, to go with the assault music he favored.

"Hello, Teddy."

"Theodore, man. *Theodore*."

"All right. How are you, Theodore?"

"Shitty." He glared at his mother and kept on stomping out through the front door.

"No respect," Caitlin said.

"He's at that age.

"He's a little shit. Hal says he needs a good boot in the ass. I'm beginning to think he's right."

"Child psychology must be one of Hal's long suits."

"Don't start with me," she said.

"I didn't mean to. I'm sorry."

"We are not going to sell the river house, if that's why you're here. I'll never agree to sell it. I don't know why you can't get that through your head."

"I'm only thinking of your best interests."

"Sure. *My* best interests."

"I mean it. Are you still working at the card shop?"

She finished her cigarette, immediately lit another. "So?"

"I know what your take-home pay is, and it—"

"They gave me a raise."

"It's still not much. With no more rent money coming in—"

"Rent money doesn't matter right now. Hal makes good wages, pays his share. We're doing okay."

"Hal isn't going to be a permanent fixture."

"How do you know he isn't?"

"You as much as said it isn't serious."

"It's serious enough for now. Besides, somebody'll rent the river house eventually. Somebody always does."

"You've been lucky, Cat. Keeping tenants for any length of time is getting harder, you know that as well as I do. The place is falling apart—"

"Oh, bullshit. When was the last time you took a good look at it? Or even drove by?"

He couldn't remember the last time. Years—before the last big flood.

"Yeah," Caitlin said, "I thought so."

"I talked to John Lacey when that hippie bunch moved out last month. And before that, when the complaints began piling up. He said it took a bad beating in the last flood. It might withstand another without major foundation work, but he wouldn't want to bet on it. He has no reason to exaggerate."

"So we'll shore up the foundation."

"*We* will?"

She just looked at him.

"All right. I'm willing to pay for it, if it means putting the house on the market."

"But not to keep it in the family."

"It should've been sold years ago, when river property was at its peak. As things are now, we'd be lucky to realize a hundred thousand for it. You can have all the money, Cat. Every penny."

"I don't want money, I want to keep the property."

"It's a drain on both of us, can't you see that? And I don't just mean a financial drain."

"No, I don't see that."

"I won't put any more of my capital into the house. Let it collapse, let the next flood carry the bloody place out to sea for all I care."

"That won't happen, no matter what the Realtor says. That house has been standing for sixty years, and it'll stand another twenty or thirty, what do you want to bet?"

Exasperation was making him edgy, restless. And the smoke from her cigarettes, the residue of tens of thousands of others that permeated the room and its furnishings, had aggravated his sinuses, giving him a dull headache. He leaned forward, the palms of his hands making dry, raspy sounds as he rubbed them over his knees.

"Cat, listen to me. That house . . . I don't want it in my life anymore. I don't want to have to think about it. I simply want it gone."

"Why?"

"For God's sake, you know why."

"Guilt wouldn't have something to do with it?"

"Guilt?" The accusation shocked him. "What would I have to feel guilty about?"

"You're the only one who can answer that. You were the survivor that night."

"What does that have to— Jesus! You don't think there was anything I could've done to prevent what happened?"

"I don't know. Sometimes I wish I'd been there instead of you."

"You couldn't have done anything, either. What's the matter with you? You were eight, I was ten . . . kids, little kids."

Nothing from Caitlin.

"I was in bed when Pa came and the yelling started. I didn't know he'd brought a gun with him. How could I know he'd bring one of his guns?"

"You told him about Ma and Fatso the time before. What'd you think he'd do if it happened again?"

"Not what he did."

"Then why'd you tell on her?"

"I couldn't stand what she was doing to him. I didn't want her to hurt him or us anymore."

"But you didn't care if he hurt her."

"That's not true. You can't put the blame on me. Or on Pa, for that matter."

"The hell I can't. He killed her, didn't he? The dirty son of a bitch killed my mother, and you, all you did was run away and hide." She was yelling now, red-faced, her eyes sparking. Quick to tantrum, as always. Keep going down this same worn-out, potholed road with her and she'd have hysterics.

"I did not run away and hide," he said.

"What else do you call it? They found you in the attic, didn't they? For all I know you were hiding up there the whole time he was killing her and himself."

"Dammit, that's not so. I went to the attic after I found them dead. I hardly remember it, I was so sick and scared—you'd have been sick and scared too if you'd seen what I saw."

"I wouldn't have hidden in the attic."

"How do you know what you'd have done? You can't know from an adult perspective."

She drew a couple of ragged breaths, coughed, then filled her lungs with more carcinogens and coughed again. The break in their heated exchange seemed to calm her somewhat. "Okay," she said, "there wasn't anything you could've done, and you don't feel any guilt. Then why're you so afraid of the river house after all these years?"

"*Afraid* of it?"

"You haven't been inside since that night. You wouldn't go back in there if your life depended on it."

"Oh, come on—"

"It's true. You won't go near the property, you keep nagging me to sell it, you want it out of your life, you don't want to think about it. Isn't that right?"

He could no longer sit still. He stood and paced the room, the smoke and dust burning in his nostrils and making his head pound.

"I won't sell," Caitlin said. "Not now, not ever. If the house collapses, gets swept away, fine, there's nothing I can do about that. But the property is going to stay in my hands as long as I'm above ground. I mean that, Cameron."

"Why? Why does it mean so much to you?"

"It's all I have left of Ma. Every time I look at a picture of her, it's like looking at a stranger."

"A monument, for Christ's sake?"

"You shut up with that kind of talk."

"The house means so much to you, why don't you go live there?" He stopped pacing to stare down at her. "Why stay here? Sell this place instead."

Bleak and painful things moved beneath the surfaces of her face. She sucked hard on her cigarette, jabbed it out in the nearest tray, pinched another out of the pack.

"You've never lived there, not one single day," he said. "You couldn't stand it any more than I could. Why don't you admit it to yourself, if not to me?"

"Get out, Cameron," she said without looking at him. "Go home to your wife and family. Leave me the fuck alone."

There was no anger left in her voice. Nor any left in him, he realized. Nothing filled the hole where it had been, a hole like an open wound. "I'm sorry," he said.

"For what? Coming here and screwing up my Saturday?"

"For trying to hurt you. Why do we always end up hurting each other?"

"Yeah, why?"

"We used to be close. Now—"

"Now we'd both be better off if we never saw each other again."

"I don't believe that."

"Well, I do." She stood ponderously, still not looking at him, the fresh cigarette dangling from one corner of her mouth. "Just don't ever say another word to me about selling Ma's house," she said, and went out of the room, left him standing there by himself in the rubble of her life.

aitlin Koski. 547 Applewood Lane, Sebastopol. Son, Theodore, fourteen or fifteen. Divorced, living with a mechanic who worked for North Analy Auto Body.

Inside the Mazda again, Nick wrote the information in the little notebook he'd bought. Neighbor watering his lawn up the block didn't know the mechanic's name and didn't know Gallagher. Wasn't familiar with the silver BMW, either.

Gallagher was still in the house across the street. Alone with the Koski woman, far as he knew, now that the punked-up kid was gone. Mechanic worked half a day Saturdays, neighbor'd said. Morning matinee with another bimbo? No surprise, if that was what it was. Just because she lived with somebody didn't mean she wasn't playing around on the side. And just because Gallagher had a wife in Los Alegres and a classy bitch in Paloma didn't mean he wasn't banging some downscale babe in Sebastopol.

That kind of crap made him sick. When you had somebody you loved, why would you want anyone else? He'd never cheated on Annalisa, would never hurt her like that. Same went for her. Soul mates. Phrase you heard tossed around, usually brought a snicker or a smart-ass remark, but he believed in it, knew it for a fact. He and Annalisa were soul mates. Put on this earth to be together, be there for each other no matter what.

Bugger over there, what was he put on the earth for? Rich, pampered types like that went around trampling on other people's lives, good people like Annalisa, they didn't give a pig's ass what happened to anybody but themselves. Men like that . . . disease carriers, like rats and roaches. Men like that—

Gallagher was coming out of the house. Alone, walking fast. Pretty short matinee, but some guys were like that. Rabbits. Gallagher figured to be a guy that operated on a time budget, too. Fifteen minutes for this meeting, twenty minutes for that one, five minutes to take a dump, half an hour for lunch, twenty-three minutes for a Saturday-morning screw. Looking at his watch as he came down the steps. Right. Time for him to move on to whatever was next up on his schedule.

Nick waited until the BMW pulled away from the curb. Then he fired up the Mazda and eased out a block behind.

am was on Highway 116, halfway to Forestville, before he realized—or admitted to himself—where he was heading. He almost veered off and turned around. Almost. Something kept him from doing it. Perversity, Caitlin's accusations, a kind of morbid curiosity—he wasn't sure just what was motivating him.

In Forestville he took the cutoff that wound through thick pine and redwood forest to Guerneville. The river, he saw as he crossed the new flood bridge, seemed even lower than usual for this time of year—a slender, silt-brown, twisting thing whose main segment was more than a hundred miles long, stretching from its headwaters near Potter Valley to its ocean mouth at Jenner, fifteen miles to the west. The Native American name for it was Shabakai. "Long snake." Sleeping snake in the summer and fall, lying placid under the early-November sun; it didn't look dangerous at all. But it could be as deadly as any rattler when it grew bloated enough with winter rains to exceed its thirty-two-foot flood stage. The last time that had happened, three years ago, the river had crested at forty-six feet and three people had died, the entire populations of Guerneville and its smaller neighbors, Rio Nido and Monte Rio, had had to be evacuated, and scores of low-lying summer homes and year-round residences had been swamped with water or mud or both.

Most of the people kept coming back. Repairing, rebuilding, replacing lost possessions. River dwellers, those who lived along the Russian

River year-round, were a special breed. Modern-day pioneer stock. The harder they were battered, the greater their losses, the more determined they became.

His grandfather, Cameron Gallagher the First, had been like that. He'd built the river house in the thirties, as a summer place, and when he'd retired from his law practice after World War II, it had become his permanent residence for the last dozen years of his life. Grandpa Cameron had been the first to die there, of natural causes. His only male offspring, Paul, had inherited the house but none of Grandpa's hardiness or spirit. A weak man, Paul Gallagher. And a lousy attorney because he'd had no passion for the law, had taken it for a profession because it was what Grandpa Cameron wanted; *his* burning ambition had been to own an antiquarian bookshop. Pa, the bookish wimp. A quiet introvert driven to booze by a hot-pants wife he couldn't handle and to violence when he'd had Rose's infidelities shoved in his face once too often. He'd deserved better than he got. Not that what he'd done to her and himself and by extension to his son and daughter was forgivable, but he wasn't the monster Caitlin tried to make him out to be.

Cam could feel depression moving in on him as he drove west out of Guerneville. First Caitlin and now this unwise decision to revisit the dark center of his past—another wallow in the same old mental sewer. His headache had worsened, too. Please, Jesus, not a migraine, he needed to be able to drive home. But it didn't feel that bad. No thrusts of pain down through his sinus cavities and into his eyes, no nausea or dizziness or gathering weakness in his limbs. Tension, nothing more.

Better turn around anyway, head home. But he didn't do it. The compulsion to see the river house again was still on him. Beloit had suggested he do it at one of their sessions, he remembered. "Often, Mr. Gallagher, the wisest course is to confront the creatures that inhabit one's nightmares. They are seldom so terrifying when faced directly in the light." Psychobabble with a core of truth. He'd told Beloit he'd do it, but he hadn't. It had been too easy to find excuses not to follow through.

Well, he was following through now. Up to a point, anyway.

Monte Rio. Moscow Road. And finally Crackerbox Road near Duncans Mills. A little enclave strung out along its mile-and-a-half, dead-end length, mostly on high grassy banks crowded with pine and rock maple and wild grape. A jumble of architectural styles and sizes, from country cottage to rough-log cabin to rustic homes on large lots. And a third of the way west of the Duncans Mills bridge, across the road from a steep and heavily wooded slope—

The river house.

Cameron Gallagher I's pride. Paul Gallagher's folly. Cameron Gallagher II's bane.

He swung off the narrow road onto the grassy verge in front. God, yes, the place was run-down, much worse than Caitlin's property in Sebastopol. Tall grass and shrubs and tangles of blackberry vines choked the once neat front yard. One of the tall old pines on the riverbank had come down in a past storm; most of it had been chopped up for firewood, evidently, but its heavy, root-webbed base had been left to rot in and out of the hole where it had stood. Near it were scattered bits of branches and sprays of chain-saw dust and chips that made him think of the carcass leavings of predators. The open-fronted garage on the other side of the house looked as though it might not survive another winter, even if the house did; in any case it wouldn't be long before it collapsed into a jumble of rotting boards like the gardening shed beyond it. A handyman hired by Riverbank Realty in Guerneville came in once a month, but even if he was competent, there was only so much one man could do in seven or eight hours every thirty days. And the last tenants, an unreconstructed hippie and his brood, obviously hadn't cared enough about their surroundings to bother with even minimal upkeep.

Cam rubbed at the ache above the bridge of his nose and behind his eyes, drew a deep breath before he left the car, and walked over to what was left of the front fence. Slats missing, picket tips broken off, inward sags here and there, the gate hanging from one hinge . . . Christ. From there he stood looking at the house itself.

Scabrous. That was the first word that crossed his mind. A once handsome two-story modified Victorian that had been allowed to deteriorate into something resembling an Addams Family summer home. Or a haunted house out of an Edwardian ghost story. Off-white paint faded, peeling, worn off in spots and splotched with mildew and water stains in others; shingles gone from the roof, pieces of trim dangling loose or gone completely, a section of the porch railing ripped away. Grandpa Cameron would've been appalled. But then, Grandpa Cameron would have been appalled at most of what had gone on in this place over the past three decades.

The window in the near attic dormer drew his eyes; he could not quite make himself turn away without looking at it. The glass was streaked and dirty and had a jagged crack in it. The streaks made him think of tear stains, the dirt of dried blood, and in spite of the day's warmth he felt a faint chill. A corner of his memory lifted and let him see the interior of the attic the way it had been that night twenty-five years ago, the shapes massed and crouching in the gloom, the huddled figure on the mattress. Violently he shook his head, yanked the memory flap closed again.

I shouldn't have come here, he thought. Why the hell did I come here?

He got back into the car. Thinking then that what he ought to do was hire somebody to torch the place, give the insurance money to Caitlin, and be done with it that way. Or do the job himself, some dark night when he could screw up enough nerve. Just jerking himself around: He wouldn't do either one. Not made that way. Cam Gallagher, law-abiding citizen. Cam Gallagher, gutless wonder, like his old man.

He swung into a quick U-turn, headed back toward the intersection with Moscow Road. He hadn't gone far when he passed a dark blue Mazda drawn off onto one of the narrow turnouts. A man sat hunched behind the wheel, his face averted as Cam drove past.

When he glanced into the rearview mirror and saw the Mazda pulling out behind him, he didn't think anything of it. But the blue car was still there when he crossed the bridge and turned onto Highway 116 east, still there through Monte Rio and Guerneville, still there—maintaining the same speed and distance behind—all the way to Santa Rosa. He was feeling vague stirrings of apprehension by then, and they grew sharper when the car trailed him onto Highway 101 south and matched his speed there, too, changing lanes whenever he did.

Coincidence. He kept telling himself that. But his stomach was knotted and his palms were moist when the Mazda followed him onto the Los Alegres turnout, then into town. What if it followed him home? If that happened—

But it didn't happen. He turned right on D Street, and the blue car kept going straight down Los Alegres Boulevard.

The relief he felt was out of proportion to the incident. Better watch out, Gallagher. You're getting paranoid on top of everything else. No one's following you. Of course not.

Why would anyone want to stalk Cameron Gallagher?

Sunday, Nov. 1

Dear Annalisa,

I'm writing this from a place called Los Alegres, California. A little town north of San Francisco.

Are you sitting down? Better sit down if you're not because I've got BIG NEWS. The news we've both been waiting for so long.

I found him, baby.

I FOUND HIM!

No mistake. It's him, it's really him. I knew it as soon as I saw him two days ago. It was like he'd stepped right out of the sketch.

His name is Cameron Gallagher. Big shot in the Paloma Valley wine business. He could've been in Denver that night on a business trip, or maybe he was there with a woman who wasn't his wife. He was with somebody like that the first time I saw him. Wouldn't you know he'd be that kind?

He lives here, in a big fancy house in the hills. I found out some other things about him today. I think he has AN-OTHER woman he's cheating with in ANOTHER town nearby. But I need to know for sure about that and a lot of other things about him before I decide what I'm going to do.

One thing I already decided. I'm not going to do it quick

like I thought I would when I found him. That'd be too easy. I want him to suffer like you have suffered and I have suffered. I know that doesn't sound like me but I'm not the same man I used to be, honey, not after what he did to you. He's going to suffer. And I'll make sure he knows why before I'm finished with him.

Rest easy, baby. It'll be over soon and then I'll be back with you again. If you were better now and could put your arms around me and tell me you love me too I'd do it quick and come right home to you. But I know it's going to take a lot more time for you to get well, so there's no hurry and I'll stay here and do it right. That's the best gift I can give you besides all my love, always.

Your devoted husband,

Nick

PART II

Stalk

ou have no clear idea of why you are compelled to sleep with this woman?" Dr. Beloit asked.

"No. That's why I'm here."

"Would you say she is unusually attractive?"

"Not unusually, no. Sexy. Very sexy."

"As attractive as your wife?"

"Yes, but not in the same way."

"As sexy as your wife?"

"Same answer."

"Does your wife satisfy you sexually?"

". . . Yes."

"Why did you hesitate?"

"I don't feel comfortable answering questions like that."

"Perfectly understandable," Beloit said. "Do you love her?"

"My wife? Yes, very much."

"So naturally you don't wish to see her hurt."

"Naturally. No."

"Or your daughters hurt."

"No."

"Yet a sexual liaison with Jenna Bailey could hurt them. You understand that."

Sexual liaison. Cute. "If they found out. I wouldn't let that happen."

"Are you certain you could prevent it from happening?"

"No. I'm not certain of anything right now."

"How would you characterize your feelings for Ms. Bailey?"

"Lust, I suppose. Animal magnetism."

"Nothing more than that?"

"You mean love? No."

"How do you suppose she feels toward you?"

"Pretty much the same."

"A mutual desire for conquest and gratification."

"Not conquest, not on my part."

"Have you ever had an extramarital affair?"

"No. Never."

"Do you think that could have a bearing on Ms. Bailey's interest in you?"

"That I'm married? Or that I've never had an affair?"

"Either or both. Have you discussed it with her?"

"No. But anyone who knows me knows I don't cheat. She could have found out easily enough."

"Some women find the seduction of a faithful husband to be an appealing challenge."

"I don't believe Jenna's like that."

"Could an affair be advantageous to her business relationship with you?"

"No. She's not like that, either. And neither am I. Her motives are probably pretty simple, doctor. She's horny, and she thinks we might be good together in bed."

Not a flicker of a smile from Beloit. "But it is not that simple for you, is it?"

"I don't know, maybe it is. I wonder how it'd be. Any man would."

"Do you expect she might provide something lacking in your relations with your wife?"

"I don't understand the question."

"Some sort of sexual activity you covet."

"You mean something kinky? No."

"How would you define kinky?"

"How would you define it, doctor?"

"We are not discussing my sex life," Beloit said. "We are discussing yours."

Smug, Cam thought. He moved uncomfortably in the big padded armchair. Did Beloit even have a sex life? He was a little man in his fifties, not much over five feet tall, with a blob of a head and a pushed-in face and bushy eyebrows and a hooked nose and stary eyes behind thick-lensed glasses. Mr. Potato Head. One made of punched and poorly molded Silly Putty. He was married, though. Wore a wedding ring, and on his desk was a framed photograph of a woman and two young men. Cam had never gotten close enough to examine the photo, and glancing at it now he felt a sudden urge to stand and reach over and pick it up, find out just what sort of woman would marry a Potato Head and what their progeny looked like.

Cruel, petty, and unfair. He knew it, told himself such thoughts were unworthy of him, and tried to blank his mind to all but the issue at hand.

"It has nothing to do with particular bed games," he said, "kinky or otherwise. It's just—an unfocused need, a compulsion that I can't make go away."

"There are many different types of compulsions," Beloit said. "Would you say yours falls into the category of a fatal attraction?"

"I don't . . . fatal? What do you mean, fatal?"

"As in negative reinforcement, a repressed desire for punishment."

"What? You think I want her to *hurt* me?"

"What I think isn't relevant. What do you think?"

"I'm not into pain, doctor. Physical or mental. Besides, Jenna is hardly the acid-throwing or bunny-boiling type."

Beloit looked at him steadily and blankly.

"I guess you didn't see the movie," Cam said.

"You said you aren't into pain. Are you positive of that?"

"Of course I'm positive. I'm not a masochist."

"Yet haven't you allowed yourself to be continually battered by the events of your childhood?"

"So now we're back to that."

"Do you see any relationship between your childhood trauma and your compulsion to commit adultery?"

"No."

"Take a moment to consider it."

"I don't see any relationship," he said, but he was lying. He saw it clearly enough. He'd seen it all along.

"Isn't it possible this new crisis is linked to all the others in your life, that it has the same source?"

Cam shifted position again. His eyes shifted, too, so that he was looking at the couch across the room. Did any of Beloit's clients ever lie on that couch? Probably not. It looked brand new, virginal, like a stage prop. People expected a psychoanalyst's consulting room to have a couch, so there it was.

"I'm not self-destructive," he said.

"Why did you use that term?"

"Why? It's what you think I am, isn't it?"

"As I've said, Mr. Gallagher, it is what you think that matters."

"All right, then. I just said I'm not. No way."

"Have you ever had a self-destructive impulse?"

"Suicide? No. I couldn't do that to my family."

"Yet you feel you could commit adultery."

"It's hardly the same thing."

"Do you think about dying?"

"Not much, no."

"About death in the abstract?"

"I don't know what you mean by that."

"Death as a release from pain, a source of peace."

"No. Didn't we go over all this once before?"

"We did, yes." Without consulting his notes.

"And my answers were the same?"

"Yes, I believe they were."

"Well, then? Why go through it all again?"

"Do you believe in God? In the concepts of heaven and hell?"

"Oh, come on, doctor. What do my religious beliefs have to do with anything?"

"They have bearing on your state of mind," Beloit said. "A man who believes strongly in God and an afterlife will react differently to physical and emotional stimuli than a man whose beliefs are weak or nonexistent."

I shouldn't have made this appointment, Cam thought. This is why I quit seeing him, all this glib psychobabble. He isn't helping me. He can't help me. I ought to get up and walk out of here right now.

"I believe in God," he said. "I can't tell you how strongly, because I'm not sure myself. I've never been much of a churchgoer."

"A merciful God or a vengeful God?"

"Both, I guess."

"Both?"

"Depending on circumstances."

"In your parents' case, a vengeful God?"

"I suppose so. Against my mother for her sins."

"And your father?"

"The instrument of her destruction."

"A man without sin, then?"

"I didn't say that."

"He was the object of divine vengeance, too, wasn't he? To have committed a cardinal sin and then to die by his own hand?"

"I . . . can't answer that. All I know is that my father was a victim. Just like my sister and I were victims."

"Of your mother?"

"Of her deceit, that's right."

"Do you believe her soul was consigned to hell?"

"I don't know what hell is." That's a lie, he thought immediately. I've had glimpses, haven't I?

"The Old Testament variety, let's say. Eternal damnation in fire and brimstone."

"I hope so."

"Your father's soul?"

"I don't know . . . no."

"Most religions believe murder and suicide are mortal sins, punishable by—"

"I don't care about that. What kind of questions are these, anyway, all this metaphysical stuff?"

"Pertinent questions, if you accept the fact that you have a deep, unresolved hatred of your mother and that you pity your father. That seems quite clear. Do you accept it?"

"Yes. Except for the unresolved part."

"You don't feel you need to resolve your hatred for her?"

"Resolve it how? How can I not hate her, after what she did? How can I forgive her?"

"Resolution doesn't necessarily mean forgiveness."

"Then what does it mean?"

"You loved your father as much as you hated your mother. Is that correct?"

"Yes."

"You are sorry he's dead."

"Sorry he died the way he did, yes."

"And you are glad your mother is dead."

"She got what she deserved."

"Do you feel any guilt for being glad?"

"Not a bit."

"Isn't it possible you do without being aware of it?"

"I don't buy that. Why should I feel guilty?"

"You might if at a subconscious level you feel responsible, at least in part, for what happened to your parents."

There it was again, the same baseless half-accusation Caitlin had thrown at him last Saturday. If he didn't know better, he'd think she was seeing Beloit, too. He sat forward, his hands gripping the chair arms, a band of tightness beginning to pull behind his eyes.

"What could I have done to prevent it?" he said thinly. "Tell me that. I didn't even know what was happening until I heard the shots, until it was already over and done with."

"I did not say you could have prevented the tragedy."

"You said I blamed myself—"

"I *suggested* you may feel a sense of responsiblity and guilt."

"And I told you I don't."

"Perhaps not where the tragedy itself is concerned," Beloit said, "but in the events leading up to it. Your mother's relationship with the man you call Fatso. We have already established that you knew about the affair prior to that fateful night."

Fateful night. Beloit had missed his calling; he ought to be writing scripts for bad TV psychodramas. Cam pressed knuckles tight against the bone above his eye sockets, eyes squeezed shut. When he opened them again, the doctor's Potato Head face swam fuzzily before it settled into focus.

"Yes. I knew about it."

"You told me, I believe, that you actually caught them in flagrante delicto."

"So?"

"And that you told your father what you saw."

"You bet I told him."

"When?"

"The next day. As soon as I saw him again."

"What was his reaction?"

"He was mad as hell, naturally. Wouldn't you have been?"

"Did he confront your mother?"

"Yes. I heard him yelling at her."

"You were not in the room at the time?"

"No, they were in their bedroom with the door shut."

"Did he threaten her?"

". . . I don't remember."

"Did you know he owned a handgun?"

"Yes. He used to take me shooting. Target shooting."

"Did he ever threaten your mother with the weapon?"

"I don't remember. What—"

"Try to remember. Did your father ever threaten your mother with death or physical violence in your presence or hearing?"

"I don't . . . Maybe. Once."

"Before or after you told him of your mother's affair with Fatso?"

"Before. What're you getting at now?"

Beloit took off his glasses, squinted myopically while he polished them with a monogrammed handkerchief, put them back on. "What was your exact reason for telling your father about the affair?"

"I wanted him to know."

"Why did you want him to know?"

"He was my father, she was cheating on him in his own house, our house—he had a right to know what was going on."

"What did you believe he'd do?"

"I didn't think about that."

"Not consciously, perhaps. But it is possible, isn't it, that you told him because at a deeper level you felt it would provoke him into an act of violence against your mother, the woman you hated? That you wanted him to carry out his threat, to—"

"No!"

"—to shoot and kill her because you wanted her dead?"

"It wasn't my fault! None of it was!"

"Of course not," Beloit said quietly. "The point is, such destructive desires in a child can lead to repressed feelings of guilt in the adult. Guilt in turn may lead to self-hatred, which in turn—"

"I don't blame myself, I don't hate myself." The office seemed to have grown unbearably stuffy; he couldn't get enough air into his lungs. "None of this . . . I don't like where this is going. It doesn't have anything to do with Jenna Bailey. I came here for help—"

"Help is what I am attempting to offer, Mr. Gallagher. Insight into your motivations past and present, including those regarding Jenna Bailey."

"By trying to get me to admit I have some sort of death wish?"

"By asking you to consider a possible core reason for the psychological problems that continue to plague you—an escalating pattern of self-punishment brought about by your childhood trauma and your subsequent unresolved feelings of hatred for your mother and culpability in her death. Emotional dysfunction, the migraine headaches and periods of depression, the borderline alcoholism, and now the urge to commit adultery might all be part of such a pattern. If left unchecked, the subconscious urge for punishment can lead to a disintegration of one's defenses and result in more overt acts of self-destruction . . ."

There was more, but Cam no longer listened. Babble, just babble. When Beloit finally ran down, Cam said, "Your theory, core reason, whatever it is, is wrong, doctor. Wrong. Yes, I hated Rose, she was a slut and a lousy mother and I'm not sorry she got what was coming to her, but I never wanted her dead. Never wished it, never prayed for it, never once even thought about it let alone colluded in it. I wasn't that kind of boy. I'm not that kind of man."

Big solemn eyes stared back at him, magnified by the thick lenses, like disembodied eyeballs floating in a pair of jars. Compassion in them? No, nothing in them. Nothing.

"So now we're right back where we started," Cam said. "I've still got a compulsion to sleep with Jenna Bailey, and I still don't know why. You haven't helped me one damn bit."

"I am sorry you feel that way."

"Not half as sorry as I am."

"I can't tell you what to do about your desire to commit adultery, no matter what the motivation. The decision is entirely yours. I can tell you this: If you give in to it, you will be hurt. Your wife and family are likely to be hurt as well, but you most of all. Perhaps irretrievably so." Beloit's glance sideslipped to his desk clock. He folded his hands together and said, "I am afraid our time is up for today, Mr. Gallagher."

"Just like that? Time's up, good-bye, come back next week if you haven't self-destructed by then?"

"I have another appointment at five o'clock."

"And you need fifteen minutes to get the taste of me out of your mouth."

The silent stare.

Cam's headache had worsened. "What am I going to do?" he thought and then realized he'd said the words aloud.

Beloit didn't respond to that, either. Beloit didn't know or care, bottom line, because he was one of the lucky ones, the well-adjusted ones—Beloit didn't have a head full of ghosts and furies that were eating him alive. So how could he know, really understand, what it was like to be snack food for demons?

N ick followed Gallagher for a week, off and on, varying the places where he picked him up. Sunday, Gallagher took his family down to the marina on the Los Alegres River; four of them got into a white cabin cruiser, big and shiny new, and went off down the river. His boat. Another rich bastard's toy. Nick hung around there for a while, looking things over, thinking maybe the boat and marina would work out for him. Didn't feel right, though. They had wire-enclosed ramps leading down to the slips, and you couldn't get into them unless you had a key. Only other way out there was by swimming. Besides, he was a farm boy, mountain boy, truck jockey. He didn't know diddly about boats.

Monday, Tuesday, Wednesday, Gallagher went straight back to Los Alegres after work. Goodwill let Nick off at four, so he had plenty of time to drive over to the Paloma Valley, get into position. Thing he couldn't figure was why Gallagher hadn't hooked up with the brunette with the Lexus again. Could be he'd read the situation wrong and she wasn't Gallagher's bimbo. Except the way she'd been snuggling up to him in the hotel bar, it sure looked like they were getting it on together. Must be some reason he hadn't been to see her. Made Nick curious, even though it probably didn't mean much as far as his planning was concerned.

Thursday, when he drove by Paloma Wine Systems at four-thirty, the BMW wasn't there. Left early. To see the bimbo, finally? Nick drove around for a while, didn't spot the WINEMAN license or the white Lexus, gave it up and headed back to Los Alegres, and set up on the street below where Gallagher lived, the only way up to Ridgeway Terrace. And here he came at six-ten, looking grim in the frame of the driver's window as he flashed past. Must've been a quickie, Nick thought, if he was with the brunette. Or else they'd had an argument and he was going home without it.

Friday was the same as Monday, Tuesday, Wednesday—Gallagher went straight home after work. Halfway through the hills that day, Nick turned off, turned around, and headed back to Paloma. Feeling restless, wanting to drive instead of sit and wait. Circled the square, keeping a sharp eye out, and what do you know—there was the white Lexus slotted in up the street from the Hotel Paloma. He parked a few spaces away, walked back to double-check the license number. The brunette's, all right.

He crossed to the hotel, went into the bar. She was there. Different table this time, two guys in suits and another woman with her, all of them sipping wine and laughing it up. Nick wedged himself at the bar, ordered a beer, paid three bucks for it—man, these prices—and watched the brunette.

She kept sipping and laughing, and a couple of times she put her hand on the silver-haired guy next to her, and once she leaned up close and whispered in his ear and then kissed his mouth when he turned toward her. Slut. Nick had seen her type before. Her classiness was the kind some women put on like lipstick, along with their fancy clothes. Underneath she was hard, no mistake. He could see how hard she was all the way over here. Guys like Gallagher, all they saw was the body and the hot eyes and the white smile. Didn't look any deeper. All they wanted was sex. She'd be plenty good in bed, this one. Do anything a guy wanted and some things he wasn't even expecting. But that was all it was, all it'd ever be—just fucking. Her kind only loved one person, only cared about one person. The one living inside their own skin.

Watching her made him miss Annalisa so much he could feel the hurt like fire down low in his belly, same kind of pain he'd felt when he was thirteen and his appendix had almost burst and he'd had to have an emergency operation. He turned away, looked at his beer until the pain eased and he was okay again. When he looked back at the table, one of the waitresses was over there and the four of them were ordering another round.

He maneuvered along the bar until he was next to the waitress's slot when she came up. "Four more Fenwood chard," she said to the bartender.

Bartender said, "At least they drink their own. What's the occasion?"

Waitress shrugged. "Who knows. TGIF."

Nick watched the bartender pick up a bottle. Backbar lighting was bright enough so he could real the label: Fenwood Creek Reserve Chardonnay, 1997. He shifted his gaze to the waitress, caught her eye, smiled at her.

"Is that Fenwood Creek a good wine?" he asked.

She looked him over, decided he was just being friendly, and shrugged again. "So they say. I can't afford it myself."

"Me, either, if it costs more than five bucks a bottle."

That got him a small, crooked smile. "Costs five bucks a *glass* in here."

"Ouch. All those people work at Fenwood Creek?"

"That's right."

"Dark-haired woman in the green suit. Her name's Linda, isn't it?"

"Linda?" Waitress glanced over her shoulder. "No, that's Jenna Bailey."

He repeated the name. "She somebody important there?"

"Acts like she is."

"Sounds like you don't like her much."

Another shrug. "I don't like anybody who leaves chintzy tips." Bartender put four full glasses on her tray. Waitress hoisted it without looking at Nick again, took the refills to the table.

Lull in the conversation over there as the waitress served them. And then the Bailey woman was looking up and across, straight at Nick. He saw her stiffen, the smile wiped off her mouth; she said something to the silver-haired guy next to her, and the guy looked, too. Hell. She'd noticed him watching the night she was in here with Gallagher, caught him watching again, and now she was starting to get up. Nick shoved away from the bar, pushed through the crowd. Not hurrying, not taking his time.

Outside he crossed the street, went halfway to the Mazda before he glanced back. Jenna Bailey hadn't followed him out. Nor any of the people she'd been sitting with.

Nick took the wheel. Wait around, trail her home? Better not. Might be a long time in there, might not go straight home when she left. Might be wary enough to spot him, too—ID the car, get his license plate number. He knew her name, where she worked; that was enough for now. Find out where she lived later on, if he needed to know.

It's the laughter that wakes him up.

He knows right away what's going on. Her and Fatso, downstairs in the spare bedroom. When did Fatso show up? He's not supposed to be here. Didn't Dad warn her she better not let Fatso come around here anymore?

I hate you. I hate you, Ma.

I'm gonna tell Dad about this, too. You better believe I am. Soon as he comes up tomorrow.

The laughter stops. Now it's quiet again.

I know what they're doing. How can she do it with Fatso, right here in our house? How can she do it with him at all? That time I saw them, her all white and sweaty, him with his belly and hairy ass, and she was . . . I never thought I'd see her do anything like *that.* . . .

Banging sound. Bedboard hitting the wall.

Another laugh that turns into a kind of yell.

He puts his hands over his ears, burrows down deep under the covers.

After a while he pokes his head out and listens. Quiet downstairs, but now it's raining again. Wind howling, rain smacking on the roof and against the window. Is Fatso still here?

He gets up and goes to the window. There's his truck in the yard. Jeez, is he going to spend the whole night here?

I hate you, Ma. You and him both.

He's in bed again when he hears the voices downstairs. Loud at first, Fatso saying, When can I see you again, sweet tits? Her saying, Keep your voice down, you want to wake up the kid? Then he can't hear what they're saying because the door's open and the wind is whistling in. Then the door bumps shut again. Outside, Fatso's truck starts up, and he guns the engine the way he likes to do. Damn son of a bitch Fatso. Then the truck backs out and roars off, and it's quiet again except for the storm.

But not for long.

Now there's another car in the driveway. Not Fatso's truck, engine sound's different—Daddy's car! Dad's here!

He jumps out of bed, rushes over to look. Dad's car, all right, Dad getting out and running through the rain. Door slams downstairs. Hard footsteps heading for the kitchen. "Rose? I know you're down here, I saw his truck." Thump, thump. "Right where I knew you'd be, you bitch." And then Dad starts yelling and swearing, real loud. Oh jeez, he's pissed! I never heard him that pissed before.

And she starts yelling back at him, calling him dirty names. She sounds drunk. Sure she is, her and Fatso must've been drinking whiskey. They did that the last time, too.

Her: Do what I please, don't have to answer to you, fucking bastard.

Dad: Whore, slut, right here in our house with the boy upstairs, what kind of mother are you.

Smack. Shriek. Wow, he must've hit her! Serves her right, the dirty whore.

Her: Leave me alone damn you don't you lay a hand on me again or you'll be sorry.

Dad: Had all I can stand can't take any more.

Her: Chrissake what're you doing with that, put that thing away, are you crazy?

Dad: Show you what I'm going to do with it.

Her: You don't have the guts you wimp you pisspoor excuse for a man.

He's over at the door now, opening it, looking out and listening. And then—

Bang!

Oh no, that sounded like a gun—

"Rose!" Dad's voice, different, all moany and wild like the wind. "Rose, God, I didn't mean . . . Rose!"

Little noises.

"No!" Dad again, like he's wailing. "No no!"

Quiet.

And then—

Bang!

Dad, Daddy, what—?

And he's in the hallway, at the top of the stairs. His heart is pounding like it wants to burst through his chest. He leans over the banister and stares down. Dark except for light coming from the kitchen, long pale wedge of light.

"Dad?"

Thud, thud, thud of his heart.

He's afraid, more afraid than he's ever been. He doesn't want to go down there, he's so scared of what he'll find. But he has to go, he has to find out—slow and then fast and then slow again as he reaches the bottom.

"Dad? Daddy?"

Thud. Thud, thud. Thud.

Along the hall into the kitchen. It's empty. Lights are on in the back bedroom, too, and he keeps going that way, the floor cold under his bare feet. He's shivering as he nears the open bedroom doorway—

Smell comes out at him and makes him stop.

Burned smell. Gunpowder smell.

Don't go in there, don't look!

He goes in, he looks—

Oh God oh shit!

Both of them—

Dad Daddy on the floor—

And her on the bed—

And the gun on the floor—

And bright red all over both of them, her nightgown, his head and face, wet, glistening, dripping—

Daddy's eyes are open, staring, and her eyes—

Shut no open and staring too no shut—

There's a roaring in his ears, he can't hear—

He wants to run but instead he goes to Daddy, maybe Daddy's not dead, and he bends down and looks close—

Dead dead dead.

And the gun lying there—

Don't touch it don't pick it up!

Roaring, roaring, and the fear and the cold and the blood—

And then he—

He looks at her again, he can't stop himself—

She's on the bed with her eyes shut—

Open.

She opens her eyes.

Suddenly she opens her dead eyes and she's staring back at him, right into his face—

And he's running shivering running crying running back up the stairs but not into his bedroom up the attic stairs hide in the attic safe in the attic scared cold shaking all over Daddy she opened her eyes but she didn't but she did hide hide hide!

"SHE OPENED HER eyes," Cam said. He was shaking the way he had that night, oiled in sweat. He felt sick and disoriented. "This time it was different. . . . This time she opened her eyes and *looked* at me."

Hallie held his head against her breast.

"Always before I dreamed it the way it happened. I didn't look at her again after I bent down over my father, I just ran. But this time I looked. She was dead, but she opened her eyes and stared right into my face. As if she were—"

"As if she were what, baby?"

"Accusing me," he said. "As if it really was my fault she was dead."

ight riding again.

Empty Sunday, Gallagher staying home with his family this weekend, and the restless need for motion prodding him back into the Mazda, the security of metal and leather and chrome, even before it got dark. Around and around Los Alegres until nightfall, then out onto the freeway. Friday night it'd been south, San Francisco, San Jose, Stockton, Oakland. Tonight it was north, up through Santa Rosa. Missile hurtling through the dark, lights blooming and dying, blooming and dying, laser-beam slices and neon flashes and little winking pinpricks like fireflies, like holes burning in black suede. Radio playing "Since I Met You, Baby," "Me and Bobby McGee," "Big Girls Don't Cry," "Yesterday," "Help Me Make It Through the Night," "Rocky Mountain High," "You've Got to Hide Your Love Away," "For the Good Times." Every song reminding him of Annalisa, the life they'd had together, until Garth Brooks's "Night Rider's Lament" came on and made him smile a little. Thinking part of the time—Annalisa, Gallagher, half-formed ideas that weren't ready to jell yet. Rest of the time not thinking at all, just driving, listening to the music and watching the night unfold.

Straight up Highway 101 past some place called Cloverdale, west on a back road to Boonville, north on another one to Ukiah, north again to a junction, quick stop for gas and coffee, then east on another two-laner into Lake County, Pomo County, all the way around Lake Pomo.

Dark water out there flashed the night at Clearwater Lake into his mind. Fourth date with Annalisa. Long drive, different roads and terrains, fast for a while, slow for a while, and he'd started wanting her more than he'd ever wanted any woman. Wanted her from the first time he saw her, but it was love and sex all mixed together this time, the long night ride and her sitting there beside him and the scent of her perfume and her body like some kind of aphrodisiac. Excitement building in her, too, he could see it every time he glanced over at her. She'd moved close to him, warm hip touching his, soft breast pressing his arm, heat climbing and climbing until it gave him a hard-on. Same kind of thing for her, she'd told him later, making her wet and tingly all over, making her want him as much as he wanted her.

Finally he'd stopped the car on the lookout above Clearwater Lake, nobody else around, moonlight splashed on the mountains and trees and water and sky. Soon as he shut off the engine, they were kissing. Couldn't shuck out of their clothes fast enough, he couldn't get inside her fast enough, they couldn't come fast enough, and at the same time, too, everything just about perfect even then.

I love you, Annalisa. His first words to her afterward.

I love you, Nickie. Without missing a beat.

Next day, first thing next morning, he'd gone out and bought the ring and then gone to her apartment and asked her to marry him. . . .

Back on the state road now, heading toward Williams and Highway 5, letting the good memories and the music flow through him. Hardly any traffic—after midnight by then—and the night empty and black. Then there was a burst of light as he came around a curve, somebody with his brights on and driving too fast, road narrow here, and the lights veering suddenly into his lane. He swerved, the lights veered back just in time. Close. So close the two cars nearly scraped sides as they tore past each other.

Didn't bother Nick too much after his pulse rate slowed down. He'd had close calls before, two or three. Drunks, tired people, people in too big a hurry, damn-fool truck jockeys on speed—night rider's hazards, you just had to accept them. Only one accident in the thousands and thousands of miles he'd logged in his life, that one nothing but a fender bender up in Idaho, not his fault, not much damage, cops hadn't even been called and everything settled on the spot with the other driver.

Crazy. Crazy that he burned up the highways and back roads, wore out eight or nine sets of wheels, and all he'd ever had were a few close calls and the one fender bender, and Annalisa'd gone out to the store one snowy January night, only a six-block drive, and look what'd happened to her. Wasn't right, wasn't fair, odds were all wrong, but there it was. Where the hell was the sense in a thing like that?

Wasn't much sense in anything, the way it seemed sometimes. Everything random, lot of crazy luck good and bad. Bad luck that Annalisa's car had picked that night to break down, bad luck she was in the wrong place at the wrong time a few minutes later. Good luck that nothing had happened to him on the road, that he'd been in the right place at the right time last Thursday afternoon when Gallagher showed up to meet his girlfriend. You couldn't do much about it either way, bad or good. Let it happen, take advantage of a situation when you could, don't worry about it when you couldn't.

Williams coming up. Better head south on Highway 5, head back to Los Alegres. Be at the auto court by four, get three or four hours' sleep. He didn't have to be at the Goodwill until nine tomorrow.

Funny, but he wasn't tired. Work all day, drive half the night, and he was still wide awake. Good, keen edge hadn't worn down much at all.

On the radio now, Simon and Garfunkel's "The Sound of Silence." He'd never understood that song when he was living in Denver, back when everything was right with Annalisa and him. Now he did. Now, alone, driving, holding on to the night, he knew what every word of it meant.

enna called early Monday morning.

He was on edge as it was; the sound of her voice honed it. Bad weekend. He'd had that same nightmare twice, the disturbingly altered one where the bloody Rose opened her dead eyes and stared at him, and he'd drunk too much in a futile effort to blot it out. The constant grinding ache behind his eyes had been there for days and was only partly hangover. And now Jenna.

"Well," she said, "you *are* in residence. I thought you might've gone on a trip somewhere." Soft tone but without the purr; with a veiled sharpness instead. Like razor blades hidden in silk sheets.

"I've been busy. It's that time of year."

"Yes, Cam, I know. We're busy up here, too."

"Of course you are."

"I almost called you at home on Saturday," she said.

His left hand, resting on the desk blotter, spasmed involuntarily. He lifted it, held it out; watched it shimmy slightly. "Why would you want to call me at home?"

"Not for the reason you think. You remember that man in the Hotel Paloma bar? The one who was watching us?"

"What about him?"

"Have you see him again since that night?"

"No. Why?"

"He was in the hotel bar again Friday night. Watching me this time."

". . . Are you sure?"

"Sure it was the same man? Yes. Sure he was watching me? Yes. Bryan noticed him, too. I was there with Bryan and Dennis Frane and his wife."

He didn't know what to say. He could feel his nerves crawling under his skin.

"I would've confronted him," Jenna said, "but he left before I could. Bryan stopped me from going after him. I wish he hadn't."

"Why would you want to confront him?"

"You know how I feel about weirdos, Cam."

"Maybe he just finds you attractive."

"It wasn't that kind of watching. He's up to something."

"Come on, Jenna."

"I want to know what it is," she said. "I should think you would, too."

"Me? Why me?"

"It was you he was staring at hardest the first time."

"I don't know about that. And I wasn't there Friday—"

"Don't be an ostrich, for heaven's sake."

"Jenna . . . what's the point of getting worked up over some harmless guy you've seen twice in a bar?"

"How do you know he's harmless?"

"I don't know it, but I'm assuming—"

"Yes, well, I'm assuming he isn't."

"On what grounds? He hasn't done anything to you, or to me. People look at each other, it's not a crime."

"It is if he's a stalker, a rapist. I know what I'm talking about, Cam. It happened to me once before."

"You were stalked, raped?"

"Yes. Let it go at that—I'm not going to relive the details with you. You're certain you haven't seen that man in the past ten days?"

"Positive." His mouth was dry. I need a drink, he thought. Nine-thirty in the morning, and already I'm lusting after a martini. "What do you want to do about this, Jenna? What do you want me to do?"

"Nothing," she said. Something new and unpleasant seasoned her voice, like a rancid buttering. Disgust? "I simply wanted to make you aware of a potentially dangerous situation."

"Okay, I'm aware of it. I don't happen to agree, that's all. Do you mind if we discuss something else?"

She said, "Right now we don't have anything else to discuss," and broke the connection.

He tried to get back to work, but he could no longer concentrate on the proposed new list of Oregon state regulatory requirements he'd been studying. The conversation with Jenna kept replaying in his head. Stalked and raped . . . a hell of a thing, an awful thing. It explained her hard-core fascist outlook, but it didn't mean her interpretation of a stranger's looks and actions wasn't colored by paranoia. Rape victims were often paranoid about men, strangers, and who could blame them? Still, this man hadn't bothered her in any way, by her own admission. And that stuff about the man staring hardest at him—

The blue Mazda on Crackerbox Road, the one that had followed him back to Los Alegres.

Christ, he thought, the same man? No, of course not. Somebody who happened to be going where he was, a simple coincidence. And even if it was the same man—

Even if it was—

Dangerous to him? Nonsense. Dangerous how?

Dangerous *why?*

23

F armer's name was Kells, Joe Kells. Old guy, past seventy, beanpole thin and spry for his age. He reminded Nick of his old man. Same body type, same stringy cords in his neck. Big difference was, Kells liked to hear himself talk, and the old man'd never said more than ten words a day to anybody if he could help it. Didn't have any friends, didn't even leave the farm much after Mom died. Nick never could get close to him, hadn't felt much when the heart attack killed Pa two days after Nick turned seventeen. Only three people came to the funeral, one of them the prairie neighbor who bought their land on the cheap. Neighbor said to Nick after the service, "Good man, your father. Just didn't fit comfortable in the world."

Say the same thing about Tom Hendryx's son.

He don't fit comfortable in the world anymore.

This guy Kells owned a place out in the country west of Los Alegres. Truck farm, vegetables and alfalfa. Decided to clean out his low-lying barn, he said, "before El Niño hits and floods it again like last time." Called up Goodwill, and Nick and his helper, Eladio, went out to pick up the stuff Kells was donating—old gas range that still worked, kitchen table and chairs, swamp cooler, bunch of tools and odds and ends.

Kells insisted on helping them load the truck. He talked the whole time, hopping from subject to subject. Seemed to have a good memory and said he'd lived in the area all his life. So Nick picked his spot and primed him about Gallagher. He'd taken to bringing up Gallagher's name, asking questions, every chance he got to work it into a conversation. Picked up a few things here and there, most interesting a hint of something that'd happened to Gallagher's parents a long time ago. If anybody knew the details about that, he figured maybe it was this old guy Kells. And he was right.

"Sure, I know Cam Gallagher," Kells said. "Not to speak to, we don't travel in the same circles, ha ha. Just by what I hear. Family used to be important people around here. His grandfather was mayor of Los Alegres in the forties. Didn't know him, but I knew his son, Paul. Paul was a lawyer, too. Did some legal work for me back in the sixties, land deal that got bollixed up and he straightened it out, saved me close to three thousand dollars. Poor bastard didn't deserve his fate, but hell, how many of us do? Cam Gallagher's the last of the clan. Well, except for his sister, and Paul's sister, Ida—"

Nick asked, "What happened to Paul that he didn't deserve?"

"Killed himself. Shot himself in the head."

"That right?"

"Yep. Shot his wife first. Killed her and then killed himself, bang, bang, bang. Left those two kids orphans just that fast."

"Gallagher and his sister."

"Yep. Don't remember her name. Started with a *C* like his. I think she still lives around here somewhere. Not Los Alegres, some other town."

"Why'd Paul shoot his wife?"

"Caught her cheating on him. She was a grade-A bitch, slept around before and after she was married. Everybody knew it, she didn't seem to give a fig. Rose, that was her name. Good-looking woman but a slut and a boozehound. Paul knew about her sleeping around, no way he couldn't've known. Must've loved her plenty to put up with it long as he did. But a man can only take so much. One night he up and snapped. Drove up to their house at the river when he wasn't expected, caught some fella there with her, shot her and then himself. Don't recall why he didn't shoot the lover, too. It'd been me, I'd have made a clean sweep."

"House at the river, you said. What river would that be?"

"Russian River. Gallagher family had a house up there. Cam's grandfather, first Cameron Gallagher, he's the one who built it."

"Cam still own the place, do you know?"

"Can't say I do because I don't, ha ha. Don't see why he would after what happened there. Near Rio Nido, I think it was. No, Duncans Mills. Papers called it the House of Death, they always got to make everything sound worse than it is. But it was a pretty big deal at the time. We don't get many murders around here."

"When did all of that happen?"

"Oh, must've been better than twenty years ago. More like twenty-five. Hell of a thing for those kids. Cam in particular. Scarred him, I'll bet. Don't see how it couldn't have."

"Why do you say that, Mr. Kells?"

"He was there that night, him and his mother spending the weekend at the house. Middle of winter, don't remember exactly when. She went up there to meet her lover, took the boy along as camouflage. You know, so Paul wouldn't figure she'd be up to anything with the kid in the house. Too bad for both of 'em he did figure it out."

"Did Cam see it happen?" Nick asked. "The shootings?"

"Saw it or heard it. Saw the bodies, anyhow, his own father and mother. *Had* to've scarred him, he couldn't've been more than nine or ten at the time."

"What happened to him and his sister afterward?"

"Oh, Ida and her husband took 'em in and raised 'em. Ida and Frank DeLucca. Grew grapes over in the Paloma Valley, that's how Cam got into the wine business—sort of grew up in it. Frank's dead now, been dead four or five years. Ida still lives somewhere in the valley, far as I know."

They were finished loading the truck. Nick filled out the receipt on his clipboard, gave it to the old guy to sign. "There you go, Mr. Kells. Thanks for the donation."

"Sure thing," Kells said. "Always glad to help out whenever I can. What'd you say your name was?"

"Nick."

"How come you're so interested in Cam Gallagher, anyway, Nick? You know him?"

"I'm getting to."

"Well, he's a nice enough fella, even if he does live high on the hog. I hear he drinks what he sells, but hell, you can't blame him for that. I'd drink myself if I went through what he did. Scars. You know what I mean, young fella?"

"Sure," Nick said. "I know just what you mean."

C am spent two days fighting off a vague hunted feeling every time he went out in public. Jenna's paranoia feeding his paranoia and leading to half-furtive glances at people on the streets, in cars, in restaurants, on the lookout for the face of a man he'd seen exactly once in his life, at a distance in a crowded bar. Imagining menace riding in every blue Mazda.

He didn't see the face.

He didn't see any trailing blue car.

By Tuesday night he felt like a thorough fool. One of life's serio-comic nutcases, like the ones who imagined they were alien abductees or the victims of ultrasecret government death-ray experiments. He told himself to cut it out, quit driving with one eye on the rearview mirror, quit staring at everybody as if they were lunatics ready to hurl themselves on him without provocation, jibbering epithets and wielding lethal weapons. Get a grip.

He wondered if he ought to have another session with Dr. Beloit. Decided the answer was no. What good would it do? He'd had enough of Beloit's brand of psychoanalysis; the last thing he needed was a reprise of last Thursday's fiasco. And sure as hell the good doctor would try to turn the suggestive fear of a stranger into another example of the alleged self-destructive impulses of Cameron Gallagher. He could work through this temporary kink on his own.

As for Jenna, he thought he could handle that situation, too, now. Her paranoia, like her fascist views, was a turnoff; the compulsion to sleep with her wasn't nearly as strong as it had been. Confine his dealings with her to a business environment, and he'd be able to control the temptation. He was convinced of it.

All he had to worry about now were the nightmares, and the headaches, and the depression that always came with the long, dark days of winter. . . .

ounty library in Santa Rosa stayed open late on weeknights. Nick found that out and drove up there. Librarian told him they had issues of both the Santa Rosa and Los Alegres papers on microfilm, going back more than twenty-five years. But they weren't indexed, so you had to know the approximate dates of whatever you were trying to find, then scan each issue in that period.

More than twenty years, old man Kells'd said, closer to twenty-five. Middle of winter. Narrowed it down some. Start back twenty-three years, say, work up to twenty-five, keep it to the winter months, November through February. See what that bought him.

He went into a room with the librarian. She brought out the files of the *Santa Rosa Press Democrat* for November and December of '75, January and February of '76. Showed him how to work the machine, got him started, left him alone.

Slow work, even though he only looked at the front pages because Kells'd said the shootings made a big splash. Still had to crank through the rest to get to the next day. Wasn't anything in '75/'76. And '74/'75 wasn't the right winter, either. He got '73/'74 and started in on those— and there it was.

January '74. January 4. Something stirred in him, cold and hard, when he saw the date. Same week of January that Gallagher'd hurt

Annalisa, only four days' difference. January 8, he'd never forget that date. Gallagher's month and week for disasters.

MAN KILLS WIFE, SELF AT RUSSIAN RIVER.

Paul Gallagher, thirty seven, Los Alegres lawyer. Rose Adams Gallagher, thirty-five, housewife and mother. Domestic argument ends in double shooting. Alcohol involved, infidelity suspected. Only other occupant of the house at 1600 Crackerbox Road the couple's ten-year-old son, Cameron. Boy found unharmed, hiding in attic. Second child, eight-year-old daughter, staying at the home of a friend in Los Alegres.

Nick read the article again. Read the next day's follow-up story. Few more details there: Woman shot twice in the chest, husband blew his brains out, some guy named Halloran questioned and admitted being wife's lover and also in the house that night—but Nick didn't care about any of that. Wasn't much about the kid except he was under a doctor's care.

He asked for the January '74 file of the *Los Alegres Argus-Courier*. Story in there didn't tell him much, either. One of the boy's teachers described him as "a sensitive child" and one of the brightest students at his school. Sensitive. Man oh man.

On the way out of Santa Rosa, Nick kept thinking about the coincidence—both tragedies, his and Gallagher's, happening in January only four days apart. He thought about the house where the shootings had happened—1600 Crackerbox Road near Duncans Mills. That was where Gallagher'd gone two Saturdays ago. Same house? Must be. Did he still own it? Find out.

He had ideas now. Little more information, little more planning, they'd come together and he'd know just what he was going to do.

Hallie said, "I called Caitlin just before you came home tonight. To invite her to Thanksgiving dinner."

"What'd she say?"

"What she always says. She has other plans."

"I don't know why you bother every year."

"She's family, that's why."

"Did you tell her Aunt Ida will be here?"

"Yes. She said, 'Cam must be happy about that. He was her favorite.'"

"That's not true. Ida didn't play favorites."

"I know. She didn't sound good, Cam."

"How do you mean?"

"Oh, you know, upset and stressed out. There was a lot of yelling in the background."

"Teddy?"

"No, a man's voice. Heavy on the profanity."

"Hal, the mechanic. Her new live-in."

Leah asked, "What's a live-in?"

"Never mind," Hallie said. "Just eat your supper."

"It means the new guy she's sleeping with," Shannon said.

"Thanks so much for teaching your sister what she doesn't need to know."

"I *already* know about that stuff," Leah said.

"Anyway," Shannon said, "I'm glad they're not coming. Aunt Cat's no fun, and Teddy's a creepy dork."

"That's a fine way to talk."

"Well, he is. A dork and a dickhead."

"Shannon. Watch your mouth."

"What'd I say?"

"You know what you said. This is the dinner table."

"As if I didn't know."

Leah said, "Can I have some more broccoli?"

"Jeez. She actually *likes* that stuff."

"*May* I have some more," Hallie corrected.

"Okay, may I?"

"Shannon, pass the bowl to your sister. Cam?"

"Mmm?"

"You're awfully quiet."

"Am I? Not much to say, I guess."

"You've hardly touched your food. Don't you like the casserole?"

"It's fine."

"Eat some of it, then. If you don't, after what you've had to drink—"

"Two martinis and a glass of wine. Big deal."

"Cam," she said warningly.

"Okay. Okay. Pass that broccoli over here, squirt."

"I'm not a squirt."

"Look like one to me. Cute little squirt."

"Phooey," Leah said. Then she said, "Shannon almost got run over today."

"What!" From Hallie.

"Oh, it wasn't any big deal," Shannon said.

"That's not what you told me. You said you almost got squashed like a bug."

"Shut up, you."

"What happened, for heaven's sake?"

"Well, I was like coming home from school—"

Leah said, "You're not supposed to use the word 'like.' "

"Shut *up*. I was coming home from school, you know, walking my bike up the hill—on the sidewalk, not in the street—and this blue car came flying around the corner—"

Cam said, "Blue car?"

"Yeah. It came flying around the corner, real close to the curb. If I'd been in the street, it *would've* squashed me."

"What kind of blue car?"

"I don't know, a blue car."

"Who was driving it?"

"A guy. I never saw him before."

"What did he look like?"

"Jeez, Dad, it all happened so fast—"

"Was he about my age? Thin, dark hair?"

"No. A young dude. You know, from the high school. He had a girl with him, sitting real close. I'll bet she was fooling around with him, and that's why he—"

"Shannon!"

"Well, you wanted to know what happened, Mom."

"Thank God you weren't hurt. The way kids drive nowadays—" Hallie broke off and then asked him, "Cam, what was that about a dark-haired man in a blue car?"

"Nothing important. Just . . . an overreaction."

"To what?"

"I had words with a man in a blue car the other day, at a stoplight downtown. One of those traffic things."

"You don't really think . . . ?"

"No, of course not. There's no reason to worry. It's nothing at all."

He poured himself another glass of wine.

nnalisa came to him in the night, the way she did sometimes. Warm, soft, sweet-smelling. He could feel her breath on his cheek, the touch of her hand, the satiny surfaces of her breasts and thighs as she snuggled against him.

"I'm cold, Nick. Make me warm."

"Sure. You never have to be cold when I'm here." . . .

"Oh God, Nickie, you made me come three times. Three times!"

"Let me rest awhile, and we'll try for four." . . .

"Would you mind if we had a baby? I mean, soon. I think I might be pregnant."

"Mind? You know I want to have kids with you." . . .

"False alarm. I took the test today, and I'm not."

"There's plenty of time, honey. We've got all the time in the world, make as many babies as we want." . . .

"Oh, what a beautiful watch! Oh, Nick, it must have cost a fortune! Are you sure we can afford it?"

"Absolutely. I wanted you to have something really nice for Christmas." . . .

Fingers playing in his hair. Sharp little teeth nibbling on his earlobe.

"Let's go for a night ride, Nickie."

"I was thinking the same thing. We'll make it a long one, the longer the better." . . .

"Another false alarm. I didn't want to tell you until I was real sure."

"Plenty of time, all the time in the world." . . .

"Could we go out to San Diego sometime? I'd really like to see it again, where I used to live. Show it to you."

"Sure we can. This spring. I've been with Miller's long enough, I'm pretty sure they'll let me take an early vacation." . . .

"Look at that snow come down! Brrr. I'm glad we're in here together where it's warm."

"How about we go to bed and get even warmer." . . .

"Nick, Nick, Nick, oh God Nickie you feel so good inside me."

"I love you, Annalisa, I never loved anybody the way I love you." . . .

"We're out of coffee, hon. I'm going down to the store and get some."

"Maybe I better go instead. Snowing pretty hard out there now."

"No, you stay here and read the paper, you worked hard all day. We need a few other things, too."

"Okay, but go to the Addison Grocery instead of the supermarket. It's closer."

"I will."

"And be careful. Streets are icy as hell."

"Don't worry, I'll be back before you know it."

Lips brushing his cheek, hand waving. Gone.

And gone from beside him—

—and he was alone someplace else, standing beside another bed looking down at her, hospital smells, hospital white, oh God her face, so pale, all those bruises, and the bandage around her head . . .

"Annalisa! Say something, talk to me!"

"She can't hear you, Mr. Hendryx."

"Will she be all right? She's going to be all right, isn't she?"

"We're doing everything we can, but she suffered a severe head trauma from the collision with the telephone pole."

Head trauma. Telephone pole. Annalisa . . .

"What happened, officer? Tell me what happened."

"Her car stalled about a block from the Addison Grocery. She was walking there to call for help, call you, probably. Car came barreling out of the market lot, too fast for the conditions, skidded on a patch of ice, and sideswiped her, knocked her into that pole."

"Driver didn't stop to help her?"

"Didn't even slow down. Hit-and-run. Woman who was pulling into the lot saw the whole thing. The man was in the store right before it happened, buying aspirin. Clerk said he looked drunk or sick. Caught a glimpse of the car he was driving and thinks it had a rental sticker. He gave us a good description of the man. If necessary we'll have a police artist do a sketch. Don't worry, Mr. Hendryx. We'll find him."

Don't worry don't worry. Find him find him find him . . .

"Why can't you find him?"

"I don't have an answer for you. I wish to God I did. The sketch we had made has been in the papers, on TV, and the clerk swears it's a good likeness. We've had a few calls, but—"

"What about the rental car?"

"We've checked all the agencies in the Denver area. Boulder, Fort Collins, the Springs. It's possible the car was rented out of state, if it was rented at all."

"But there must've been damage . . ."

"All the auto body shops in the state have been alerted. The truth is, there might not've been much damage. He didn't hit your wife head-on, he sideswiped her, just enough impact to throw her into that pole. No broken glass or paint samples at the scene. Small dents or bumper scrapes, maybe, but that's the kind of minor damage that goes unnoticed on rentals."

"You're telling me he's going to get away with it. Is that what you're telling me?"

"No, sir. We haven't given up. We'll keep doing everything we can until we find him."

Didn't find him didn't find him didn't find him—

—and he was back in bed and Annalisa was beside him again, warm, soft, whispering.

"They'll never find him, Nickie."

"I know it. I know they won't."

"He's going to get away with it."

"No. *I'll* find him. I promise I will, I swear it."

"But how, if the police couldn't?"

"I don't know, but I will. No matter how long it takes. Someday, somehow, I'll make him pay."

"Oh, Nick, I love you."

"Just don't ever leave me. I promised, now you promise. Don't leave me, Annalisa."

"I won't, I promise. Except now, for a little while."

"No . . ."

And gone again.

Empty darkness all around him, nothing but the night.

On Friday morning, when he checked his e-mail at the office:

```
Last chance, Cam. Call me. J.
```

Last chance. Well, that made things simple, didn't it? Ignore the message, and the Jenna crisis was history. When he saw her again, there might be some strain for a while, but they'd both get over that. It wouldn't affect their business relationship—

Or would it?

What if she was as predatory as Maureen claimed? Spurn a predatory woman, especially one with paranoid tendencies, and you were likely to make a bad enemy. Jenna could do him some damage if she felt like it—do Paloma Wine Systems some damage. Fenwood Creek was one of PWS's major clients, and she had the power to take their compliance business elsewhere. She knew a lot of people in the valley, important people in the industry, some of whom could be swayed by a campaign of lies and innuendoes. . . .

Cut it out, Gallagher.

Jenna wasn't like that. Her interest in him was temporary and strictly physical, just as he'd told Beloit—nothing more than an itch. She'd find somebody else to scratch it for her; the valley and the industry were loaded with eager scratchers. One thing about her he was absolutely certain of: She was not a one-man woman.

He thought of Hallie.

And with a feeling of relief, he consigned Jenna's message to his electronic wastebasket.

o trouble finding his way back to Crackerbox Road. Like most truckers, he'd always had a good sense of direction. Go to a place once, if he needed to find it again he could, without getting lost or having to read a map.

He noticed the scenery more this trip. Pretty area. Tall pines, red-woods, dark river snaking along, old-fashioned little resort towns. And the ocean not too far away. Mountain country, the Rockies, was what he preferred after growing up on the flat prairie east of Denver, but Anna-lisa, she'd like it here. Maybe he'd bring her out someday after she got better . . . no, that wasn't a smart idea. Wouldn't be good for her to spend any time in the place where the man who'd hurt her had lived.

But he'd bring her to southern California like he'd promised. San Diego, where she'd been born and grew up—family moved to Denver when she was sixteen. Pacific kid. Called her that once, she laughed, so he kept teasing her with it afterward. Annalisa Foster, the Pacific Kid. Always talking about going back there, not to live but for a visit. No way he could've said no to her even if he'd wanted to. All the plans they'd made for the spring trip to San Diego . . . drive at night, sleep during the day, longest night ride they'd ever taken together. Getting excited himself, talking about it that January night right before she went out to the store and didn't come back and Jesus why hadn't he gone instead? Why had he let her go out alone on such a rotten night?

Questions he'd asked himself a thousand times before, ten thousand times. No sense beating himself up with them all over again. Finished, done with, no way to go back and change any of it.

Gallagher. Gallagher was now.

Annalisa was later. She was the past and the future.

The house Gallagher'd stopped at was just up ahead. Nick pulled off as he neared it, parked behind a Geo with a banged-in rear fender. For Rent sign was still there next to the front gate, property still looked deserted. He'd only seen the house from a distance before; closer in, it was bigger than he remembered, two stories, lots of land around it. Nice once probably, falling down now. Place where Gallagher's father and mother died, all right. Number 1600. He hadn't been able to find out yet if Gallagher still owned it. But if not, why'd he drive all the way up here and stand around on the road for five minutes looking at it?

Front gate was partway open. Nick went through, waded among weeds and grass to the porch. Riddled with dry rot and termites, wonder it hadn't collapsed already. People and their houses. He ever owned one with Annalisa, and he would because she wanted one so much, a place for their kids to grow up in, he'd take care of it, keep it up. You had a responsibility to take pride in the place where you lived. Not enough people gave a damn anymore.

Overgrown path to one side that led around back. He followed it past a snarl of berry vines, a collapsed shed—and there was a woman back there, sitting on what was left of a rear stoop, smoking a cigarette, looking down a grassy bank at the river. He pulled up short, then started to back off, but she heard him and swiveled her head his way. He stopped again. She didn't get up or change position, just sat there watching him.

"I didn't know anybody was here," he said.

"Just me and the birds."

"Thought I'd take a look around." Smile. "Saw the For Rent sign, and the property seemed deserted—"

"You interested in renting it?"

"Doubt I can afford it."

"It's cheaper than you might think."

"You the real estate agent?"

"No, the owner. Well, one of the owners."

"Mind if I ask your name?"

"Caitlin," she said. "Caitlin Koski."

Nick kept reaction from showing in his face. Piece of luck—big piece. She was the woman Gallagher'd visited in Sebastopol. Not another bimbo after all, but his sister. One of the newspaper stories about the shootings said Gallagher's younger sister was named Caitlin, he remembered that now.

"Come on over here," she said, "so we don't have to yell."

He went to where she sat. Wasn't much to look at, not half as pretty as Annalisa, but she'd probably be all right if she washed her hair, put on some makeup, dressed in something besides jeans and a sloppy sweatshirt. Then she turned her head a little more and he saw the fresh bruise on her temple, a big red welt below her ear.

"I know," she said, "I look like I got mugged. I've been sitting here feeling sorry for myself."

"Did you?"

"Did I what?"

"Get mugged."

"No. At least not by a stranger after my money."

"What happened?"

"Fight with my boyfriend last night. Ex-boyfriend. I threw the prick out this morning."

"I'm sorry," Nick said.

"Yeah, well, he's no loss. Too free with his hands."

"You call the cops on him?"

"What for?"

"Man hits a woman, he ought to be in jail."

"Now, that's a refreshing attitude. But it wouldn't change Hal's ways any. Only make him mean enough to come after me once he got out." She didn't sound bitter or angry, just matter-of-fact. Been through crap like that before, he thought. She had that beat-up-by-the-world look. "You know my name—what's yours?"

"Nick. Nick Hendryx."

"Well, Nick, this is a good property, even if the house doesn't look like much. Plenty of room inside and out, three bedrooms, two baths, fully furnished, and half an acre of land. Nice view and a private beach. You have a family?"

"No."

"Married?"

"Long story about that."

"Uh-huh. We've all got one, right? So you're alone?"

"For now."

"Kind of a big place for one person, but maybe you like a lot of space to rattle around in."

"Sure," Nick said. "What's it rent for?"

"Eight-fifty. That's cheap for riverfront property."

"Cheap for a house anywhere. Lease or month-to-month?"

"Either way. I'm flexible."

"How much up front?"

"First month plus five hundred security deposit."

"I don't know. Thirteen-fifty's a lot of cash."

Her eyes moved over him. Taking his measure and liking what she saw. He could tell that from the way her face changed some, softened. She didn't seem so hangdog anymore, either.

"We could work something out on the security deposit," she said.

"Would the other owners go for that, Mrs. Koski?"

"Caitlin. I haven't been Mrs. Koski in years."

"Maybe they wouldn't want to budge on the deposit."

"Don't worry about that. Only other owner is my brother, and he doesn't give a shit . . . doesn't care about this place. I do, so I'm the one who makes the rental decisions."

"How come he doesn't care, your brother?"

"He's got more money than he knows what to do with, for one thing."

"There another reason?"

"It's personal."

"Sorry."

"So am I. But it's not your problem." Her eyes kept moving on him.

Nice eyes, best thing about her—big, brown, direct. "So what do you think, Nick?"

"About what?"

"About living here."

"Well, I'd have trouble swinging even the first month's rent right now. I just moved into the area, just got a job. Most of my savings are long gone."

"Where're you living? Here at the river?"

"No, in Los Alegres."

"Where my big brother lives." She took out another cigarette, offered the pack to him. He shook his head. Popped an M&M to show her he had a vice, too. "I guess you wouldn't want that long a commute."

"I don't mind driving," he said. "Thing is, job I have isn't much. Doesn't pay much."

"So you're looking for something better?"

"Yeah. Or a second job to bring in more money."

"Planning to stay in the area, then?"

"Like to. Weather's better than Denver."

"That where you're from, Denver?"

"Mile High City, that's right."

She got to her feet, smiling at him. He knew that kind of smile. "A man who's willing to work two jobs, wants to settle in one place, says he's sorry when he doesn't have to, and doesn't believe in smacking women around. I didn't know they made guys like you anymore."

Didn't know what to say to that, so he just shrugged.

"You'd make a good tenant," she said.

"Thanks. But I just don't see how I could swing it."

"Like I said, I'm flexible. And nobody's exactly been eager to rent the place, this late in the year. How about a look inside? The grand tour."

"Sure, if you don't mind."

"Then maybe we can go somewhere, have a cup of coffee, see what we can work out. Sound like a plan?"

"Sounds like a plan," Nick said, smiling.

is monthly Sunday-morning golf game didn't go well. Nine holes at the Paloma Valley Country Club with Toby Charbonneau, Lloyd Edmonds, and Pete Hines of Stellar Vineyards. Cam couldn't keep his mind on either the game or the usual banter and shop talk; his thoughts wandered, touching on Jenna and Beloit and the phantom stalker and then shying away again.

He shot a very poor seven over par—triple bogey on the eighth hole. That had always been the trouble with his golf, a lack of concentration. The Los Alegres club pro had told him once that he had a natural swing and a good feel for the subtleties of the game, and that if he worked at it, learned how to focus properly, he could be a scratch player, perhaps win a tournament or two. Smoke in the wind. He had enough difficulty staying focused on the important things in his life. Golf was recreation, a means of doing business—nothing more.

They broke for lunch, with the intention of playing the back nine afterward. It didn't happen because of the weather, heavy clouds all of a sudden, cold wind, light drizzle. "El Niño taking an early leak" was the way Toby put it.

When the foursome broke up after lunch, Lloyd walked out to the car with him. "You seem kind of spacey today, Cam. Troubles?"

Lloyd was one of his better friends. Better, not best—he had no best friends, he thought wryly. No one he was close to except Hallie. No one he could talk to about serious matters except Hallie and his succession of shrinks. Lloyd was a good listener—six-figure-per-annum attorneys had to be good listeners—and Cam had known him since high school, went fishing and played golf with him, got together with Lloyd and Janet and their two sons for family outings. But their conversations were limited to subjects that were either superficially personal or impersonal, like sports and politics. Lloyd knew about the Gallagher Family Tragedy, as people used to call it, but neither of them had ever mentioned it, not once in twenty years. As if it were some sort of unspeakable secret.

He said, "Lot of things on my mind, Lloyd."

"Nothing serious, I hope."

"No. Nothing serious."

"You okay to drive?"

"I didn't have that much to drink."

"Not what I meant. Funny thing about driving—you need to keep your mind on the road."

"I'm okay," he said. "You know me, buddy. Mr. Cautious behind the wheel. Never an accident, never a citation."

"Yeah, well, first time for everything."

Mr. Cautious, he thought as he drove home—carefully, observing all the traffic laws. In one sense, that was a good name for him. Steady, plodding, not a reckless bone in his body. The closest he'd come to any sort of rash act was Jenna Bailey, and now that was a closed issue. Yet in another sense, the name didn't fit him at all. A genuine Mr. Cautious was well adjusted, conservative, rock-solid; nobody who drank as much as he did, who had his history and was as screwed up inside as he was, could ever be any of those things. It was as if he were two people, one living inside the other, wanting to be the other. Like the putative thin man inside every fat one.

Hallie had taken the girls to lunch and a movie; the house was too quiet without them. He poked around among the CDs, found one that more or less suited his mood, and put it on. A drink? Better not. He sat and listened to the music, but restlessness popped him back up again after a few minutes. Reading, watching TV, doing homework—none of it appealed. Damn rain, he couldn't even go outside and putter in the garden. Here comes El Niño. Here comes winter.

He wandered aimlessly around the oversize family room, stylishly decorated in Danish modern—a far cry from the dark, solid furniture he preferred. Pottery lamps, decorative pottery bowls, handwoven curtains, all in harmonious beige and blue. Even his chair—Dad's chair, the family called it—was a blue contoured thing that wasn't as large or as comfortable as he'd have liked. Hallie's tastes, Hallie's choices, right down to the geometric Mondrian prints on the walls. Well? He'd said it didn't matter to him how they decorated their new home, and it hadn't at the time or for years afterward, but now for some reason it did.

The room was Hallie's. And the kids': schoolbooks and video games scattered around, one of Shannon's sneakers peeking out from under the sofa. There wasn't one item in it that had his stamp, that reflected his personality in any way. It was as if he were an intruder here.

He passed through the other rooms, and it was the same thing. Even the bedroom, even the brass-frame bed—Hallie's. Hallie's house, the girls' house. The only room he could call his own was his study, and even that seemed somehow impersonal. What did it say about him, really? Computer that he used for work or to idly surf the Internet when he was in the mood. Model of a sailing ship that somebody'd given him so long ago he couldn't remember who it had been. Wine posters—freebies from people in the industry. Rolltop desk that Hallie had bought as a surprise birthday present after he'd admired it in an antique store. Shelves of books that he hadn't read in years or meant to read and kept finding excuses to avoid. Was all this *him*? Was any of it him?

Who am I? he thought. Mr. Cautious? Mr. Wanna-be Normal? Mr. Fucked-in-the-Head? Mr. Nobody?

I don't know, he thought. I don't know who Cameron Gallagher really is.

And maybe that's because the real Cameron Gallagher died along with Rose the whore and Paul the suicidal weakling the night of January 4, 1974.

Mr. Impostor. A man with no identity at all, posing as a dead man.

31

Finding a second job wasn't as easy as finding the first, because this one had to pay well. Night or day work, didn't matter, but night was better so he could keep the Goodwill driving job. He spent all week hunting, lunch hours and evenings and part of one afternoon off. Every place he went was a bust.

Then on Saturday morning he walked in on the right one at the right time. Poultry processing outfit north of Los Alegres, driver needed for P.M. deliveries. Guy in charge, Mr. Statler, told him the job had already been filled but he was in luck because the driver they'd hired had busted his leg, guy's wife had just called with the news. So the job was Nick's if he could take out a load of dressed birds to Modesto right away tonight. Nick said sure. Mr. Statler gave him a tour of the plant, went over his routes and schedules. Saturdays and Sundays, Wednesdays and Thursdays—two different routes, south to the Central Valley, Modesto, Turlock, Merced, places like that, north to Chico, Red Bluff, Redding, each route twice a week and almost all of it night riding. The other bonus was the salary. Twenty-two an hour. Almost as much as he'd make if it was a union driving job.

So now he had something to tell Caitlin Koski. Perfect timing there, too. She'd rent him the house now for sure—not that he'd had any doubt of it. Wanted him for a tenant, but that wasn't all she wanted. Made it plain she was interested in *him*. Supposed to see her tonight, talk some more about the house. Call her, switch the date to next week, next Friday, offer to take her out to dinner. Play her along and get her to open up about Gallagher.

He didn't like stringing anybody along, especially a single mother with a load of problems, but it had to be done. Funny. In a way he liked her, too. Wasn't physical, she wouldn't have attracted him even if he didn't love Annalisa so much. But she had those pretty eyes, that direct way of looking at you. And a direct way of talking, no b.s., nothing hidden. He admired that. It was how he'd been, tried to be anyway, before all the hurt and suffering. Now he had to make compromises, like it or not. For Annalisa's sake.

Caitlin Koski. Another one who'd been hurt plenty in her life, and not just from being smacked around by some asshole's big fists. Look at her up close, spend a few minutes with her, you could see the scars. He felt sorry for her. Liked and felt sorry for the sister of the man who'd nearly killed his wife. Crazy, wasn't it?

Maybe not. Caitlin hadn't been in Denver that snowy January night. Wasn't her fault. She'd suffer some for it in the end, couldn't be helped, but not too much—she wasn't close to Gallagher. Wouldn't be anything like Annalisa's suffering. Or his.

He shook his head, driving, thinking about all this. Should feel pretty good, getting the night hauling job for good wages, getting the house at the river, getting close to paying Gallagher back. But right now he didn't, much.

Sad. That was how he felt right now.

Kind of sorry-sad that there had to be so much hurting for almost everybody in this life.

Over the next couple of weeks Cam worked hard at being Somebody. Mr. Rock-Solid, Mr. Normal, Mr. Good Husband, Father, Provider. He spent long hours at the office, and the fact that Jenna neither called nor e-mailed him made it easier to stay focused. The one time she phoned PWS on business, she'd asked specifically for Maureen.

He quit playing hunted man, studying faces and watching for blue Mazdas. He eased off on his drinking. He made love to Hallie with renewed vigor, easin' round the side each time to keep the damn jockey out of their bed. He went to Leah's pre-Thanksgiving dance recital—she had an eight-year-old's unshakable certainty that she was destined to be a great ballerina—without having to be coaxed. He bought Shannon the new computer she'd been lobbying for for months (*she* wanted to be a software development engineer). He made arrangements to attend a four-day wine festival in San Diego in early February with Hallie, not telling her so he could spring it as a surprise when the time came.

Even the weather cooperated. Late fall had always been his favorite time of year, and the last half of November was particularly nice this year. Sunshine and cloudless skies, most days, even on Thanksgiving. And the leaves turning in the vineyards a brighter, shinier red-gold than usual, as if they'd been sprayed with lacquer. The prospect of winter didn't seem quite as bleak as it had. The predicted two hundred inches of El Niño-spawned rainfall seemed an empty threat, the stuff of doom-sayers and the disaster-hungry media.

The nightmares left him alone; so did the more severe headaches. He seemed to have more energy. He even began to look forward to Christmas and all its trappings with a kidlike exuberance.

There hadn't been much joy in Christmas when Rose Adams Gallagher was above ground. His father had tried to make the Yuletide season festive for Caitlin and him, six-foot trees groaning under the weight of ornaments and lights and tinsel, mounds of presents, caroling with and for the neighbors. But Rose had invariably found ways to spoil the good times. Complaints, snide little digs ("You don't need a pair of roller skates, Cameron, you're so clumsy you'd probably break a leg"), fits of pique when she didn't get her way, booze-provoked quarrels that led to shouting matches. The last holiday before she died, she'd turned up missing at the family's traditional Christmas Eve gathering; went off somewhere in the early afternoon—to celebrate with one of her boy-friends, no doubt—didn't come home until long after everyone was in bed, never explained or apologized to him or Caitlin; Paul had told them she'd been visiting a sick friend, but it had been such a bitter and obvious lie that Cam hadn't believed it for a second.

The Christmases afterward hadn't been much better. Aunt Ida and Uncle Frank had tried, but they'd been childless before and were resent-ful of being saddled with two young kids, ashamed that the kids were issue of a murderer and the town slut, and the combination of resentment and shame had made growing up in their Paloma Valley house an expe-rience without much laughter or fun, even on holidays. He'd vowed that his own children would not have that cross to bear, and he'd kept the promise. Even during his worst periods of depression, Shannon and Leah had had happy Christmases, Easters, Thanksgivings.

One day at a time. He'd tried that philosophy before; now, at least for the present, it was working—he was almost the Somebody he longed to be.

One day at a time.

om Foster? It's Nick."

"Nick! Lord, it's good to hear your voice."

"Yours, too. Guess it's been a while."

"Too long. We've been worried about you."

"No need. I'm taking care of myself."

"Where are you, honey?"

"California."

"California's a big place."

"Little town out here. Mom, how's Annalisa?"

". . . Oh, Nick. She . . . I wish . . ."

"Is she any better?"

"No . . . the same. Same as before."

"I miss her so much, I had to call."

"I know you do. So do we."

"What do the doctors say?"

"Oh, they . . . you know how doctors are."

"But they're still hopeful, right?"

"Yes. Still hopeful."

"Does she recognize you and Pop yet?"

"No. She . . . no."

"Does she say anything at all?"

"No."

"Can she feed herself, get out of bed?"

"No. Nick, honey . . ."

"Insurance hasn't run out or anything yet?"

"Not yet, no."

"So the money situation's okay?"

"Yes."

"You sure? I can send you some if—"

"It's all right, Nick. We have plenty of money."

"Well, that's good. How's Pop?"

"He's the same. You know Pop."

"Still working ten hours a day at the store?"

"And more. It helps keep his mind off . . . you know."

"How about you? You doing okay?"

"Managing. I wish Pop were here, I know he'd like to talk to you. Why don't you call him at the store?"

"Maybe I will."

"Or I'll have him call you. What's your number there?"

"Public phone, Mom, like always."

"Nick . . . why don't you come see us? Come home?"

"That's one of the reasons I called. I am coming home."

"Oh! That's wonderful news. When?"

"Middle of January, about, if everything works out."

"How do you mean, everything?"

"Some things I have to take care of."

"What things?"

"For Annalisa and me. Things that'll help her get better."

"Can't you tell me what they are?"

"Not now. They're private, Mom."

"Couldn't you come for Christmas? We'd love to have you here for the holidays."

"I'm working two jobs. I couldn't swing it."

"What sort of jobs? You don't mind my asking?"

"No, I don't mind. Driving jobs. One of them pays pretty well, but I've got some expenses."

"Is there anything you need? Anything we can send you?"

"Annalisa is all I need. Annalisa to get well. . . . Mom? You crying? I didn't mean to make you cry."

"It . . . I'm all right. It's not you, honey."

"Don't feel bad. She'll get well. She will. You have to believe that as much as I do. Don't ever stop believing it."

"Nick?"

"Yes, Mom?"

"We pray for you. Every day Pop and I pray for you."

"That's good, but Annalisa's the one who needs your prayers. All our prayers. Pray for her, okay?"

"I do. You know I do."

"Sure, I know."

"Will you call Pop now? Talk to him?"

"Maybe not right away. I've got to work tonight."

"Nick . . ."

"In a few days. When I can."

"When will I hear from you again?"

"Christmas, maybe. Before the middle of January."

"And you will come home then? Promise?"

"If I've done what needs to be done by then."

"Can't you just give me a hint what—"

"Good-bye, Mom. Give Annalisa all my love. And don't stop praying for her."

The message to call John Lacey at Riverbank Realty was waiting when Cam returned from lunch on the first day of December. Some damn fool decided to rent the place after all, he thought. He called Lacey back, but not until he'd dealt with two other messages and signed a batch of letters Gretchen, his secretary and receptionist, had left on his desk.

"Have you spoken to your sister recently, Mr. Gallagher?"

"No, I haven't. Why?"

"Well, she's found a tenant for the house."

"*She* has?"

"Yes. She called this morning and asked me to draw up the rental agreement."

A note of disapproval in Lacey's voice prompted Cam to ask, "Is there some problem with that?"

"Not exactly a problem. It's just that she made the arrangements herself, without consulting with me. Or with you, evidently. And she wants to waive the security deposit."

"For what reason?"

"She wouldn't give a reason, except that she personally vouches for the renter."

"Renter. One person, for a house that size?"

"That's right. A man named Hendryx, Nicholas Hendryx."

"I see."

"Do you know him, Mr. Gallagher?"

"The name isn't familiar, no."

"His current address is South City Apartments, Los Alegres."

South City Apartments was a fancy name for the semisleazy auto court down near the freeway. Terrific.

"What does he do for a living?" Cam asked.

"Two places of employment," Lacey said. "Goodwill Industries and North County Poultry Processors. Works as a truck driver for both."

"How long has he been in the area?"

"Less than a month."

"Have you met him? Spoken to him?"

"Neither. Mrs. Koski said it wasn't necessary, that she'd bring him in to sign the agreement when it's ready."

"Do you know anything else about him?"

Lacey didn't. Nick Hendryx had no local ties, no family he was planning to have live with him, no credit rating. His only references were Caitlin and his current employers. The employers spoke well of him, but as Lacey pointed out, less than a month on the job wasn't much of a test of dependability. Not enough for the security deposit on the house to be waived.

"Was she adamant about that?" Cam asked. "Waiving the deposit?"

"Yes. Very."

"I suppose Hendryx wants to move in immediately."

"On the fifteenth."

"All right," Cam said. "I'll talk to my sister and get back to you, probably tomorrow."

"You do understand my reluctance? The property is a difficult rental, particularly at this time of year and with the El Niño business, but under the circumstances . . ."

"I understand, John, and I appreciate the call. You'll hear from me soon."

Ah, Caitlin, he thought as he hung up, why won't you ever learn?

HE CALLED HER as soon as he got home.

"I figured I'd hear from you tonight," she said. "Lacey called you, right?"

"Why did I have to hear it from him, Cat?"

"I don't need to ask your permission to rent my house."

"Our house."

"You don't give a shit about it. I do."

"This man Hendryx. Is he somebody you know personally?"

"What difference does that make?"

"I'm just curious. He hasn't been in the area long—"

"Why don't you just come out and ask me if I'm sleeping with him?"

"Cat, don't make this any more difficult—"

"You're the one who's making it difficult. I'm not sleeping with Nick, but maybe I will. Soon."

He smothered a sigh. "What about Hal? What does he think about this?"

"Hal's history. Two weeks gone and already forgotten."

"What happened?"

"Next question," she said.

"Okay, fine. Tell me about Hendryx."

"He's a nice guy, he works hard, and I like him. That's all you need to know."

"Why does he want to live at the river? He works two jobs down here, and it's a longish commute."

"That's his business, not yours."

"The house is my business, Cat. Whose idea was it to waive the security deposit?"

"Mine."

"But he suggested it."

"No, I suggested it. He offered to pay the deposit, went out and got a second job so he could afford to pay it, but I said no."

"Why would you do that?"

"I told you, he's a nice guy and I like him."

"Then why not just move him in with you and Teddy? Why does he need a big house like that all to himself?"

Silence.

"Caitlin?"

"You're an asshole, big brother, you know that? Sometimes you're the world's biggest asshole."

"I'm only trying to look out for your best interests—"

"Here we go again. Same old bullshit."

"All right, it's bullshit." Clash and conflict, every time he spoke to her. Exasperation made him say, "I can put a stop to this, you know. Rental agreement has to have both our signatures."

She said, "You do that, and you'll regret it," in a voice as cold and hard as he'd ever heard her use. "I mean that, Cameron."

"Nick Hendryx must've really gotten to you."

"If he has, it's my doing, not his. And not in the way you think. He's not Gus or Hal or any of the others. He's different."

"How is he different?"

"You wouldn't understand."

"Try me."

"No. Are you going to sign the agreement?"

"I'd like to meet him first."

"No."

"Why don't you leave that up to him?"

"I said no. The house is empty, and I want it rented to Nick Hendryx. Period. Are you going to sign the agreement?"

He didn't want to argue with her anymore. Aggravation, sadness, a sense of loss—they were all his dealings with Caitlin ever seemed to bring him. "If it'll make you happy," he said.

"What'll make me happy is you not giving me crap all the time."

"That's not my intention, Cat. I hate us always being at each other's throats."

"You think I like it?"

"Why can't we be good to each other?"

"Good? What's good? You tell me."

He took a breath before he spoke again. "Hallie and the girls and I would like you and Teddy to spend Christmas Eve with us this year. I thought I'd invite you this far in advance so—"

"Sorry," she said. "Other plans," she said, and the line began an empty buzzing in his ear.

ix o'clock Tuesday night. Nick was getting ready to head out, eat supper, go for a night ride, when somebody knocked on the door. Court manager or one of his neighbors—who else? He went over and opened up.

Gallagher was standing there.

Cameron fucking Gallagher, right there in front of him.

He stared, and Gallagher stared. Like they'd both come face to face with something unexpected, something out of the dark. Nick went cold and empty at first. Couldn't think, couldn't figure how Gallagher knew where to find him, what he was doing here. Days since he'd seen him. Too busy with Caitlin and the two jobs to do much trailing.

Gallagher said in a voice jammed with surprise, "You're the man who—" The rest of it didn't come out. He made a sound in his throat. "Are you Nick Hendryx?"

All of a sudden Nick filled with heat and a wild urge to grab Gallagher by the throat, choke him until he turned black. His hands twitched; he had to slap them down hard against his sides. His face had a tight, frozen feel, as if, if he moved a single muscle in it, it'd crack like glass.

Again, "Nick Hendryx?"

"That's right." Words pumped loose with only his throat moving, not his mouth. "Who're you?"

"Cameron Gallagher. I've seen you before."

"That so?"

"In the Hotel Paloma bar. About a month ago."

"Wouldn't be surprised. I get around."

"I . . . was with a woman named Jenna Bailey."

"So?"

"Do you know her?"

"No."

"The blue Mazda there. Yours?"

"What if it is?"

"I was just . . . You don't know me?"

"Said I didn't." Had himself under control now. Wouldn't crack and put his hands on Gallagher. Later. Later. "Listen, what do you want? You selling something?"

"No. I came to . . . I'm Caitlin Koski's brother."

"Oh, so that's it."

"She didn't send me, if that's what you're thinking. It was my idea."

"Sure it was. Meet the guy who's going to rent your Russian River house?"

"Right." Gallagher hesitated, maybe thinking about asking to come inside. Didn't do it, and that was good because Nick would've said no. Close himself up with Gallagher in a box like this one, and he might not be able to hold on to his cool. "Well . . ."

"Why you'd ask about my car?"

"It looks familiar. Were you at the river, our house up there, a few weeks back? A Saturday afternoon?"

"Might've been. Why?"

Gallagher shook his head. "Have you known my sister long?"

"Not long. Met her at the house."

"Are you seeing her? Socially, I mean."

"Didn't she say?"

"Not exactly."

Nick put a smile on. "Wondering what my intentions are?"

"Just wondering."

"She's a nice woman, your sister. I like her."

"She said the same about you."

"Too bad she doesn't say it about *you*."

"What do you mean?" Frowning. "What did she say about me?"

"Nothing much." Not as much as he'd tried to find out. Woman was hard to pry information out of. "Just that the two of you weren't close. That about right, Mr. Gallagher?"

"Yes." Something in his voice—hurt maybe. "About right."

"You have some objection to me renting your place?"

"No, no objection. But I can't help wondering why a single man would want to live in such a big house."

"I like space, lots of it," Nick said. "And the rent's cheap for a place that size. Cat tell you I took a second job so I could afford it?"

"Yes, she told me."

"When I see something I want, I go for it. Been that way all my life. Back home in Denver and everywhere I've been since I left."

No reaction. Chin up and down once, that was all.

"You ever been in Denver, Mr. Gallagher?"

"A couple of times."

"How'd you like it there?"

"I didn't have a chance to see much of it. I was there on business."

"What time of year?"

"I don't remember exactly."

"January? Lots of snow and ice on the streets in January."

No reaction. "I suppose so."

"Don't you know? Never been there in January?"

"No. Once when it was snowing, but I don't think it was January."

Hell it wasn't, you son of a bitch. "My wife's still there," Nick said. "Still in Denver."

"Oh, so you're married." Mouth twitched, nothing else.

"Happily married, that's right."

"Does Caitlin know that?"

"She knows. I told her." Not much, just enough.

"And she doesn't mind?"

"Not the way things are, she doesn't."

"What way is that?"

"My wife's in a hospital up there in Denver. She got hurt one night, real bad, and still hasn't got better."

Hesitation. "I'm sorry to hear that."

"Uh-huh. You're sorry."

"I mean it. Some kind of accident?"

"Some kind. Hit-and-run kind."

No reaction.

"Head injuries from being thrown into a telephone pole. Put her into a kind of coma."

Son of a bitch said again, "I'm sorry. What do the doctors say? About her chances for recovery?"

"They say she might. I know she will."

"You must love her very much."

You'll find out how much. "That's right, I do."

"Why aren't you . . . I mean . . ."

"Still in Denver with her?"

"I don't mean to pry into your personal affairs . . ."

"Nothing I can do for her there. She's got the best doctors, her folks to watch over her. Out here I can do her a lot more good."

"You mean by working, making money to pay the hospital bills?"

Nick didn't answer that. Just smiled, thin and tight.

Smile made Gallagher uneasy, but he tried to cover up. "Did they ever catch the hit-and-run driver?"

"Never did. But he'll get caught. Someday he'll pay for what he did to Annalisa. Someday soon."

Chin up, chin down. Phony expression of sympathy to hide what he was feeling underneath. Nick's hands twitched and clenched. Hunger to rip Gallagher's face off flared again for a few seconds, but he held it in check. Kept his voice steady, the smile in place.

"Well," Gallagher said, and *his* voice didn't sound so steady. Sweating inside if not out. Getting the idea. Trying to figure a way out, maybe, standing here, but there wasn't any way out. And maybe getting that idea, too. "Well, I hope you're right about that."

"No doubt about it. So what do you say, Mr. Gallagher?"

"Say about what?"

"Your house at the river. Not going to stop me from renting it, are you?"

"That wasn't my intention in coming here."

"Now that you know about me, I mean. Married man with a hurt wife, hit-and-run victim, keeping company with your sister."

"I can't stop Caitlin from seeing whom she pleases."

"Didn't answer my question."

"No, I'm not going to stand in your way. Or my sister's way. All I ask is that you treat her decently."

"I always treat women decently. *I'd* never hurt a woman."

"Good. That's good." Nervous now, couldn't stand still. See the fear in his eyes. "Well, I'd better be on my way."

"I'll be seeing you, Mr. Gallagher."

"I don't think it'll be necessary. I'll have the rental papers sent to me, save myself a trip to Guerneville. You can move in on the fifteenth as planned."

"Be seeing you anyway, one of these days. Before too long."

Nothing to say to that. Chin up, chin down, and away to his BMW with shoulders hunched, moving fast.

Nick watched him drive out of the courtyard. Thinking he couldn't've done a better job of handling Gallagher if he'd arranged this meeting himself. Should've faced him, put on the pressure sooner. Now that it was on, he'd keep it that way. Keep the bugger off balance and guessing until the time was right. Because what could he do about it, any of it? Guilty of felony hit-and-run, couldn't go to the cops. And he wasn't the type to pick up a gun, some other weapon, and go hunting. Not him, rich big shot like him. He wouldn't run, either. Guys who lived the kind of life he did didn't know how to run.

He'd be right here, squirming, still trying to figure a way out, when Nick was ready for him.

I am poured Bombay gin over ice cubes in two glasses, making one a double, added a drop of vermouth and a twist of lemon peel to both, and brought the smaller drink to Hallie. They were in the sunroom, where they always had their predinner cocktails. Private time, just the two of them, no kids allowed.

He sat in the other armchair and sipped, sipped again, sipped a third time before he lowered the glass. The gin cut a fiery swath through him, but it didn't soften the hard edges the way it usually did. It would take more than one or two martinis to do the job tonight.

He said, "I stopped at South City Apartments on the way home, to see the man Caitlin rented the river house to. That's why I was late."

"Did you talk to him?" Hallie asked.

"Yeah. I talked to him."

"And?"

"Odd. A damned odd duck."

"In what way?"

"Forthcoming enough, but not quite . . . I don't know, a little off somehow. Sly. Things going on under the surface."

"You don't think he's—?"

"Dangerous? No. No, I don't think so."

"You don't sound too sure," Hallie said. "Lord, Cat's taste in men. Another weirdo."

Dangerous. Weirdo. Cam took a longer pull at his drink before he said, "He's married. Came right out and said so."

"Uh-oh. But why would he admit it?"

"It's no secret. Cat knows, at least he said he told her. His wife's in a hospital in Denver. Some sort of hit-and-run accident that left her in a coma."

"Poor woman. Why isn't he in Denver with her?"

"I asked him that. He said he could do her more good out here."

"Did he mean money?"

"No," Cam said. "I don't know what he meant."

In his mind he kept going over the conversation with Hendryx. Why tell *him* about the wife, the accident? Why ask him if he'd ever been in Denver in January? Why say the hit-and-run driver, never caught, was going to pay someday soon? It was as if—

As if he suspects me, Cam thought.

But that's crazy. Why would he suspect me? In Denver twice in my life, never had an accident there or anywhere else. January. Ice and snow. One of the trips it was snowing, but it wasn't January. I don't think it was January. Christ, the blackout that time, the blood on my hands and shirt . . . but that was just a nosebleed, and it didn't happen in Denver. Portland. It was Portland. . . .

What's the matter with me? Thinking like that, as if I'm trying to convince myself I couldn't be guilty. Beloit, that quack, would say I *want* to be guilty, him and his goddamn self-destructive impulses. I had nothing to do with what happened to Hendryx's wife. If that's what he thinks, he's got me mixed up with somebody else.

Has he been following me? That one time, it could've been him and his blue Mazda. Him in the hotel bar, too. But why would he be stalking Jenna? That doesn't make any sense. All of it, just coincidence. But why is he fooling around with Caitlin, married man with a brain-damaged wife? Why does he want to rent the river house? He must be up to something—

"Cam!

He blinked, spilled a little of the martini on his pant leg.

"For goodness' sake," she said, "where were you?"

He shook his head. Brushed at the wet spot.

"The expression on your face . . . as though something was hurting you."

He swallowed what was left in his glass, went to the liquor cart for a refill.

"Cam?" Concern in her tone. And the old undercurrent of uneasiness that said, Lord, what is he doing to himself now? "Are you all right?"

"Yes," he lied.

"That man Hendryx seems to've really upset you. Is there something you haven't told me?"

He longed to spew it all out—Hendryx's inexplicable attitude, his own paranoid fears, Beloit's death-wish nonsense, even the near affair with Jenna. Unload it on Hallie, purge himself the way Catholics purged their sins in the confessional, find peace and absolution through her. But the words wouldn't come. Everything was locked up tight inside him, and he couldn't tear any of it loose no matter how hard he tried.

"No," he said. "No, there's nothing."

enwood Creek winery. Medium-size place, oak trees and vineyards all around, big asphalt parking lot on one side. Upper end of the Paloma Valley, near the village of Fenwood.

Nick turned off the highway, drove down a short lane into the lot. Time by his watch was 4:35. Sign said the tasting room closed at five, so there were only a couple of cars parked on the visitors' side. More cars in the employees' section toward the back, next to the warehouse. White Lexus was parked there, front slot, as if the Bailey woman was looking for a fast getaway once quitting time rolled around.

He came back, parked near the entrance. That was the only way off the winery grounds. Besides, he had a long sideslant view of the Lexus from there.

Half hour passed. A few people straggled out and got into their wheels and drove off, none of them the brunette and none paying any attention to him. Five-twenty, and four more filed out of a door to one side of the tasting room. Brunette was among them, the one who locked up. They walked in a bunch to the employees' section. Dark by then, but Nick hunkered down anyway when the Lexus rolled past; he wasn't ready for her to see him yet.

He let her and the car behind her reach the highway before he swung out of the lot. She turned south, the other car following, Nick following that one a hundred yards back. When she got into the middle of Fenwood, she cut off at a supermarket. Nick did the same, holding at the road end of the lot where he could see the Lexus and the market entrance.

She stayed in there for a while. Regular shop, not just one or two items. Probably meant she lived fairly close by, which made it easier for him. For all he'd been able to find out, she might've lived in Santa Rosa or Paloma or Los Alegres. She wasn't listed in any of the local phone books.

Fifteen minutes, and she came out pushing a cart with two or three bags in it. Loaded the bags into the trunk. He stayed put until she was back on the highway and rolling south again, another car behind her, before he followed.

They rode half a mile. Then she turned again, west on a side road that hooked up into the hills. Another half-mile, another turn. Narrower side road, with a steep incline after a few hundred yards. Partway up the incline, her brake lights flashed; she cut into a driveway, stopped along-side a mailbox. Nick went on past without slowing. Up over the rise, out of her sight, he found a place to make a U-turn. Waited five minutes at the roadside, timing it by his watch, then drove back at an easy twenty-five.

His headlights picked up the mailbox and number painted on its side: 4100. Driveway led back through trees to a house with lights show-ing now; he had a glimpse of the Lexus parked in front as he slid past.

Down at the intersection with the first side road, he stopped to check the signs. Black Oak and Madrone Way. 4100 Madrone Way.

Okay. He'd found out what he needed to know about Jenna Bailey. Now he could start turning up the heat.

That Saturday Cam took the *Hallie Too* downriver for the last time until spring. The weather was cold and overcast, but with no immediate threat of rain, and he needed to be alone, on water, the salt wind in his face. Free for a little while.

He navigated down through the Black Point narrows into San Pablo Bay and cruised along the eastern shore almost as far as the Carquinez Straits before he turned back. The bay was whitecapped, but the XLC slid through the chop smoothly and with little roll. She was such a sweet boat. Fine-tuned MerCruiser diesel, V-berth that slept four comfortably, plenty of extras, a heat and defrost system that would keep the cabin warm and dry under the worst conditions. He could have afforded a bigger, more luxurious craft than the Skagit, but not one that suited him and his needs more perfectly.

It was late afternoon when he maneuvered into his slip at the Los Alegres marina. When he had all the lines tied, he locked everything down inside the cabin, began tarping the deck and superstructure for the winter. The marina was sheltered; even at high tide—Los Alegres River was really a saltwater estuary—and in the heaviest of storms, there was little threat of damage here.

He was almost finished with the tarping when he noticed the man watching him from up on the seawall. He stiffened, shaded his eyes. The distance was too great for him to make out the man's features, but the build was thin and wiry—and the car beside him was blue.

Fear gripped him first, then dissolved under a sudden and violent surge of anger. All right, Hendryx, he thought. Let's get this out into the open right now.

He jumped off, ran along the float to the caged ramp, ran up the ramp and out onto the seawall. And then stopped, breathing hard, his hands clenched with such force he could feel the bite of his nails. A tic began to spasm on his cheek.

The blue car was a Toyota.

And the man standing beside it was nobody he had ever seen before.

. . . COLD, DAMP, DARK. Smells of mold and mildew, rain and dust and mouse turds. Sound of the rain outside, beating on the roof, wind-flung against the dormer windows. He hears it dripping, a leak somewhere inside one of the walls. Drip. Drip. Drip. He doesn't dare shut his eyes because then it won't be rain he'll see and hear dripping, it'll be something else wet, glistening. Something bright red.

Blood.

Downstairs, on the bed. Blood.

Downstairs, on the bedroom floor. Blood.

Downstairs, her dead eyes open and staring.

Downstairs, in the red-blood night . . .

aitlin said, "He really pisses me off sometimes. Showing up like that at your motel, checking up after I told him to leave you alone."

"Well, it's his house, too," Nick said.

"Cameron hates the river house. It wasn't you he was checking up on, it was me."

"Why would he do that?"

"He thinks I don't know how to run my own life. Always trying to tell me what to do, what's good for me. He's the last one to tell anybody how to live."

"Why d'you say that?"

"He's twice as fucked up as I am, that's why."

"Seemed normal enough to me."

"Yeah, well, he puts on a good front. Underneath he's a mess. Booze, depression, bad headaches—a bagful of neuroses. He's been in and out of therapy most of his life."

"On account of what happened to your folks?"

"Mostly, I guess."

"Must've been pretty hard on him, being there the night it happened. He see any of it?"

"He says he didn't. Says he was in his room."

"Don't you believe him?"

No answer to that. Caitlin sat staring into the fire. They were on the couch in her living room, Presto-log burning blue and green and yellow in the fireplace, him nursing a beer and her working on her fourth glass of wine. Cheap white wine out of a box—"I like it and it drives my brother up a wall, him and his wine snobbery." Just the two of them in the house tonight. The kid, Teddy, Theodore, was staying at a friend's place, she'd said when Nick got there. Fine with him. He didn't like the kid much. Snotty and loud and already doing drugs at fourteen—stoned on what was probably coke one of the other times Nick had come over. Caitlin didn't seem to notice. Too wrapped up with her own problems. Kid was his, he'd have kicked his ass black and blue.

Theodore being gone made things easier. No music blaring out of his room, Caitlin relaxed and drinking enough to loosen her tongue. But he wondered if she'd arranged it. Twice she'd tried to get him to sleep with her, came right out and asked him the second time. That was when he'd told her about Annalisa. Only way to keep her from pushing him for sex, he'd figured, and still be able to hang in there with her. Worked so far. Sympathetic, said she understood—mother in her coming out for him if not for Theodore. And tonight she was finally opening up about Gallagher. Do what he had to to keep her on that track, off the other.

He asked the question again. Why'd Gallagher say he wasn't a witness if he was?

She lit a cigarette. Nick didn't like that habit in a woman, smell of tobacco on her breath, secondhand smoke biting in his lungs, but he hadn't said anything to her about it. Wouldn't. Wasn't his place. She wanted to give herself cancer, that was her choice.

"He's a coward," she said.

"You mean that? A coward?"

She meant it, all right. Sticking in her craw and needing to be spit out. Once she got the piece of it loose, rest of it came in a glob. Everything he wanted to know about Gallagher and the shootings.

Police'd found him hiding in the attic, she said, lying on a mattress in his own urine, half out of his head. Screamed and bawled like a baby—she'd found that out years later, wormed it out of the aunt who'd raised them. Gallagher hadn't called the cops, guy who'd been sleeping with the mother went back and saw the bodies through a window and made the report. All Gallagher'd done was run and hide in the attic and piss all over himself.

But that wasn't all. "Hadn't been for my big, brave brother," Caitlin said, "that whole goddamn bloody night might never've happened."

What she meant by that, Gallagher'd told his old man about the mother's affair. Caitlin said if he'd kept his mouth shut, the father might not've gone up to the river house with a gun, and her parents'd still be alive today. Nick said maybe it would've happened anyway, sooner or later—mother'd had a lot of affairs, right?

"So she slept around, so what?" Caitlin said. "He could've divorced her. Sex isn't any reason to kill somebody, is it? Infidelity?"

"No, neither one."

Finished her wine. "I need a refill. You ready for another beer?"

"Not right now."

She went into the kitchen, came back with her glass poured to the top. "Drinking too much myself," she said. "Alcoholism runs in the family."

Nick asked, did she think Gallagher'd wanted their mother to get killed? She said she didn't know. Question wasn't new to her; heard it before, inside her head if nowhere else. Maybe he hadn't wanted her dead, exactly, she said, but he'd wanted her punished some way. And he hadn't wanted the father to kill himself because Gallagher'd loved him— it was only the mother he'd hated. Other way around for Caitlin. Loved the mother, still did. Felt sorry for her, too. Trapped in a loveless marriage, father was as gutless as the son. Cat didn't blame her for getting what she needed someplace else, she blamed the old man for driving her to it. Nick didn't buy that. Women cheating were no better than men cheating, no matter what the reason. But he didn't say so.

He asked, how come she and Gallagher still owned the river house, after what'd happened there? Question he'd asked her before. Hadn't got a straight answer then, but he got one tonight, her words a little slurred from all the wine. Gallagher had his way, she said, house'd've been sold a long time ago. She was the one keeping it in the family, all she had left of her mother and her childhood. Couldn't bring herself to live there, she said, but at least she wasn't afraid to go inside. Gallagher was. Hadn't set foot in the house in twenty-five years, hadn't even been on the property so far as she knew. Probably go to pieces if he did set foot inside, she said, curl up in a little ball and pee all over himself again.

Nick left her alone after that. Wasn't anything more he needed to know. Both of them sat quiet for so long, he jumped when she leaned over and put her hand on his knee.

"I'm a little drunk," she said.

"You're entitled."

"Little drunk, and I want to lie down. Nick?"

"Yeah?"

"How about . . . I'd really like . . ."

He didn't say anything.

"Stay with me tonight. Okay?"

Still didn't say anything.

"I don't want to be alone," she said.

"Cat, I told you—"

"I know. Poor wife. Understand, really do, but I'm not talking about sex."

"No?"

"No. Might not believe this, but sex isn't that important to me. Don't even like it much. Just that sometimes . . . some nights I need to be close to somebody. Need to be held. You know?"

"I know," he said.

"Don't have to get undressed or go in the bedroom. Stay right here on the couch, in front of the fire. Hold each other, that's all."

He didn't say anything.

"Nick? Don't you need to be held? Sometimes? Your wife like she is, so far away?"

Hurt in him began to well up again. "Sometimes."

"Tonight? Just tonight, for both of us?"

He sat rigid. She didn't touch him, didn't keep talking, but it wouldn't've mattered if she had. Brain had stopped working, everything was feeling now. So much feeling he turned to her, looked at her—pleading in her face, firelight moving on it, softening it, making her almost pretty—and he couldn't help himself, he put his arms around her and she came in close and before long they were lying stretched out and he was holding her thin body against the length of his. Couple of minutes like that, good like that, and he felt her shoulders start to shake, wetness on his shirt and skin. She was crying. Holding on to him tight and crying with no sound into his chest.

Nick shut his eyes. And as soon as he did Annalisa was there, smiling, the firelight flickering on her face and making her even more beautiful. Then he was holding her just as tight as she was holding him, telling her, "Shh, baby, it's all right, it's going to be all right," and brushing and kissing away her tears.

"I love you, Annalisa," he said, and she stiffened and then slowly relaxed again, clinging to him. After a while she stopped crying, and when she went to sleep he drifted off himself, keeping Annalisa warm and safe in his arms.

T he rains started the second week in December. One heavy two-day storm that dumped more than an inch on Los Alegres and the Paloma Valley, a succession of gloomy, drizzly days afterward. Here comes El Niño. The weather people were saying it, so everybody else was saying it too. Get the sandbags ready, folks, it's going to be another long, wet, floody, muddy winter.

The migraines started again that same week. The first one came on Sunday, while Cam was playing an interactive video game with Leah and Shannon. Relatively mild; he took the medication the neuresthenic specialist had prescribed, lay down for an hour in the darkened bedroom with cold compresses over his eyes, and he was all right again. The second attack, on Friday morning, was more severe. He was at PWS, in the warehouse chewing out his foreman, Dave Tabor, over a mishandled shipment of Taliaferro varietals, when the symptoms all seemed to hit him at once. Violent stabbing pain behind his eyes, acute nausea, dizziness, confusion, the sudden descent into black nontime. His next awareness was of lying on the couch in his office, Maureen there and fussing over him. The medication helped, but the pain lingered with enough intensity to keep him down. He finally had to ask Maureen to drive him home in the BMW, one of the other other employees to follow and bring her back.

Hallie made him promise to see the specialist on Monday, and he went and had the usual checkup and listened to the usual lecture about lifestyle changes and relaxation techniques and drastically reducing or eliminating his intake of alcohol, and left with a prescription for some new drug that had proven effective in helping other migraine sufferers. What he really needed was a new head. The one he had now was Abbie Normal, like the monster's brain in *Young Frankenstein*.

Gray days, gray thoughts, restless black nights. Not even the pleasant activities of the Christmas season—present buying, tree selection, tree trimming—cheered him as much as they had in the past. He had no more contact with Caitlin, so he didn't know if she was still seeing Hendryx, but the rental agreement showed up in the mail from Riverbank Realty with Cat's signature already on it. The agreement was written month-to-month; normally that kind of arrangement went against his better judgment, but not in this case. Having Nick Hendryx for a tenant for a minimum of thirty days was bad enough. Anything longer, guaranteed, would have been that much harder to take.

His temper shortened, and his depression grew. One evening after supper he snapped at Leah for putting the TV volume up too loud. Shannon jumped to her sister's defense, and he growled at her too, and then at Hallie when she tried to play peacemaker. The bickering that followed scraped his nerves raw. It was either get out of there for a while, or he'd end up drinking too much and making the situation worse. He had the good sense to go for his car keys instead of the gin.

He didn't drive far, just down to McLear Park half a mile from the house. It was a large park, a city block wide and three city blocks long. Old shade trees, sprawling lawns where he and the family still picnicked now and then, horseshoe and tennis courts, a softball field, a children's playground. And a baseball diamond where semipro teams sometimes played, where he'd played Little League for two years—second base, good field but a poor hitter. He sat in the car for a time, until there was a break in the light rain. Then he went walking, following the park's network of muddy paths.

It was the right place for him tonight. Nobody around, house lights and traffic sounds at a distance, the cold air both bracing and soothing. He walked for a long time, back and forth through the grounds, completely around the park twice. The tension in him gradually eased, and by the time he stopped to rest behind one of the dugouts, his depression seemed to have eased, too.

He stood with fingers hooked through the wire mesh screen, looking at the eroded pitcher's mound and the rain-puddled infield and sweeps of outfield grass. After a time he could almost hear the crack of ball against bat, the cries of players and the cheers of spectators, the smack of a line drive hitting his glove. Echoes from far away and long ago. Long, long ago.

Longer than January 4, 1974.

In one sense, he hadn't come far since that terrible night. In another, he'd come a long way. Damaged, yes, problems, yes, but he was still in the game, still in there swinging. And he had so much to be grateful for— Hallie, his daughters, PWS, a combination hobby and escape valve like the Skagit cruiser. So much to live for.

Rose and the old man hadn't destroyed him. Neither had Jenna. And so far he hadn't destroyed himself.

Death wish? No, by God. No.

I can beat this, he thought. Hang in, go on, and beat this. And I will. I *will*.

Nick took possession of the river house on the fifteenth, as scheduled. Checked out of South City Apartments that morning, so all he had to do after work was drive to Guerneville and pick up the key from the realty guy. He'd already paid the first month's rent with a money order. Only month's rent—he wouldn't even be there that long.

He stopped at a Safeway and bought coffee, a jumbo package of M&Ms, and a few other things, then drove out to Crackerbox Road. Raining again tonight, and in the wet dark the house had a wasted look. Big, hulking thing, hunched and ugly, like a huge shadow caught among the dripping trees. Annalisa wouldn't have liked it at all. Bright new houses with big yards and plenty of flowers, that was what she liked. Carnations and roses. Her favorites. Pink, white, red, yellow. He'd bought her carnations, bouquets of them, every chance he had. Single roses, too, long-stemmed, on special occasions. Made her eyes shine every time, that smile of hers light up. Marigolds were another flower she liked—bright and sunny like herself. Planter box full of them in the kitchen window of their apartment. He'd tell her, "You'll have a whole acre of carnations and roses and marigolds someday." Meant it, every word. Someday, when she was well again, he'd give her everything she ever wanted.

He got out in the rain to open the driveway gate, drove through and into the open garage. Chinks, ball-size holes, in the roof and walls, so there wasn't an inch of dry in there. He was dripping like the trees by the time he made it into the house with his battered suitcase and the bag of groceries.

House had been closed up so long it had a dank, musty smell. Dry rot—floors were spongy with it. Cold, too, and damp from the rain. Caitlin'd showed him where the thermostat was; he turned it up past seventy. First blasts of air out of the wall registers stank of moldy dust. But the furnace was in decent shape, even if the rest of the place wasn't. Wouldn't take long for it to warm up the house's old bones.

Went for a walk-through, switching on lights and shutting them off again, to familiarize himself with the layout again. Downstairs—living room with a fireplace, kitchen, bathroom, small bedroom, screened rear porch with a washer and dryer and an old chest-type freezer. Back bedroom was where the shootings had happened. Nothing in there now except a rollaway bed, a dresser, and a couple of old chairs.

Upstairs, two bedrooms and another that might've been a study once—had built-in bookcases on one wall. Nick put his suitcase in the front bedroom. He'd use that one because the windows had a view of the road out front. Bed in there was an iron-frame job, frame painted white and banged up, mattress and box springs lumpy, sagging. Mattress was made up with clean sheets and pillowcases, thermal blankets, an old comforter. Caitlin. She'd offered to drop off the bedding and some towels, spares from her linen closet, and she'd ended up making the bed for him. How'd she guess this was the room he'd pick to sleep in?

Locked door in the upstairs hall, between the bathroom and the rear bedroom. Way up to the attic. Two keys on the ring from the Realtor; second one fit the lock. Inside was a narrow staircase, thick smells of dust and mildew. A pull string dangled down from a light fixture screwed into the wall, but nothing happened when he yanked on it. Bulb must be burned out. Meant none of the tenants before him used the attic much, if at all.

He went down and outside, fetched his utility lantern from the Mazda's trunk. Beam showed him layers of crap on the risers as he climbed into the attic, more of the same up above. Low, tight space, roofline slanting down sharp on both ends. Only place you could stand up straight was in the middle, and even there the rafters were only a couple of inches above the top of his head. He pulled another light string—another dead bulb. Then he stood shining the lantern beam around.

Wasn't much to see. Spiderwebs. Small, dirty windows in the dormers at either end, front one with a crack in it. Few scraps of rickety furniture, one of those old steamer trunks with a caved-in side, pile of magazines in a corner that'd been torn into shreds and used for nests by rodents or something.

He stayed put for a minute or two, listening to the rain on the roof, a dripping somewhere inside one wall. Feeling a little of what Gallagher must've felt the night his folks died. Something skittered behind him, but when he swung the light that way he didn't see anything. Rats? He didn't like rats, they were the one fear he and Annalisa had in common. But it didn't sound like rats. Nothing for the buggers to eat here, and they wouldn't nest in a place that didn't have a food supply close by. Mice, or maybe a squirrel. He could live with either of them.

Went back down, shut the attic door but left it unlocked. Pad of writing paper and a pen in his suitcase; he got them out, took them down to the kitchen. Put some water on for coffee, made himself a peanut butter sandwich. Then he sat at the Formica-topped table to write Annalisa a letter and make up a list of the things he was going to need.

e shouldn't have gone alone to Fenwood Creek's annual party the Friday before Christmas. He'd asked Hallie to go with him, but there was a benefit at the senior center that same night, and she couldn't, wouldn't cancel out of it. He couldn't, wouldn't snub the Fenwood people by not showing up for the party, so he rationalized his way into driving up there by himself. He'd only stay for a few minutes, have one glass of wine, limit his schmoozing to Bryan Collins, Fenwood's owner, and Dennis Frane, their sales head. Say hello to Jenna, be polite, then walk away as quickly as he could.

All well and good, but it was still a mistake. He knew it for certain as soon as he walked into the festively decorated tasting room and the first person he saw among the crush of bodies was Jenna.

She was talking to somebody and didn't see him, so he was able to maneuver around on her blind side and across to the long serving counter. Jumpiness in him, nerves suddenly drawn tight. Why? He was over his yen for her, he really was. It was just that—

Just that I need a drink, he thought.

What they were pouring tonight was among their cellar best. The '95 Carneros chardonnay (medium dry, butterscotch and toasty oak accents, ripe fruit underneath, short finish). The '93 petite sirah (full-bodied, warm smoky nose, hint of cloves and raspberries, balanced tannins). And the '92 private reserve cabernet, their second-finest red this decade, the '91 private reserve cab already long bought up and laid down by connoisseurs (rich texture, black cherries and pepper, crisp acidity, long, fruity finish). Fine, dandy, but he wanted a *drink*. A Bombay martini, cold and crisp, rich flavor of juniper berries, whisper of vermouth, hint of lemon peel, long, warm finish.

The servers, two men and two women, were all wearing Santa Claus hats and red and green jackets. Cute. One of the women came over to him, the white pompon on the droopy end of her hat bouncing. "Merry Christmas, Mr. Gallagher. What can I get for you?" He knew her but he couldn't remember her name. He mumbled a "Merry Christmas" and asked for a glass of the private reserve cab.

They'd opened the banquet room, as they did every year, to accommodate the crowd. Hot and cold hors d'oeuvres, a five-piece band with one male and one female vocalist batting out spritely holiday favorites, people standing or sitting at tables, even two or three couples dancing. He went that way because it was away from Jenna. Acquaintances spoke to him, and he spoke to them; it all ran through him like water through a colander, nothing left but a few words here and there like misty droplets. "Deck the halls with boughs of holly, fa la la la la . . ." He finished his wine, went back for a refill. Dennis Frane came up, lingered, wandered off again. "I'm dreaming of a white Christmas . . ." He drank the second glass of cab, much faster than he should have. Better eat something, he hadn't had any food since lunch. But none of the hors d'oeuvres appealed to him. He looked for Bryan Collins, couldn't pick him out, and returned to the serving counter for a third glass of cab. His head was beginning to ache a little. "Oh, you better watch out, you better not cry . . ."

"Cam. When did you get here?"

Jenna, at his elbow. He turned slowly, pasting on a smile. "Well, hello. Little while ago."

"I've been watching for you, but I didn't see you come in."

"I didn't see you, either," he lied. Except for a smile that seemed as artificial as his own, she looked fine. Green dress, tight, showing off the deep swell of her breasts; not too much makeup, and the dark hair worn upswept, fastened with a jeweled comb, decorated with a sprig of holly. "You look festive."

"I don't feel festive." She took his arm, steered him away from a laughing couple who were pushing up to the counter. "We need to talk," she said.

"About what?"

"Not what you might think. It's important, Cam."

"All right. Go ahead."

"Not here, with all these people. Alone."

His mouth had a puckered feel; he drank more of his wine. It might have been two-dollar-a-bottle plonk instead of twenty-eight-dollar-a-bottle, award-winning cabernet sauvignon. "I think I'm free for lunch on Monday," he said.

"It won't wait until Monday."

"When, then?"

"Tonight. As soon as I can get away from here. My house, you know where it is."

The wine's acidity had set up a burning in his empty gut. He said, "I don't think that's a good idea, Jenna."

"Don't you? Well, I do. It's important, Cam."

"*What* is?"

"I think I can get away by eight." She pressed something into his hand. Key. "You won't have to wait more than half an hour, if you leave now."

"Jenna, I don't want to play any games with you. Can't you just tell me—"

"At the house. Alarm's on and the pad is just inside the door. Remember to disarm it—the code is two thousand and one. And this isn't a game."

"All right, but—"

"Here comes Bryan," she said. "Half an hour," and she moved away to let silver-haired Bryan Collins step up and take her place at Cam's side.

He spent five minutes chatting with Bryan and somebody else who joined them, and when he managed to work free, he couldn't remember a word of the conversation. The key felt hot against his palm as he made his way into the chilly drizzle outside. He felt silly and manipulated, like a reluctant conspirator in a game he didn't understand.

Not a game, she'd said, but was that the truth? One last attempt at seduction? It didn't seem like her; she was openly aggressive, not cryptic and devious. But he couldn't be sure. The simple truth was, he didn't know Jenna at all.

The only other explanation he could think of was the dangerous misfit business again. Nick Hendryx? Or some other phantom stalker? Her paranoia at work, if that was it.

Unless something had happened, something overt to stir her up.

I don't want to know, he thought. Asking for trouble if I go to her place, no matter what this is all about. Stay the hell away from her!

He started the car, left the packed lot, and turned south on the valley highway. Going home. Telling himself he was going home all the way to Black Oak Road, right up to the time he made the turn and headed into the hills to Jenna's house.

cross the road, parked in shadow in front of a closed-up nursery, Nick watched the silver BMW roll to the stop sign at the winery entrance. All sorts of lights on over there, building lights and grounds lights, making everything bright as day even through the light rain. Gallagher's wheels, that BMW. He'd know it anywhere even without the WINEMAN license plate. And Gallagher alone inside. Hadn't stayed long at the party Fenwood Creek was having. Less than forty minutes.

Nick had watched him drive in. Parked here over an hour, since he'd followed the Bailey woman from the winery to her house and back again. She'd gone home to change for the party, different outfits going and coming. Spotted him on the return trip, he'd made sure of it. Second time this week he'd made sure—goose her a little more, turn up the heat on Gallagher through her. She must've told him about it by now. Over there at the party, maybe. Now it was time to shift back onto *his* tail, show himself to Gallagher, too, at some point. See where he was headed now, then decide.

Nick waited until the BMW was a few hundred yards down the highway, rolled out behind it. Gallagher wasn't in any hurry, but he wasn't poking, either. Slowed down through Fenwood village, sped up again once he was on the other side. Going home?

No. Turning off on Black Oak Road.

Heading for 4100 Madrone Way. Finally connecting with his piece on the side. Him leaving the party first, then her following a little later. Keep tongues from wagging, that way.

Fine. Perfect.

Nick swung off onto Black Oak. Smiling as his lights burrowed ahead into the dark.

clutch of seconds after Cam pulled into Jenna's driveway, the headlights that had been behind him threw the wet pavement, the flanking oak trees, into bright relief and then funneled past without slowing. He couldn't tell what kind of car it was or how many people were inside; it was merely a quick-moving shadow, rain-blurred behind its lights. One of Jenna's neighbors. Somebody with no interest in him at all. Christ, but she had him spooked again.

He tried to even his breathing, relax his body, as he went the rest of the way up the drive. The tension remained. Blood beat in his temples in a steady rhythm; his stomach still burned from the acidity in the wine.

Two night spots were mounted on the front wall of the redwood-and-fieldstone house, another on the attached garage, laying patches of misty brightness across a paved parking area and the upper end of the drive. He parked the car as close to the house as he could without blocking the garage. Raining harder now; he ran to the door.

Inside, a blinking red light drew his attention to the alarm-system pad, and he remembered Jenna reminding him to disarm it. What had she said the code was? For a few seconds his mind was blank. Come on, before the damn thing goes off! Two thousand and one, that was it. The movie, the millenium, easy number to keep in your head—most people's heads. He punched out the four digits. The red light winked off, and a steady green one came on.

He shucked his trench coat, hung it in the hall closet. He'd been here twice before, once with Hallie for a dinner party shortly after Bryan Collins hired Jenna away from a Silverado Trail winery, the second time earlier this year, by himself, for an afternoon wine-and-cheese party. Small, two bedrooms, one of which she'd turned into a home office, but a pricey hunk of real estate nonetheless. Bryan paid his management people top salary, as he could afford to do, given Fenwood Creek's growing reputation and annual volume of sales.

There was a wet bar on the far side of the living room. Jenna wouldn't mind if he helped himself to some of her gin. He found a bottle of Beefeater's, but when he opened it and caught a whiff of the content it nearly made him gag. Pour even a short one on top of the red wine, no food, and he'd be drunk or sick or both when she got here. And he still had a long drive home on a rainy night.

Common sense, Gallagher. In this, in everything you do here tonight.

He screwed the cap back on the Beefeater's, went to sit on a white leather sofa. The decor was mostly white or off-white—carpet, whitewashed brick fireplace, alabaster sculptures, marble-topped tables. Virginal. He wondered if Jenna had decorated it this way as a kind of private joke, or if that was how she saw herself, as a chaste person underneath the earthy, sexually aggressive exterior. Or, Lord, maybe she just liked white.

Five minutes. Ten. He could feel himself growing more and more wired; only the throbbing in his head, the fiery hurt in his stomach, kept him from making another trip to the wet bar.

He sat listening to the rain and the heavy thud of his pulse. Trying not to think. Trying to sit and wait patiently.

Come on, Jenna. Come on, come on, come on!

arked and waiting again. This time on a muddy turnout next to a
creek, fifty yards or so on the downhill side of the Bailey woman's
driveway. Relaxed. Telling Annalisa inside his head, "Prod him
tonight, get him worked up and worrying, then back off again. Stay away
from him and the bimbo until after Christmas. It's like catching a trout,
baby. Set the hook, yank him, let him have some slack, yank him again,
watch him wiggle and squirm, then reel him in."

One pair of headlights passed, but they were high-set, and he knew
it was a pickup or a four-by-four, not the white Lexus. Ford Bronco,
right. Twenty minutes. Rain stopped, but the wind kept whacking
around in the trees. Half an hour. She was taking her time getting here
to meet Gallagher. Probably couldn't get away from the Christmas
party. Somebody important at the winery, Ms. Jenna Bailey. Product
manager. What did a product manager do? Had something to do with
sales, like Gallagher and his company had something to do with sales.
Perfect match. Sell each other a bill of goods, manage the hell out of
each other's products every chance they got.

Thirty-five minutes, and here came another pair of lights up Madrone Way from Black Oak. Passenger car lights this time. Nick watched
them grow and spread, glaring like a couple of searchlights. Brights on.
Far reach of them gleamed off the wet metal of the Mazda's hood while
the other car was still better than a hundred yards downhill. Another few

seconds, and the car's speed slackened all of a sudden, and right after that there was a splash of red in the darkness behind the beams—brake lights. They went off again quick, but then, with maybe fifty yards separating him and the one coming, the brake lights flashed again. Driver braked hard that time because the headlights wobbled as the car slid a little on the slick pavement—

Lights veered toward him, straight across the road toward the Mazda.

Nick tightened up behind the wheel. First thought: Shit, not another drunk. Second thought: Cop? By then the other car was off the road and plowing to a stop a few feet from the Mazda's front bumper, high beams turning the misty windshield into a silver-flecked blaze. He threw an arm up to shade his eyes. Through the glare he saw the driver's door open, somebody come out fast and run around between the two cars.

Bailey woman.

Coattails blowing in the wind, hands in the coat pockets, face twisted into an angry grimace.

Last thing he'd expected. Supposed to see him sitting here and drive on past, all worried and scared, and instead here she was, bearing down on him like Rambo's sister. He should've started the engine, backed up and driven away and left her standing there stewing. But he didn't think of that in time, not until after she was at his window. She thumped on the glass with a closed fist, leaning down so her face, a white-streaked blur, was peering in at him. Still time to get out of there, but he just sat still. That was his first mistake.

Second mistake, reflex, confusion, some damn thing, was opening the window. Soon as he did that, and she was looking at him square on, eyes black and shiny-hot in the light glare, she took her other hand out of the coat pocket and showed him what was in it.

Gun.

Little flat automatic pointing into his face.

"All right, you bastard, I've had all I'm going to take of you stalking me," Spitting the words like a cat spits. "Get out of that car and do it quick or I swear to God I'll shoot you dead and claim self-defense."

ore than twenty minutes of waiting now. And the acid burning in his gut seemed to be getting worse. He shoved up from the sofa, feeling shaky, sweaty all of a sudden, and walked slowly into the kitchen for a glass of water. The first wave of nausea hit him as he reached the sink. Belly roiling, he stumbled into the nearby guest bathroom. Had just enough time to drop to his knees in front of the toilet before the wine came up in a thin, sour spurt like diluted blood.

He was weak and dizzy when he finished. He pulled himself up over the vanity sink, washed his face with cold water. It didn't help. Roaring in his head—it felt huge, balloonlike, as if it were expanding and contracting like something attached to a bellows. He staggered out of the bathroom, made it back to the sofa before the pain erupted. Bright, stabbing pulses down through his sinus cavities and into the backs of his eyeballs.

Migraine.

Bad one.

Oh God no not now not here—

Medication, one of the new pills the specialist had given him . . . he fumbled the vial out of his coat pocket, but his hands shook so badly he couldn't get the cap off. Vertigo had him then; he fell back against the cushions. Swirling, swirling, as though he were caught in a vortex. Disoriented, couldn't think, and the darkness closing in—

ick got out of the car. What else could he do? Woman backed off
as he opened the door, watching him, the little gun steady in her
hand. Classy surface had rubbed off her; she was all cold, hard steel
standing there. Not an ounce of bluff in what she'd said about shooting
him. She'd meant every word.

"You've got me wrong," he said.

"Like hell I have. What was the plan? Stalk me for a while and then
break in and rape me, kill me? Or do you just get your jollies scaring
women because you can't get it up any other way?"

The plan, Nick thought, the plan is *Gallagher*, damn you. He said,
"I'm here because I'm having car trouble—"

"Bullshit, buddy. I saw you following me earlier tonight. I've seen
you half a dozen times, hanging around, watching me."

"What're you going to do?"

"What do you think? Call the police and have your sick ass thrown
in jail."

"You can't do that. I haven't done anything to you."

"No? Harassment is a crime. Even if the charge doesn't stick, they'll
have your name and address, and if you ever try anything with me again
they'll know right where to look. Or I will. I was stalked and raped once,
I won't let it happen a second time. I'd kill you or any other asshole who
tried it in a New York minute."

"Look, lady, can't we—"

"No, we can't. Start walking."

"Walking where?"

"Up the road away from your car."

He did it.

"Stop there. Keep your back to me."

Did that, too. Behind him he heard her moving in the other direction, back to her car. For her purse and keys and to shut off the headlights— night went dark again. He listened to her walk back up behind him.

"Move," she said. "Up my driveway to the house."

Couldn't let her take him into the house. Gallagher was in there, and maybe he'd talk her out of calling the cops and maybe he wouldn't. Might just let her do it, try to get out from under that way. Run a bluff if Nick said anything about the hit-and-run. Sketch wasn't proof Gallagher was guilty, and besides, Nick didn't want the law to punish him. Not anymore. Justice was in his hands now, the right punishment all arranged. Spoil everything for Annalisa if he let this woman take him inside.

"Move, I said."

He moved, but slow. Little short steps.

"You want to get shot? You will if you don't hurry it up."

Widened his strides, but not by much. Head down, looking for something, anything, to turn the situation around. Low spot alongside the driveway, puddled rainwater filling it, ground on either side looked muddy. He angled that way, but not all at once.

Bimbo was closer behind him now than she had been. Not close enough for him to pivot and make a grab for her, but close enough for what he had in mind. He was going slow again, and she muttered something that sounded like "Fucking bastard." Getting impatient with him. Good. Impatience made you careless.

He was on the edge of the road when he reached the puddle. Almost to the end of it, he let his left foot slide off, splash into the water so she'd hear. Made a noise like he'd slipped and then went down sideways to one knee, putting both hands on the soft ground the way you would to break a fall. She stopped, still close—stopped and was saying "Don't you try anything—" when he twisted up and around and pitched the handful of mud he'd scooped up.

Gob of it spattered her in the face, tore a surprised cry out of her, threw her off balance. Gun went off, pop! like a cork coming out of a bottle, but he wasn't hit. He was onto his feet and at her by then. Slapped the automatic out of her hand, dodged a slash of her nails, punched her jaw with a short-armed right. Solid, scraped-knuckles blow, felt it all the way up his arm—made him wince because it was the first time in his life he'd ever hit a woman. She grunted, fell over backward as though her legs'd been chop-blocked from under her. Hit the pavement flat on her back, smacked-meat sound that must've been her head slamming into the asphalt. Twitch, jerk, another twitch, and she was still.

Breathing hard, Nick looked up the driveway and both ways along the road. No headlights, just some house lights among the trees—hers and others a couple of hundred yards uphill, her nearest neighbors. Gun hadn't made much of a bang, and her yell had been too low to carry. Gallagher'd've shown himself by now if he'd heard.

He looked for the automatic. Found it, dropped it into his coat pocket. Pocketed her purse, too, little beaded thing. Then he went to the woman, bent over her. Gurgling sounds in her throat, but she lay as still as before. Coat and dress had bunched up around her thighs, long white legs, black panties. Nick pulled the dress and coat down to cover her.

"Why'd you have to come on like Rambo's sister?" he said. "Why didn't you just go on home to Gallagher like you were supposed to?"

Then he slid his hands under her back and legs, swung her up, deadweight in his arms, and carried her to the Mazda.

C oming out of a blackout was like waking up with a bad hangover. Slow, groggy awareness. Pulse thudding in his ears, queasiness, tingly weakness in his limbs, burning thirst. Cam lay motionless with his eyes shut, trying to gauge the severity of the attack. Bad enough, but he'd experienced worse. The day at the office, when Maureen had to drive him home. The night in Portland when he'd had the nosebleed.

He opened his eyes to slits. Soft lighting that didn't assault the retinas; ceiling beams. Jenna's house, Jenna's living room. Had she come home and found him passed out?

He moved his head experimentally. Pain, but not the crippling kind. Dull thrumming. Function?

In inching movements, he sat up. The pain seemed to hold steady. He was still on the sofa, and he seemed not to have had another nosebleed or done any more vomiting. He listened to a heavy quiet broken only by the faint, distant ticking of a clock; the rain must have stopped. The house had the same empty feel as when he'd let himself in. Nor was there any purse or coat, anything to indicate that Jenna was here.

How much time had he lost?

He focused on his Rolex. Nine-fifteen. Little more than an hour.

Where was Jenna? Even if she hadn't been able to get away from the party until it ended at nine, she should be here by now. It was only a fifteen-minute drive from Fenwood Creek.

He felt in his pocket for the vial of migraine capsules. It wasn't there, and he remembered he'd had it in his hand just before he blacked out. He found it between two of the cushions, managed to get the top off without spilling any of the capsules. He tried to swallow one dry, but it wouldn't go down.

Teeth gritted, he pushed to his feet. Brief wave of vertigo, then he was all right. A little wobbly but not in any immediate danger of falling down. He walked slowly across the living room, into the bathroom. Too many mirrors in there; it wasn't easy to avoid looking at his reflection, but he managed it. He swallowed the capsule with tap water, using the toothbrush tumbler, drank two more full glasses, and then splashed cold water over his face and neck. Better. He swished Scope around to rid his mouth of the foul aftertaste of wine and vomit. Then he held his hand up to eye level, palm downward, and watched it for a few seconds.

Steady. Steady enough to drive, once the capsule did its work and the pain eased, if he was very, very careful. Thank God for that. If he'd been laid low and Jenna had had to drive him home . . .

Nine-twenty-five. And still no sign of Jenna.

He couldn't imagine why she was so late. Perhaps she'd called to explain, decided when there was no answer that he'd left or hadn't come here at all. Didn't matter right now, anyway. He couldn't wait for her any longer. Driving home was all he could cope with. Bed, sleep, a new day, then he'd find out what Jenna wanted from him.

He retrieved his overcoat, put the key she'd given him on the hall table. She'd have another; nobody gives an only house key to another person. He pushed the Set button on the alarm pad, went out, and pulled the door shut behind him.

For a minute or two he stood sucking in the cold night air, letting the wind dry his clammy skin. The thrumming in his head was muted and tolerable now. Keep the window down, and driving shouldn't be a problem. BMWs practically drove themselves; all you had to do was steer.

Down the driveway, turn right, and he was on his way—until his headlights picked up the car slewed off onto a turnout a short distance downhill. White, a white Lexus like the one Jenna drove. There were a lot of white Lexuses on the road these days, but still . . .

He braked, cut off onto the turnout in front of the parked car. The license plate was clearly visible in his lights: JENNA B. Her Lexus, all right, but what was it doing here?

Confusion, a vague sense of alarm, prodded him out. He tried the driver's door, found it unlocked. The Lexus was empty. Nothing of Jenna's on the seats, no signs of anything disturbed. He shut the door, looked around the turnout, up and down the road. Footprints in the muddy earth that weren't his. Tire tracks that also weren't his. Made by the Lexus or another car? He couldn't tell.

His frayed nerves began to jump again.

What had happened here?

Where was Jenna?

S he was dead.

Lying curled up in the trunk pretty much the way he'd laid her in, on her left side, only now her eyes were open and glazed over, staring. He touched the side of her neck, cold, Jesus, no pulse beating there, nothing. Dead.

Nick leaned against the open trunk lid. Wind blowing in through the doorless front of the garage, the gaps in the walls, picked at the hair on his neck like bony fingers. Carbon monoxide? No, wasn't anything wrong with the exhaust, and her face'd be bright red and it wasn't, it was milk-white under the smears of mud and blood. Suffocation? Not that, either. Enough air in the trunk, and he'd put the piece of duct tape across her mouth, not her nose. He'd even been careful not to wrap the tape too tight around her hands and feet.

Sticky mat of blood on the dark hair behind her ear, glistening in the pale trunk light. Smacked-meat sound of her head hitting the asphalt . . . was that it? Hard blow on the head could kill somebody—almost killed Annalisa. That had to be it.

She'd been alive when he put her in the trunk, he was sure of that. Couldn't leave her lying there on the road, somebody might come along any second, she'd put the cops on him as soon as she woke up—*had* to take her along. Kept trying to decide on the long ride to the Russian River what he'd do with her, hazy idea of keeping her locked up until he was ready to deal with Gallagher. Hazy, crazy idea, but it was all he could come up with. Except killing her, and he wouldn't've done that. Kill Gallagher, yeah, Gallagher deserved to die, but not a woman. She hadn't done anything to him except wave the automatic in his face and he couldn't blame her for that. Foulmouthed bimbo, stone-hard bitch, but she was still a woman, and he didn't believe in hurting women unless there was no other choice, like when he'd had to punch her face. Maybe he'd've had no other choice if he'd kept her prisoner. But he hadn't wanted to think about that.

Now it didn't matter. Now she was dead. And the thing was, he hadn't killed her, not really. Wasn't his fault she'd hit her head so hard. Sure, he'd punched her, knocked her down, but she was the one to blame for that, her and her little gun. He'd acted in self-defense. Banging her head was an accident. A freak accident.

Besides, admit it, it was better this way. Better for him and Annalisa. With the woman dead, he didn't have to run the risk of keeping her locked up for a couple of weeks. Dead, she wasn't a threat to his plans for Gallagher. Look at it that way. Don't think about it any other way.

"I'm sorry," he said to her, "I didn't want to hurt you, it was a freak accident. But it's better this way."

He shut the lid, locked the trunk and the car. Raining again, big drops like pellets of ice; he plowed through wet grass and weeds to the house, let himself in. Cold in there, even though he'd left the thermostat set at sixty-eight. He turned it up to seventy-five, went around switching on lights to chase away the dark—night was usually his friend, but not this night. Finally settled in the kitchen because it was the warmest room in the house.

Only he couldn't get warm.

Sat at the table drinking hot coffee, wall register blasting hot air at him, and his skin felt like frosted glass, and shivers and chills ran all over his body.

He kept thinking about the Bailey woman out there in the car, cold and dead. And how she must've died from hitting her head on the pavement, severe head trauma from being thrown into the telephone pole—

Pavement. *Pavement.*

Smacked-meat sound, cracked her skull, twitch and she was still.

Like Annalisa.

Severe head trauma.

Like Annalisa.

No, *not* like Annalisa. Annalisa was alive, her head trauma hadn't been fatal and she was going to get better but Jenna Bailey died but Annalisa wouldn't die wouldn't die wouldn't die!

He sat there shivering. And then crying, all at once, fat tears rolling down his cheeks, bawling the way he had in the hospital the night of the hit-and-run, and he didn't know right then if all the grief leaking out of him was for Annalisa or the dead woman in the Mazda's trunk.

PART III

Flood

All weekend Cam worried. About Jenna and what might have happened to her. About whether or not Nick Hendryx had had anything to do with it. About Hallie, if he should tell her about Jenna and what her reaction would be if he did. About himself, what his responsibilities were—legal, moral, personal.

He called Jenna's home number twice, Fenwood Creek twice. She wasn't home, she wasn't at the winery. No one there had any idea where she might be.

He called Caitlin to make sure she was all right. Teddy answered, told him she was out somewhere, he didn't know where; the kid's voice said he didn't much care. Sure she was okay, why wouldn't she be? Hendryx? How should he know if she'd been with the dude Friday night? Yeah, he'd tell her Uncle Cameron called, making the word *uncle* sound like an obscenity.

Monday, first thing at the office, Cam called Fenwood Creek again. Jenna wasn't there. Hadn't called in, simply hadn't shown up, her assistant said, and that wasn't like her. Mr. Collins was on his way to her house to see if maybe she was ill or something.

The rest of the morning crawled by. A few minutes before noon he rang Fenwood Creek again, but Collins wasn't there or wasn't taking calls and his secretary had nothing to report about Jenna. He left a message for Bryan, then waited in an agony of suspense until Collins finally returned his call at two-thirty.

It was as bad as he'd feared. Jenna's car was still parked on the turnout, her house was empty, and there was no indication she'd been home since Friday night or of where she might be. Collins tried to downplay the implications, but he was as upset as Cam had ever heard him. More upset than a boss over a missing employee, it seemed, which led Cam to wonder if the usually unflappable Collins had been or still was one of her lovers.

Bryan had notified the county's criminal investigation department. So it was almost certain an investigator would be around to talk to Cam eventually. Someone at the Christmas party must have seen Jenna and him talking, possibly even seen her slip him the house key. The wise thing would seem to be for him to go to the authorities before they came to him. But he was afraid of them getting the wrong idea. If she'd been kidnapped or murdered, and the identity of the person responsible remained in doubt, his presence in her house the night of the disappearance would make him a prime suspect. Angry lover, sudden violence, that kind of scenario. In any case there would be bad publicity, the sort that could harm his family, harm PWS.

The other option was to wait it out. Hope Jenna was found quickly, alive and well; and if she wasn't found, play dumb and innocent—exactly what he was—when the CID got around to him. But that was just as potentially disastrous. If the investigators caught him in a lie, they'd be even more suspicious of him. At the very least, even though he had no conclusive information about her disappearance, he could be charged with obstruction.

He didn't know what to do about Hendryx, either. He called Caitlin again on Sunday, and this time she was home. His excuse was a futile plea for her to change her mind and spend Christmas Eve in Los Alegres. He managed to steer the conversation around to Hendryx, and she said no, she hadn't been with him Friday night, he'd been away on an overnight haul. Why was he so interested? Cam said he thought he'd seen Hendryx in the Paloma Valley; she said maybe he needed glasses. And that was the end of that.

So he still had no idea whether or not Hendryx was involved. Jenna hadn't mentioned him at the party, or at any time since their phone conversation weeks ago. Her early suspicions had no foundation, at least so far as he knew, and neither did his. If he sicced the law on Hendryx and the man was innocent, Caitlin would never forgive him—it would destroy what was left of their fragile relationship.

Yet what if Hendryx was guilty? What if he was a stalker, a rapist, something even worse? It was possible; anything was possible. Caitlin might be in jeopardy, Cam Gallagher might be. Would telling the county CID about Hendryx eliminate the threat in that case? Not necessarily. There was no guarantee anything could be proven against him. And the authorities nosing around might even provoke him into some sort of retaliation. . . .

What was right? What was best for Hallie and his daughters, Caitlin, himself?

He didn't know; he couldn't decide. And what made it worse was the nagging fear that no matter what he did, something bad would come of it.

Week before Christmas, Nick went for long rides every night. Saturday and Sunday was a chicken run down to the Central Valley; but he had Wednesday and Thursday off with pay, part of North County Poultry Processors employees' Christmas package. Wednesday and Thursday off at Goodwill, too—no pay, because they didn't schedule any pickups right before the holidays. So he drove north and south, east and west, once as far downstate as Bakersfield, another time all the way to Truckee through a Sierra snowstorm.

Better in the car, moving, following the open road. He felt invulnerable, exercising the same control over his life and destiny that he had over his wheels—like the psychologist'd said in the article about night riders. Rained most of the time he was on the road, and that was all right, too. Tires humming, wipers shushing back and forth, radio playing soft, all of it soothing and the night so dark you couldn't see much except the shiny black-and-white surface ahead, as if the world had shrunk all the way down to a narrow strip that kept on curling and unwinding under the headlights. Thinking sometimes about Annalisa, sometimes about Gallagher and how spooked he must be about his girlfriend, how he'd be figuring Nick must've had something to do with it but be too afraid to go to the cops on account of the hit-and-run charge hanging over his head. Didn't think about the Bailey woman except in little blips and black flashes. Mostly didn't think about anything, just kept driving with the heater turned up as high as it would go.

Couple of times he slept in the car. Partly because he got tired and didn't trust himself to stay alert without some rest, but mainly to avoid going back to the house. He didn't like being cooped up there. Before long he'd have to stick close to the place, like it or not. Work to be done, preparations to make. But not yet, not until after Christmas. Enough time would've passed by then, and the house wouldn't keep reminding him of the dead woman, making him feel bad when he ought to feel good because it was almost over, he could count the days until he was back home.

Home. Sometimes the word was a pulse in his head: home home home home home home. Other times it was the wind and the tires on pavement and the engine whine, one long steady hum: hommmmmmmm-mmmmme. Denver. Annalisa. Mom and Pop Foster. He missed them all so much. The missing and the wishing and the wanting got so bad late one night that he stopped at a pay phone, middle of nowhere, and called up the Fosters. Just couldn't help himself. Mom answered, all shook at such a late call. It choked him up so much hearing her voice, he could hardly speak, and she thought it was some crank caller and almost hung up on him before he could get the words out.

He apologized for calling so late, said he needed to hear a friendly voice, asked how Annalisa was. Mom said she was all right, just the same, and when are you coming home, Nickie? Like I told you last time, he said. Next month. Sometime after the first week in January.

"Can't you come for Christmas?" Mom asked again. "Annalisa, she needs you—I know she does. And we need you, Pop and me, to be here with us. This year more than ever."

"I want to be there, Mom. You know how much I want to. But I can't. Not yet, not until I'm finished here."

And she started to cry, and he hung up—had to hang up because it hurt too much listening to her cry like that in the middle of the night a few days before Christmas. But talking to her made him feel better, too.

Love always made you feel better, even when you had to hear it and feel it from a long way off.

Love and night rides, they were what he needed right now. To chase away the cold, chase away the dead woman, give him the strength to get through the next two weeks. And make him ready inside his head when it finally got to be time for Gallagher.

On Wednesday morning a county CID lieutenant named Dudley showed up at PWS. Cam went cold and tight inside when Gretchen buzzed and told him who was waiting. He sat for a couple of minutes to compose himself; made sure his face was sweat-free before he told Gretchen to send the lieutenant in.

Dudley was tall, thin, flat-faced, and polite. And his visit was strictly routine; that became apparent in the first thirty seconds. He was questioning everyone, he said, who knew Jenna and who had spoken to her at the Fenwood Creek Christmas party. He knew nothing about the key, had no suspicion that Cam had been in her house that night—and Cam didn't enlighten him. The desire to unburden himself was there, but he didn't have the will or the courage to go through with it.

At least he didn't quite lie to Dudley. No, Jenna hadn't said anything to him about her plans for the rest of that evening or the weekend. No, he had no idea of what might have happened to her. No, he knew of no one who had threatened her or held a grievance against her or who had cause of any kind to want to harm her. Sins of omission. No justification for it, yet there was also no justification for putting himself and his reputation on the line. Cold comfort in that fact—the coldest kind.

Dudley was gone in less than fifteen minutes. Cam sat limp at his desk and began worrying all over again. He'd heard enough on the valley grapevine to know that both Bryan Collins and Dennis Frane remembered the man at the Hotel Paloma bar, how irritated Jenna had been when she saw him; but they knew nothing about the man, couldn't provide a detailed description. Lieutenant Dudley hadn't mentioned him, so he didn't know that Cam had been with her that first night, but he'd certainly be investigating that angle. Suppose he found someone to whom Jenna had confided her fears of being stalked, who knew about the connection to Cam?

Fingerprints—that was another source of apprehension. He'd surely left some in her house; suppose they found one and identified him? Could he get away with claiming it was an old one, from the time of the wine-and-cheese party? The odds were in his favor that if identifiable prints hadn't been found by now, there weren't any. He'd read somewhere that it was not as easy to lift clear latents off any surface, even glass, as TV and mystery novels made it seem. But still. Still.

Suppose the driver of the car that had been behind him when he turned into Jenna's driveway was found? Suppose the driver remembered the BMW, all or part of the license plate?

Suppose, suppose, suppose . . .

He didn't believe the few minutes with Lieutenant Dudley would be the end of it. Any more than he believed, now, that Jenna would be found unharmed. No happy endings here. Not for her, not for him, either. The waiting, the gut sense of impending disaster, made him feel as though he had been squeezed into a hot, airless box. Keep on living in that box, he'd suffocate or drown in his own sour juices.

He had to get out. Make a decision, take some kind of action while there was still time. He didn't know what yet, only that he'd have to do it soon. He could not go on this way.

ick spent Christmas Eve alone with Annalisa.

Before supper he picked a small branch off one of the pine trees, gathered up a couple of the bigger, nicer cones. Arranged them on the kitchen table, added two of the red Christmas candles he'd bought, and lit the wicks. The framed photo of Annalisa went between the candles and among the pine needles and cones. Pretty. Just right. Even prettier when he shut off the overhead lights and it was only the candle glow shining soft on her face, on that little private smile of hers that made him think of the Madonna in all the religious pictures he'd seen.

He ate there with her, a can of Franco-American spagetti because it was something she'd always liked, and afterward he put the card he'd bought next to her. It was a nice card, not too sentimental—perfect. Later he'd mail it to Mom and Pop Foster for them to keep with all his letters, so she'd know he was thinking of her and how much he missed her on this special holiday.

He sat at the table until midnight, warm for the first time in days, not from the furnace but from her eyes shining in the candlelight. Before he went up to bed he sang her favorite hymn, "Silent Night," like they used to do together back home. Voice was rusty, but he remembered all the words. And her voice, sweet and clear in his memory, seemed to join in and make it almost like a duet on the last couple of verses.

When they were done he said, "Merry Christmas, honey," and picked her up and kissed her. "Merry Christmas."

She smiled back at him as if she knew this was the last holiday they'd ever have to be apart.

Silent night, holy night.

The river was rising.

All the rain over the past three weeks, all the runoff from the mountain creeks that fed into it, had swollen it into a foamy brown swirl that ran high and fast against its banks. It was still five or six feet below flood stage, but if the rains continued—and the forecasters were saying they would, ballyhooing El Niño in loud voices and scare headlines—this would be another serious flood year on the Russian River. The residents of Guerneville, Rio Nido, and Monte Rio were already preparing for it. Cam drove past boarded-up houses and cabins, sandbagged storefronts, emergency evacuation equipment ready and waiting on high ground.

It had rained heavily on Christmas Day, off and on over the weekend; now, at noon on Monday, there was a thin, windblown drizzle out of low-hanging cloud cover so dark and restive it was like a black-dyed substance simmering in an enormous cauldron. The slick highway was mostly deserted. He passed only two other vehicles, one a county sheriff's cruiser, between Guerneville and the turnoff to Crackerbox Road.

He drove with his mind shut down and a tight lid on his emotions. He'd turned himself off twenty-four hours ago, when he had made up his mind to come up here—the only way he'd be able to go through with it.

Some of the homes along Crackerbox Road were empty, battened down for the winter. The few that appeared occupied wore ground girdles of sandbags—useless barriers, like matchsticks stacked in front of a drainpipe, if floodwaters exceeded the forty-foot level. Behind the homes, the muddy river churned and eddied, half-submerging scrub trees and vegetation along the lower sections of both banks; the surface boil was less than a dozen feet below Highway 116 leading out to Jenner, the only main road through the flood zone. The highway, and Crackerbox and Moscow Roads on this side of the Duncans Mills bridge, would be inundated and impassable at a forty-foot-plus crest. The only means of transportation in and out of the area then would be boat or helicopter.

Neither Hendryx nor Riverbank Realty's handyman had done anything to fortify Gallagher's Bane. Waste of time if they had. The house squatted crumbling and dripping in its nest of evergreens and tall weedy grass. Ancient, decayed, near death with its wet eyes staring blindly, waiting to die and have done with it. This winter might just do the trick. El Niño's one good deed. Tear the frigging place down, break it up, scatter its moldy bones along the riverbanks all the way out to the beaches at Jenner and Goat Rock, where the Russian River met the ocean.

He crawled past, looking. The open garage was empty; so was the mud-rutted drive and the expanse of roadside in front—no sign of the blue Mazda. As expected. Hendryx was at work at the Goodwill in Los Alegres. Cam had made sure the charity was open today, the Monday after Christmas, before leaving to drive up here.

A copse of pine separated the property line from its nearest west-side neighbor. He left the car in among the trees and walked back. No one around that he could see, only a few house lights to cut into the midday gloom. He stopped at the front gate, shoulders hunched inside his topcoat, chin ducked, looking up from under the brim of the rain hat he wore at the house's blank face. Shifting his gaze after a few seconds to the river running behind, to a torn-off tree limb with thin bare branches like spider's legs caught and bobbing in the current. When the limb swirled out of sight, he opened the gate and went through, heading first to the garage.

Nothing to find in there. Nor among the grass and weeds between the garage and the collapsed shed, between the shed and the rear porch of the house, or on the long sloping riverbank, or under the trees. He didn't admit it to himself until he was on his way to the front porch, but what he'd been searching for was freshly turned ground. A grave— Jenna's grave. The notion seemed a little foolish now, but that was part of his relief at finding nothing of the sort.

The stair risers sagged and creaked under his weight as he climbed onto the porch. At the door he took the spare key, the one he'd never used, out of his pocket. And stood there with the key in hand, aware of a faint weakness in his knees, the hard, irregular beat of his pulse.

I don't want to go in there.

I'm not afraid of this goddamn house!

He slipped the key into the lock, blanking his mind again. Turned it, turned the knob, opened the door, and for the first time since that bloody long-ago night, he entered the river house.

Cold draft from somewhere, even after he shut the door. It produced a shiver as he stood in the murky hallway. He smelled damp, mold; heard the wind in the eaves, the rain on the roof, a steady dripping high above. His breath shortened, caught in his throat. He had an intense urge to turn and run out. He fought it, leaning against the wall. Same wallpaper, pattern of little blue flowers, forget-me-nots, the paper damp and sticky against his fingers and palm as if the paper, the wall, were bleeding—

He shoved upright again, forced himself to walk through the archway into the parlor. Different furniture, old and dusty and uncomfortable looking. Caitlin's choices, or the Realtor's? Ashes in the fireplace, no other indication that Hendryx spent much time in here. Back into the hallway. A deep breath, another, and he started up the stairs.

Runners worn through in places, loose riser halfway up, creak, creak, creak. Then he was on the second floor, walking toward the rear past the bathroom door, past the attic door. Into the back bedroom. His room twenty-five years ago—mostly his, except when Caitlin threw a fit about having to sleep downstairs all alone and Pa let her have her way. On those nights he'd had to sleep down there behind the kitchen, in the room where—

No.

Twin beds here once, now a queen with a scarred wooden headboard. Mattress bare except for a yellowed plastic covering. Musty, unused. He opened the closet. Empty. The dresser drawers. Empty.

Back along the hall to the bathroom. Old leather toilet kit, shaving gear, not much else. No medications or personal items of any kind, man's or woman's.

Front bedroom. This was where Hendryx slept. Sheets on the bed, pillowcases, thermal blanket, and a comforter—unmade and not very clean. The closet's contents were two shirts, two pairs of pants, and a lightweight windbreaker on hangers, all cheap and worn, and a pair of scuffed shoes and a cardboard suitcase on the floor. The suitcase was empty. So were the pockets of the windbreaker.

On top of the dresser was a framed wedding-reception photo of Hendryx and a round-cheeked blond woman, pretty in a homespun way. His wife, the victim of the hit-and-run. The dresser and nightstand drawers contained nothing but dust and lint. No ashtray, alarm clock, books or TV or radio. Hendryx didn't smoke or set an alarm or read or watch sitcoms or listen to music or talk radio. What did he do with his time?

Into the hallway again. The only place left up here was the attic. At first his legs refused to take him there. And when he finally did get them moving, he had to fight himself through every jerky step. His breathing was labored again when he reached the door. It had a lock now, not new, but it hadn't been keyed. He opened the door, his teeth clamped so tight muscle pain flared along his jawline.

A pull cord hung from the wall fixture, same as when he was a boy; he tugged on it. Dead bulb. Murky shadows above, beyond the top of the stairs. Rain on the roof, dripping in the walls. Cold, damp, dark. Smells of mold and mildew, rain and dust and mouse turds. Voice crying in his memory, whimpering in the dark, saying things he didn't want to hear.

There was cold sweat on his face, under his arms. Nothing up there but ghosts. Hiding place for ghosts and terrified children and he did not, did not, did not want to go up there—

Wimp, pisspoor excuse for a man—do it!

Push-pull, push-pull. It raged inside him for a little time, a silent bitter struggle; then, almost convulsively, he was through the door and on the stairs.

Enough daylight filtered in through the dormer windows to let him see that the attic had been cleared out. Empty space except for dust and droppings, no Jenna, and he turned and went back down, quickly at first and then more slowly as he reached the bottom. There. Not so bad, was it?

Bad enough.

He shut the door and descended to the first floor, mopping his face with his handkerchief. Kitchen. Same appliances, or ones that looked the same. The only difference was the dinette table; this one was chrome and yellow Formica. And on it—a pine bough, two fat cones, two half-burned red candles, and a color photograph of Hendryx's wife in a tarnished silver frame.

Shrine, he thought. Like a shrine.

For a reason he couldn't name, it made him uneasy. What kind of man worships a woman enough to create a shrine to her, yet maintains a relationship with another woman? The psychotic kind capable of stalking and kidnapping a third?

Cam stepped into the rear hallway, eyes avoiding the bedroom, and had a look around the screened porch. Washer, dryer, freezer, an ancient cracked oilskin hanging from a nail—nothing. Downstairs toilet. Nothing. Now the bedroom. Come on, come on, one quick look and you're finished, you're out of here, you never have to come back again.

The bedroom door was ajar. He stood in front of it, his breath making faint rattling sounds in his throat. He put his fingertips against the panel, pushed, and then clutched at the jamb, cringing, expecting to see blood and death, in reality or in flashback images.

He saw a room, just a room.

Four walls, small unfamiliar rollaway bed, bare unstained floor—an empty room.

He turned away. A few seconds later he was out through the front door, locking it behind him. On the weedy path, sucking cold fresh air, feeling the rain on his upturned face. Through the gate, on the road, into the copse of pines, into his car.

He sat there, feeling . . . what? As though he'd run a long gauntlet.

Calm, almost numb. And acutely relieved. No sign of Jenna, nothing of hers to implicate Hendryx in her disappearance. But it went deeper than that. Beloit: Confront the creatures that inhabit your nightmares. Well, he'd confronted the house creature, and it hadn't been half so terrifying as he'd imagined. Bad moments, but he'd fought through them, he hadn't run away.

The sense of helplessness was gone. He was still in a box, but he was out of the attic. He wasn't hiding anymore.

onday was Nick's day to go shopping.

On his lunch hour he walked down to a women's store, one of those boutique places, on the same block as the Goodwill. Looked at some earrings, bought a long dangly pair made of beads and shiny stuff. They'd've looked good on Annalisa, so he figured they'd look good on Caitlin. She'd driven up the river on Christmas Day, surprised him with a present—silver key chain with a doodad that had a chunk of real turquoise in it—and he'd felt bad about not having something for her in return. He'd give her the earrings on New Year's Eve. Asked him to spend it with her, kind of wistful and sad, and he didn't have the heart to refuse her. Annalisa wouldn't mind when he told her, about that or about the earrings.

After work he stopped at a hardware store on the north end of Los Alegres, then a furniture store in Rohnert Park, then a building supply outfit in Santa Rosa. Mazda wasn't built for hauling, so he had to make two trips to the river house—drop off one load, go back to the building supply for the lumber. Took some roping and red-flagging, but he got everything tied on, no problem.

He lined up everything he'd bought, all the items on his list, in the front room. Good thing he'd always been handy. Worked construction building tract houses that one summer before he joined the army. Some-day, when he and Annalisa had their own home, he'd have a workshop in the basement or garage, all the latest woodworking equipment, and he'd make things for her—tables, bookcases, one of those little catchall desks, maybe something big and fancy like those glass-fronted cabinets that held dishes and had drawers for silverware and table linens underneath. He could almost hear the whine of the power saws as they cut through fine-grained oak and mahogany and walnut, almost see and smell the flying sawdust. Man, he could hardly wait.

Job here ought to take him about three days, be finished by New Year's Eve, New Year's Day. Part of this week off from both his jobs, same as last week, so he'd have plenty of time. That'd be a real pleasure, too—hammering and sawing and banging nails and tightening screws again—because it wasn't just scut work. It was work that had to be just right, because it meant more than any he'd done in a long time.

New Year's Eve.

The Edmondses' annual party at their hundred-year-old Cherry Valley Victorian. Same dozen couples, same trite, traditional trappings—balloons, noisemakers, party favors, trays of cholesterol-laden canapés, salads, cold cuts. The usual crystal bowl of champagne punch and plenty of hard liquor, but Cam steered clear of it all. He was twitchy just being there; hadn't wanted to come, but he couldn't think of a valid excuse to cancel out, and it was a way to take his mind off things for a few hours.

It had been a long, empty week for him. No word on Jenna, no more contact with Lieutenant Dudley, and yet the vague sense of foreboding remained. Hallie knew something was bothering him, but beyond a few tentative overtures, she left him alone. Waiting for him to come to her. If only he could find the courage; he desperately needed to talk to somebody, and she was the only one who really understood him. But would she understand about this? That was the question that kept him mute.

The one positive thing to come out of recent events was that he seemed to have lost his reliance on alcohol. He'd had very little to drink since Jenna's disappearance. Shocked sober. Shocked right out of his bleak, Rose-haunted indulgences, and into looking at himself and his life in a new, more objective way. The box he was squeezed into now wasn't the first, merely the latest in a long succession. He'd been sweating and thrashing in dark boxes, mobile coffins, for the past quarter of a century, and booze had only helped to keep him locked in. If there was a way out of this one, out of the others, he'd never find it at the bottom of a bottle.

The party ebbed and flowed around him. He circulated, wearing a happy face like a mummer's mask, listening, talking little. The main topics of conversation, predictably, were El Niño and Jenna Bailey.

"They're predicting a chain of storms through most of next week. Heavy rain, high winds."

"Just listen to it whacking down out there right now. Whole state's in for heavy flooding. Rivers and lakes are already brimful."

"You believe that big slide down in Pacifica the other day? Three houses, wham, right off a cliffside into the ocean."

"That hill back of Rio Nido is liable to take out a few more houses the mud didn't get last time. Whole slope is liquefied, they say."

"U.S. Geological Survey estimates losses from slides alone at a billion dollars again this year. Add another billion for general flood damage. You know what that means. Somebody's got to pay for all the federal and state disaster relief, and that means us, the poor taxpayers."

"Remember when they said the 'eighty-six flood was the flood of the century on the Russian and Napa Rivers? How many have there been since? Four in the last thirteen years, right? At least two of 'em with higher crests than in 'eighty-six."

"Weather Service guy said on TV the other night there's a chance of worse winter weather next century, all across the world. Longer storm chains, floods, slides, coastal erosion, you name it."

"Bad enough right now, here. We might as well be living in Oregon or Washington State."

"Global warming, that's the reason. More and more scientists agree on that. What they can't agree on is what to do about it."

"Well, I can give them one answer. Start building a fleet of arks."

Laughter. The kind with a hollow core and a tiny wiggling undercurrent of fear.

"Anybody hear anything new on the Jenna Bailey kidnapping?"

"How do you know it was a kidnapping? It's possible she went with some guy voluntarily."

"And left behind everything she owned and a job that must pay close to six figures a year? You ask me, some sexual predator got her. One of those wrong-place-at-the-wrong-time things."

"Either that, or it was some guy she knew—one of her lovers past or present. Papers keep hinting she was hot stuff. You knew her pretty well, didn't you, Cam? Was she hot stuff?"

"One of the county CID investigators is a friend of mine. He says they found a shell casing near where her car was abandoned. Ejected from a thirty-two automatic. She had a thirty-two registered in her name."

"What do they think it means, Lloyd? She took a shot at the guy who grabbed her?"

"Most likely scenario, since it was her gun."

"Any chance she hit him?"

"They didn't find any blood at the scene. But they're not ruling out the possibility."

"What else hasn't the sheriff's department released to the media, Lloyd?"

"Nothing, except there were two other handguns in her house. A twenty-two in the kitchen and a three-five-seven Magnum in her bedroom nightstand."

"That's a lot of firepower for one woman. What was she, a gun nut?"

"Well, she lived by herself. And she'd been raped once before, don't forget that."

"That's right. Five or six years ago, wasn't it?"

"Six. On the Silverado Trail where she used to work."

"They catch the guy? Maybe it was the same one this time."

"No, it wasn't. They caught him, all right. Convicted on serial rape charges—she was his third or fourth victim. He's still in San Quentin."

"Guns aren't the answer. All of hers didn't do her any good, did they."

"Her own fault, if it was somebody she knew. Women who sleep around like that are just asking for trouble."

"Oh, you men. You think being friendly is an invitation to some jerk to commit rape."

"We're not talking friendly here, we're talking promiscuous. Women with hot pants send out signals that give the wrong guys the wrong ideas."

"Crap. Rape is hardly ever the woman's fault. And it isn't a sex crime, it's a crime of violence against women. Some sicko's idea of a power trip."

"A sicko with a deep-seated sense of inadequacy, probably. It's a well-known fact that most rapists have an average chubby of two and a half inches."

"Ha ha. You're disgusting, you know that, Walter?"

Cam moved away from the group, feeling sickened. Disgusting was the word, all right, not just for Walter but for all of them. Talking about Jenna as if she were a piece of meat, an inanimate object created for their amusement, instead of a flesh-and-blood human being with good and bad qualities, hopes, dreams—a soul—like everybody else. Alive or dead, she deserved better than this. Empathy and compassion, for God's sake, if nothing else.

He found himself standing in front of the liquor buffet. But just looking at the stuff set up a reaction in his stomach; he poured another glass of ginger ale instead. Hallie was talking to Janet Edmonds, he noticed, and from the glass in her hand, he realized she was also drinking ginger ale. It occurred to him that she'd been watching him and following his lead. And that led to a sudden sharp insight: Not just tonight—on most social occasions, and even when it was the two of them alone—she drank when he drank. When he couldn't stand himself and drank too much as a blotter, she couldn't stand him, either, and drank too much in self-defense and to blot out what he was blotting out. His pain was her pain, his release was her release. It should have worked the other way as well: her pain his, her release his. But it hadn't, not often enough. Selfish. All their married life he'd been selfish, and so whenever he tried not to hurt her, he'd only hurt her more.

The insight gave him something more than understanding; it gave him strength. He asked her to dance as an excuse to talk to her alone.

"Do you mind if we leave before midnight?" he asked.

"Not having a good time?"

"No, but that isn't the reason. I . . . need to talk to you. It's important, Hallie."

"All right." No hesitation, no questions. "I'll make an excuse to Janet, and we can leave right away."

They were silent in the car. At home he made quick work of paying the sitter, then sat Hallie down in the living room and told her everything except how close he'd come to having an affair with Jenna. The first few words were difficult, but once they were free, it was like removing an obstruction in a reservoir valve: the rest spilled out in a rush until the tank was dry.

She listened without interruption. And when she finally did speak, it was in quiet tones without anger or censure.

"Why didn't you tell me this right away?"

"I was afraid to. Afraid of what you might think."

"About you and Jenna."

"Yes. I didn't have an affair with her, Hallie. I've slept with exactly one woman the past thirteen years—you."

"I believe you. I can take anything, go through anything with you, except that. Another woman would destroy us."

"I know that," he said. "And there'll never be one, I swear that to you." The promise was as devout as a prayer.

"Then you never have to be afraid with me, darling. Not about anything, ever."

New Year's Eve.

Sebastopol. Alone with Caitlin, Theodore away somewhere for the night. Cat happy, dressed up nice with her hair combed and makeup on, bustling around the kitchen like Annalisa used to do, eyes all bright and shiny when he gave her the package with the earrings. Dinner— ham and sweet potatoes. Wine—only a couple of sips for him, three or four glasses for her. Music, not too loud. Sitting together on the couch, her head on his shoulder, her fingers playing with one of the earrings that she'd gone and put on right away, chattering and laughing about nothing much. Something else Annalisa used to do.

Midnight. On TV they watched the ball drop in Times Square in New York City, and she wanted to kiss him and he let her, New Year's Eve after all, just the one little kiss, even though he could see she wanted more. Another glass of wine for her, and she begged him to hold her the way he had that other time. In the bedroom where it was more comfortable. He wouldn't've done it except that he felt like being held, too, tonight.

Lying in there with her, all their clothes on but their shoes, holding her in the dark. Not enjoying it much at first, letting it go on to please her. Liking it better after a while. Warm, sleepy, relaxed.

Until her hand moved, brushed his thigh, moved again and settled gently between his legs.

Her voice, wine-thick: "It must've been a long time for you. Such a long time."

Didn't answer. Didn't feel anything except suddenly all bunched up inside. Lifted her hand, pushed it away.

"Can't I do something for you, Nickie?"

"Don't call me that."

"We don't have to make love. I can use my hand—"

"No."

"Or give you head. Would you like that?"

"No." Pulled away from her, sat up and swung his legs off the bed.

"Nick? I'm sorry, I only wanted to—"

"I have to go," he said.

"Go? You mean leave?"

"Right now."

"No, please don't, please stay with me."

Slid his feet into his loafers, walked out into the front room. Picked up his jacket from one of the chairs.

Behind him: "Don't go, Nick. I said I was sorry, it won't happen again, I swear it won't."

Didn't look at her. Zipped up his jacket and headed for the door. He needed to drive now. Wrap the night and the Mazda tight around himself.

"Nick! I only wanted to do something nice for you!"

Something nice for him. She didn't understand. Nobody understood, not even Mom and Pop Foster. Nobody knew how alone he was, what he needed, what really mattered to him. Nobody in the whole world except Annalisa.

"You're no better than your brother," he said to the woman, and went out and slammed the door behind him.

he call came a few minutes before ten on Monday morning.
He'd just gotten off the phone with Lloyd Edmonds. Making an
appointment to see Lloyd at his office at one this afternoon. That
was the first thing he and Hallie had decided he should do, consult with
an attorney to determine his exact legal position. It could wait until
today, they'd decided; the Edmondses had left on New Year's morning
for Placerville, to spend the weekend with Janet's parents, and it hadn't
seemed necessary to upset their holiday plans. Enough time had passed
already that an extra couple of days wouldn't make any difference.

If Lloyd's advice was that he should go to Lieutenant Dudley, as it
probably would be, then that was what he'd have to do. Hallie's opinion
was that he wasn't guilty of anything, really, except poor judgment.
Lloyd would also likely advise him to offer up Nick Hendryx's name,
hold nothing back, and so he'd have to do that, too, in spite of Caitlin.
All or nothing—that was the only way out of the box.

He was thinking this when Gretchen buzzed and told him he
had a personal call. Important, the man had said. He said all right and
picked up.

"Nick Hendryx, Mr. Gallagher."

He was so surprised, all he could say was, "Yes?"

"I think it's time we had a talk."

"Talk about what?"

"Don't you know? I think you do."

"If you mean Caitlin—"

"How about I come by your place of business about four-thirty? I've got a delivery over your way, and I should be done by then."

"I wasn't planning to be here this afternoon."

"Be a good idea if you changed your plans. I think you'll want to hear what I have to say."

"If you'll tell me what it's about—"

"You never having to worry about me again in a few days. Or about your sister and me."

". . . Are you going somewhere?"

"That's right. Going home pretty soon."

"Why the sudden decision? Something to do with your wife?"

"Everything to do with her."

"Is she better?"

"She will be. Four-thirty, Mr. Gallagher. See you then."

Cam put the receiver down, frowning. Hendryx's words had had the odd undercurrent again, as if there were hidden meanings in what he'd said. If so, he couldn't decipher them. Should he meet with Hendryx? Lloyd might urge him to talk to Lieutenant Dudley immediately . . . but shouldn't he find out what Hendryx was up to before he did that? If he was going to tell Dudley about him? The lieutenant would certainly want to know what the man's plans were and why.

Besides, what harm could there be in meeting Hendryx here at PWS and giving him a chance to explain himself?

59

ate Monday afternoon. Almost time.

Watching and waiting, Mazda parked on Blackwell Road under the trees near the closed-up animal shelter. Excitement building in him, hot and cold at the same time. Rain pounding down and smearing the windshield so that he had to keep the window open in order to see out.

Five-ten by his watch.

Clear look from here at Paloma Wine Systems inside its chain-link fence. Lights on in the office wing, pole lights reflecting off puddles in the lot in front. Only two cars left there now, Gallagher's BMW and a little foreign job. Everybody else had cut out right at five.

Five-fifteen. Woman came out through the office door, umbrella fanning open. Foreign job belonged to her. She fired up the engine, exhaust smoke pumping out white and thick, headlights jabbing on, car gliding through the gate and out onto Blackwell and past where he was and gone.

Five-twenty.

Five-twenty-five.

Sweating over there, Gallagher? Wondering if I'm coming or not? Wondering if I'm really planning to let you off the hook? You'll find out pretty soon. You're all mine now. Now you start to pay for what you did.

Five-thirty.

Last of the office lights went out. Gallagher'd had enough of sitting and sweating. Almost time. Nick got the Mazda's engine humming, switched the wipers on but left the headlamps dark.

Office door opened, Gallagher walked out. Stood hunched there, big black bird shape, wind flapping the tails of his coat. Locking up.

Nick put the tranny in gear, the headlights on. Rolling when Gallagher turned away from the door and half ran for the BMW. Rolling through the gate, the Mazda's high beams stabbing Wineman, pinning him tight against the driver's side of his car. Sliding to a stop, close but not too close, angled so the lights still held him in a freeze. Hit the trunk release. Hit the door handle. And Nick was out and moving, not too fast.

"Hendryx. I'd about given up on you . . ."

Didn't answer. Kept going, away from Gallagher and along the Mazda to the rear. Lifted the trunk lid all the way up. Reached in and caught up the tire iron, hoisted the Bailey woman's automatic out of his coat pocket at the same time, turned around with the gun and the iron where Gallagher could see them. Still moving, cutting the distance between them in half.

Gallagher said, "Oh my God." Scared now. Knew he'd been suckered, but not why yet.

Nick said, "Come here. Get in the trunk."

"What? Hendryx, for God's sake—"

"Get in the trunk."

"I don't . . . what're you . . ."

"In the trunk. Last time I'll say it."

"No. What's the idea? I won't—"

"Yeah, you will. By yourself, or I'll shoot you and put you in. Or bust your kneecap with this iron and put you in."

Gallagher made a sound like a moan. Eyes bulgy and glistening slimy-white in the light, like raw oysters. Plenty scared now, all right. Piss-in-his-pants scared.

"Three seconds. One. Two . . ."

Gallagher moved. Slow and jerky, bent forward a little, guy walking into a stiff wind that wasn't there. Stopped and stared into the trunk.

Headlight beams on Blackwell Road. Nick said, "Hold it. Stand still."

Stood still himself, body turned sideways to shield his hands from the road. Beams swam past without slowing.

"Now take off your coat. Throw it inside."

Gallagher did it.

"Get in. Facedown, feet together, hands together behind your back."

Did it. Not much room in there, had to twist and curl his body to bring both arms around behind him.

"What're you going to do?" Voice muffled against the carpet mat. "Where're you taking me?"

Nick put the gun away, the tire iron down. Then he said, "To death row," and went to work with the roll of duct tape.

60

e wasn't afraid.

Stunned, dismayed, desolate, but not afraid. In a way that was the most shocking thing of all, the utter absence of terror. He had just looked at death again, felt and smelled and tasted it, different face, different circumstances, but with the same awed disbelief as that night twenty-five years ago—and yet, except for the first minute or two after Hendryx's arrival, he was quite calm. His own death staring back at him, looming in the dark that surrounded him, and all he felt was a kind of drugged numbness inside and out, as if he'd been given a massive shot of novocaine.

He lay cold and cramped, the car moving, stopping, moving, jouncing. He could hear the tires making serpent hisses on the wet pavement, the hum and rumble of other cars passing. The rough carpet abraded the side of his face; he lifted his head, wiggled his body until he was lying with his weight against his bound hands and his face upturned. The tape Hendryx had pressed across his mouth made breathing difficult. His nostrils twitched with the odors of dust, carpet fiber, grease, and oily metal; the combined smells seemed to act as a clog, so that he was unable to draw enough air through his nasal passages.

Suffocate in here.

The thought came and went. Leaving nothing in its wake.

His hands and arms began to go as numb as his mind. He maneuvered his body again, just enough to take the weight off his arms. He flexed his fingers, tried to catch hold of a tape edge to peel it loose. Couldn't manage it; Hendryx had bound his wrists crosswise and too high up for his fingers to find purchase. He went through another painful shift, until he was once more in a facedown position, then tried to work the tape off his mouth by rubbing it back and forth across the matting. All the effort earned him was another abrasion. The tape was stuck tight, more than one strip that stretched around under both ears.

A brief surge of anger and desperation prodded him into heaving, twisting contortions—a futile attempt to free his hands and legs that left him as tightly bound and more cramped. Then he was calm again, as empty of emotion as before. He lay motionless, the skin prickling between his shoulder blades.

After a while the constant uneven motion of the car made him sick to his stomach. He tasted bile, felt it in the back of his throat, and thought: Keep it down—puke, and I'll strangle. He shut his eyes, formed a vise grip with his teeth, locked the muscles in his throat. Lay like that, fighting the nausea. And even then, at the worst internal roilings, what he felt was an empty detachment, as though he were witness to an experiment involving somebody else.

The nausea passed, but the ride went on and on. No more stopping and starting; moving smoothly and steadily, not fast, not slow. Going where? Wherever Hendryx took Jenna? He took her, all right.

Took her and killed her.

Kill me, too. Last words before he shut the trunk . . . wind tore up the second, but the first was *death*.

Hallie . . . the girls . . . Caitlin? Dear God, no.

Must've been planning this all along. And I let him get away with it, walked right into it. Damn stupid fool.

Other thoughts came and went. Some more than once. But none lingered or produced much of a reaction in him except where his family was concerned. Then there were no thoughts, his mind as barren as a wasteland. He vegetated in the cold clotted black, shifting now and then, flexing his fingers to keep the circulation going as much as he could. Listened to the rain, the hissing passage of other cars, the steady throb of his pulse.

Waiting.

Two more thoughts came to him at wide intervals, like wanderers in the wasteland that appeared, passed by, and were gone again.

One: This must be what it's like to be buried alive.

And the other: Pretty soon, when we get to where we're going, when the numbness wears off, I'll find out what kind of man I really am.

61

omething going on. Nick knew it even before he saw the flashing lights of the roadblock.

Hard, driving rain, howling wind gusts strong enough to shake the Mazda. Almost no traffic on the river highway, standing water in low places that forced him to slow down to thirty or less. Nearly all the houses and stores beyond the big Korbel Winery complex dark and closed up. River swollen to a level where it covered low-lying vineyards and fields, turned trees into black jutting shapes like the ones you saw in swamps. So when the cop cars swam into view, their flasher bars making yellow and red smears, he knew they weren't there for him. An accident, maybe—something to do with the weather.

They were set up on both sides of the bridge that led across the river to Rio Nido, two cruisers on this side blocking the westbound lane. Reflector cones came up blurry in his headlights, then a cop wearing a yellow rain hat and slicker and waving a six-cell flashlight. Nick slowed to a crawl. Thinking: Gallagher makes any noise back there and they make me open the trunk, I'll shoot him soon as I raise the lid. What happens to me doesn't matter, long as he dies.

He braked to a stop, and the cop followed his flash beam around on the driver's side. Nick put on a little smile, slid the window down. Wind whipped icy rain against his face as the cop bent to look in at him. Didn't shine the flash in his face, just held the beam on the door so enough light reflected up between them to let him see. No, none of this was for him. Or for anybody in particular.

"Are you a resident of this area, sir?"

"Sure am."

"Evacuation orders came through a little while ago. River's rising fast—flood stage before noon tomorrow and more storms on the way. No one allowed in or out except emergency vehicles after nine A.M. at the latest. What's your location?"

Nick strained to hear before he answered. Nothing from the trunk. Gallagher must be passed out or too scared and confused to know what was going on. Or maybe the rain was making too much racket; Nick could barely hear the cop. *Any* reason Gallagher was quiet, okay, except him lying dead in there like the Bailey woman.

"Crackerbox Road near Duncans Mills," he said.

Cop said, "High risk of road closure in that area. I'd advise you to evacuate as soon as possible, before dawn to be safe."

"Thanks, officer."

"Better leave to the west, as long as you can get across the bridge over there. Highway should be open to Jenner all night, and One south should be okay, too. Drive carefully."

Nick nodded, put the window up, eased out around the cruisers and across the bridge past the cops and cars and light swirls on that side. Then he was alone again, traveling again, sealed off from the wet outside.

Evacuation orders, floods. He'd heard people talking about it, noted the rain and the river rising halfway up the bank behind the house, but it hadn't meant much to him. Never seen a flood before. Hadn't figured it'd happen so soon—too focused on Gallagher. Didn't bother him, though, any of what the cop had said. Shame people had to leave their homes, lose possessions, but things like that happened, floods and hurricanes, all kinds of natural disasters. Wasn't anything you could do except get through it in one piece if you could. No, he wasn't worried. Would've been if tomorrow was January 4, because then he'd've had to change everything around at the last minute. But the fourth was today, and the only thing that was important about today was that he had Gallagher.

Everything ready and waiting at the river house. Be there pretty soon, and that was where he'd stay, evacuation orders or not. They couldn't force him to leave unless they knew about Gallagher, and he'd make sure that didn't happen.

No reprieves for the condemned prisoner. Place and time of the execution was set, and come hell or high water, Cameron Gallagher was going to die right on schedule.

am was suspended between consciousness and unconsciousness when the car stopped again, with enough of a sliding lurch to rouse him. He might have been riding in the trunk for minutes or hours—he had lost all track of time. His body, his limbs, had a frozen feel. Shivers racked him; he had almost no feeling in his hands and feet. His head ached from the exhaust fumes and the hot-oil stench. Breath whistled in his nose, rattled in his throat, ached rawly in his lungs.

All of that, and still his emotions remained as frozen as his skin.

Door slam, but the engine continued to idle. He waited for the trunk lid to open; it didn't happen. Before long Hendryx was back behind the wheel, and the car was splashing and rocking forward along what felt like deep ruts. A sudden bump threw him around in the tight space, bounced his head off a metal surface. His grunt of pain died behind the tape gag. The car rolled a few more feet, there was another bump, and then it stopped once more, and this time the engine shut off.

Storm sounds. Then another door-slam and heavy, muffled steps. And the trunk lock released, the light in there came on as the lid was raised—not bright, but after the pitch-blackness it made him squint. The way he was folded up on his right side, he couldn't see Hendryx. Just as well.

"End of the line, Gallagher."

Hands pulled roughly at the tape binding his ankles. Even when they were free, he couldn't move either leg except for little painful spasms in his thighs. There was no sensation at all below the knees.

Hendryx left his wrists tied, the tape in place over his mouth. The hands bunched in his clothing, tugged and turned and lifted him out of the trunk, scraping one hip on the lock mechanism, banging his head again. Hendryx held him propped against the car, his useless legs dangling to the floor, standing close enough to breathe tooth rot into his face.

Cam turned his head aside, sucked cold, fresh air to clear his head and lungs. Garage—he could make out walls, roof, rough plank floor. Beyond Hendryx and the doorless front there was nothing but sodden blackness. Gusts of rain-laden wind blew in and started him trembling again.

"Stand up. Walk."

He shook his head stiffly, shook it again. Hendryx mistook the gestures for refusal, yanked him away from the car, and then released him and gave him a shove. His dead legs collapsed immediately and he was on the wet floorboards looking up. Hendryx hauled him upright, but the same thing happened as soon as he was released.

"Can't you walk?"

Cam wagged his head.

"Drag you, then. We're not waiting around out here."

Hendryx lifted him once more, without much effort; more strength in that wiry body than it looked to have. They moved out of the garage into the rain and wind, one of Hendryx's arms tight around his waist and the other gripping his arm, his feet dragging through wet grass and puddles like miniature lakes. House shape ahead, no lights. No lights anywhere. Swaying trees. And a loud pulsing, roaring noise—fast water somewhere close by.

Floodwater.

River house.

Jesus, why *here*?

It seemed to take a long time to reach the porch. By then Cam had some feeling back in his legs—muscle twinges, the pins-and-needles tingling that meant blood was flowing again. The numbness inside was wearing off, too. Sharpening awareness, muted feelings of rage and hate. No panic. Whatever fear lived in him ran as deep as the currents in the swollen river behind the house.

They were at the door. Hendryx held him braced with shoulder and knee while he keyed the lock. Inside then, the door slapping shut behind them. As cold and dark inside as it was outside. Furnace must be off . . . no gas or electricity? Power lines must be down all over the area. There were always power outages during storms with high winds—

But not here, not yet. Hendryx flipped the switch, and the hall light came on. Cam blinked, squinted as they crossed into the front parlor. The light clicked on in there, too.

Hendryx carried him to the overstuffed couch, pushed him down on it. Rolled him over, lifted his legs so he was lying flat on his belly with his ankles raised over one of the armrests. He heard the tearing sound of the tape being unwound from his wrists, but he had so little feeling in his hands and arms he wasn't sure when they were free. Fingers pawed at his scalp, found purchase in his hair, yanked his head up; other fingers tore the tape off his mouth.

Hendryx let go of him, moved away. Then, "All right. Sit up and look at me."

No, he thought, stay like this for now. Gesture of defiance. But he didn't obey the impulse. Too helpless, too submissive lying here this way—don't give the bastard the satisfaction.

He couldn't use his hands or arms, and his legs weren't much help, either; he was like a limbless man, a carnival freak performing a trick in a sideshow. Squirming, flopping with hips and torso—contortions and gyrations that left him panting when at last he heaved himself into an upright sprawl. He expected to see his captor laughing at him, enjoying his discomfort, but Hendryx was sitting rigidly in a chair a few feet away, wearing a fixed expression of brooding implacability.

"You know where we are, Gallagher?"

Nod. His throat was too sore, his mouth too dry, for words yet. He worked at producing saliva, at straightening himself on the cushions.

"How does it feel to be back home again after so many years?"

Cam looked away, remembering his visit here last week. If he hadn't come then, if this really was his first time in the house since January of 1974, would he still be so calm? Facing a private hell was one thing when you were alone, in control of the situation. And another when you were at the mercy of a madman.

He stared at his hands lying at his sides. Lumps of dead meat, enormous bloated useless things. A little tingling had begun in his forearms, but that was all. Only his feet felt alive, buzzing furiously and starting to ache.

"I asked you a question, Gallagher."

He licked cracked lips, managed to swallow. The words he forced out were a frog croak. "Isn't my home."

"Was once. Is again, now."

"Why'd you bring me here?"

"Don't you know?"

"I don't know anything." His voice was stronger. "Who you are, why you're doing this."

"Today's January fourth."

"What does that—?"

"Your twenty-fifth anniversary."

Cam stared at him.

"You remember what happened twenty-five years ago tonight, Gallagher. Your father, your mother. You."

January 4. He'd blanked completely on the date. The shivers were at him again as he said, "Caitlin. She told you about it."

"That's right. She told me everything."

"I don't . . . what does my family have to do with you bringing me here?"

"Anniversaries," Hendryx said. "Two in January, four days apart."

". . . I don't know what you're talking about."

"Punishment for your crimes. Perfect timing."

"*What* crimes?"

"Father, mother, sister."

"For God's sake, I was ten years old, none of what happened was my fault—"

"Not what Caitlin says. And what you did to Annalisa, that was *all* your fault."

"I don't know any Annalisa—"

"My wife. Woman you ran down in Denver and left to die. January eighth. Your second anniversary."

What he was feeling now was surreality, as if he were caught in a new nightmare made up of old body parts. "This is crazy," he said. "You're crazy, Hendryx. I've never been in Denver in January, I told you that once—I've never hit anyone with a car, never had even a minor accident."

"Keep on lying, it won't do you any good. I *know* you're guilty."

"What makes you so sure?"

"Your face. Damn ugly face."

"Christ, what're you talking about now?"

"Police sketch." Hendryx stood, withdrew something from his coat pocket, advanced with the gun in one hand and a rectangle of laminated plastic in the other. He extended the plastic close to Cam's eyes. "This one."

Pen-and-ink drawing of a man's head and face. Similar shape, similar features, same hairline—but it wasn't him. "It's not me," he said. "Somebody I resemble, that's all."

"You," Hendryx said.

"It could be anybody! It's not me!"

Hendryx put the sketch away, backed up, and sat down with the automatic on his lap. His eyes were like holes burned into the set planes of his face. The fury in them was old, stoked and brooded over for a long time.

"You," he said again. "You're guilty and sentence has been passed. Execution date is the eighth. Four days on death row, then you get what's coming to you."

Hold on, stay calm. But he could feel the undercurrents of panic flowing closer to the surface.

"You're going to kill me, just like that?"

"Execute you."

"Without a trial."

"You don't deserve a trial. Not after what you did to Annalisa."

"You wouldn't hurt *my* wife?" Working to keep his voice steady, controlled. "My daughters or Caitlin?"

The look Hendryx gave him was almost pitying. "I'm not like you, Gallagher. I don't hurt innocent people."

"How can I believe that? I know you did something to Jenna Bailey—"

"Wrong. Did it to herself."

"You kidnapped her."

"No. She tried to shoot me."

"You must've given her a reason."

"Told you, it was her fault."

"Did you try to rape her? Is that it?"

"Rape—! What d'you think I am?"

"What did you do, then?"

"Never mind. Shut up about her."

Cam let a few seconds pass before he said, "My family, Hendryx. You swear you'll leave them alone?"

"You. Just you."

"The condemned prisoner."

"That's right.

"How am I going to die? Shoot me down in cold blood?"

"Don't know yet. It won't be in cold blood, no matter what. Execution isn't murder."

"A lot of people believe it is."

"I don't care what a lot of people believe."

Cam took a breath, let it out slowly. Outside the wind seemed wilder, buffeting the house and shrieking in the eaves as if it were frustrated at being denied admittance. His left hand was pins-and-needles now; he was able to move it, then lift it onto his lap. Coax the sausage fingers into massaging the lump that was his right hand.

"Even if I was guilty," he said, "I haven't committed a capital crime."

"What?"

"What you think I did, the hit-and-run. Your wife's still alive, you said."

"Yeah. In a hospital bed, not herself anymore, suffering on account of you. That's the same as killing her."

"Hendryx, listen to me—"

"Just the same."

"All right, what about you? You've committed two capital offenses, worse ones than mine. If I deserve to be executed, so do you."

"Bullshit. What d'you mean, capital offenses?"

"Kidnapping, that's one. Two counts, Jenna and now me. You killed her, that's two, and now you want to—"

"I didn't kill your slut."

"My— What do you think she was to me?"

"Bimbo, piece on the side."

"I wasn't having an affair with her. Is that what you think? Jesus, is that why you hurt her—another way to punish me?"

"Don't you listen? She did it to herself."

"Where is she? If she's dead, you're responsible—"

"Shut up about her! I didn't kill her, I'm not responsible!"

"Okay. Okay, I believe you. Why won't you believe I'm not responsible for hurting your wife?"

In a single convulsive movement Hendryx was out of the chair. His face was blood-dark; a tic jumped along one cheekbone, as if something beneath the skin was trying to tear loose. The gun was in his hand again. Small weapon, small caliber . . . Jenna's missing .32?

"That's enough talk," he said. "Get up."

"What're you going to do?"

"Put you where you belong, where I don't have to listen to you anymore. Get up off there."

"I can't walk yet—"

"Walk or crawl, one or the other. Now!"

Argument was futile; it had been futile all along. You can't reason with a madman—how many times had he heard that said? Any more resistance might provoke him into using that gun.

It took Cam three painful tries to stand. His legs were wobbly, still tingling, but he could stay up on them, and he could walk in an awkward, shuffling gait. Hendryx kept his distance—no more help from him. Partial feeling in his left hand, enough so he could use it as a brace against the end table alongside the couch. He made it from there to the hallway arch, leaned against the jamb.

"Upstairs," Hendryx said.

It was like climbing a steep wall. Each riser was a little piece of agony, even with the banister for support. Movement took all his concentration, and that was just as well—he didn't want to think anymore right now.

His legs felt weak and sore when he reached the second-floor landing, but the stinging sensations were gone. His left hand felt almost normal. His right had regained some feeling as well.

Hendryx put on the upstairs hall lights. "You know where the attic door is," he said.

Cam's pulse skipped; his step faltered, and he had to brace himself against the inside wall. Attic. Should've known that was where Hendryx would put him. The haunted place, the nightmare place.

The attic door was shut. He was a few feet from it before he realized that a pair of heavy, new-looking iron brackets had been mounted one on either side of the frame. And that a three-foot length of two-by-four was propped against the wall.

Hendryx stepped around in front of him, pulled the door open. Enough light penetrated the shadows within to show Cam that there was no longer even a dead bulb in the wall fixture.

"Inside. Everything's ready for you."

A draft from above gave him a whiff of the fetid smells of dust, mildew, mouse turds. It brought a tight shriveling to his groin. "Hendryx, for the love of God—"

"Get in there." He waited until Cam had half-dragged himself around and through the narrow opening. "This is where you belong," he said then. "Death row cell for the next four nights and days."

And the door slammed shut and the two-by-four clattered into the iron brackets, trapping him once more in utter blackness.

ray dawn, storm still blowing wild outside.

Nick got up, got dressed, walked down the hall to listen at the barred attic door. Quiet up there. He imagined Gallagher hiding in the dark, Little Jack Horner crouched in a corner. Image put a smile on his mouth.

He went on to the back bedroom, whistling "Who'll Stop the Rain?" between his teeth. Tune Annalisa'd always liked. I'll stop it, honey, he thought. Not here but where you are, inside of you. Pretty soon now. Comin' home to you. Blue skies, nothing but blue skies from now on.

Beads of moisture on the window. He rubbed it off, looked out. River was flooding big-time, all right. Surprised him a little to see how far over its banks it was on this side, lapping at the top of the slope, some of the grassy yard underwater already. Another foot or two, and it'd be climbing the back steps. On the far side it was up to within a few feet of the highway. Not a river anymore, a muddy brown running lake. Fast current, eddies, white scum along the edges, half-submerged trees, logs and branches and all kinds of crap swirling and dancing along. Low clouds, black-bellied, and the rain coming down so heavy it was like a silver curtain.

He watched a high-wheeled truck with its lights on easing along the highway, plowing up spray. Some kind of rescue vehicle? He'd better get cracking.

Went into the bathroom first to take a leak. Flipped the light switch, and nothing happened. Power must've gone out during the night. No wonder it was so damn cold in here. He'd turned the furnace up over seventy before he turned in.

Downstairs he tried the lights in the hall, just to make sure. Yeah, the power was out. He shrugged into his coat, stepped out onto the porch. Front yard looked like a swamp, so much water and hillside mud on Crackerbox Road you could hardly see the asphalt. Weren't any rescue crews around here yet, but somebody could come along before the day got too old and the flood closed all the roads.

One thing he had to do and do quick was move the Mazda. Leave it where it was, and anybody showed up, they'd figure the house was still occupied and come banging on the door, trying to get him to leave. More important was keeping the car safe. Lane into the garage was under at least an inch of water. Wouldn't take much more of a rise for the garage floor to be under, too. Another eight to ten feet, the Mazda'd be floating. Water would screw up the brakes, knock out the electrical system—he wouldn't be driving it anywhere when the flood level went down.

Down the road a ways somebody'd built a house high among the pines on the opposite side. Long driveway leading up to it. Place looked closed up for the winter—shutters over all the windows, no lights showing any of the times he'd passed it after dark. It was on ground higher than the roof of this house; river'd have to rise another forty or fifty feet to do any damage up there. No way that'd happen. Mazda'd be safe up there.

He slogged across to the garage. Whistled "My Baby Loves Me" as he started the car, backed it out. He felt good this morning. Weather didn't bother him, flood didn't bother him, nothing bothered him. New day, only three left until the execution. And in less than a week he'd be with Annalisa again. Gallagher's talk talk talk had gotten to him last night, but he'd been tired and a little stressed out. Bailey woman's death was a freak accident, he'd already settled that. And the punishment he'd designed for Gallagher was exactly right.

What could be more right than doing what had to be done for the woman you loved?

am lay shivering in the dark. The only way he'd known it was morning was by the faint, thin line of gray at the rear wall. Hendryx had closed off both small dormer windows with inch-thick boards screwed to the wall, half a dozen flathead screws to each piece to prevent them from being torn loose. The boards across the front window were fitted tightly together so no light showed through; the gap between two at the rear window, near the top, was a quarter of an inch at its widest, where the wood on one length had warped. The thread of daylight that shone there barely penetrated the thick gloom. All it was good for was as a peephole on disaster. By rising up on his knees and flattening one side of his face against the boards, he could look out and down at the river ripping madly at its banks.

He had crawled all over the attic, front to back, side to side. Not last night—this morning, a little while ago. Last night he'd huddled at the bottom of the stairs, unable to bring himself to climb up until cold and muscle cramps forced him into it; and when he'd got up here, he'd found the mattress near the top of the stairs and been too exhausted to do anything but crawl onto it. What little sleep he'd had had been fitful: jerk awake, doze, jerk awake, doze. It was the biting cold and the thin line of morning that had started him moving again.

Except for mice in the walls, spiders and their webs, the mattress was the only thing in the attic other than himself. The rest of the floor space and the walls were bare. Not even a bucket to use as a toilet. The mattress was child-size—he understood why without letting himself think much about it—and it felt and smelled new. Hendryx had meant it literally when he called the attic a cell. A death row cell in a prison run by a lunatic.

There was no way out of this box. His keys and penknife were gone; so were his belt with its thin-edged buckle, the few coins he'd had in his pocket. Hendryx had removed all of that in the PWS lot, after he'd finished trussing him up. Hadn't seemed to be much sense in it at the time; now it was plain that Hendryx had been making sure there was nothing on him that could be used to work on the screws.

The door downstairs was the only possible exit. He had no chance of breaking it down with the two-by-four securing it. And Hendryx was not going to open it between now and Friday, the eighth—not to bring him food, not for any reason. Solitary confinement. Without even bread and water for the condemned prisoner. When that door finally did open again, it would be with care and cunning, to take him on his last walk or to carry out the death sentence right here. He'd be too weak to resist by then. No food or water for four days, nothing but his damp suit and shirt to shield him from the bitter cold, his throat already parched and scratchy. . . . He might not even be able to crawl.

His one hope lay in outside help. Hallie knew about Hendryx; so did Lloyd now, after yesterday's consultation. They'd tell the authorities, may already have done it. But there was no proof that Hendryx was responsible for his sudden disappearance, any more than there'd been in Jenna's case. The police couldn't mount an official investigation anyway on a missing person's report until twenty-four hours had elapsed. Worst of all, there was the storm and the flooding river. All day yesterday there'd been countywide flash-flood warnings, reports of massive evacuations under way along the Russian River, and forecasts of a string of powerful storms over the next three days. By now, or very soon, the roads in and out of the area would be closed. As long as the heavy wind and rain continued, rescue boats couldn't operate, and helicopters couldn't fly safely. Even if rescuers did show up here, he had no way to signal them, and Hendryx couldn't be forced to evacuate or to let anybody inside the house without a search warrant.

His only hope was no hope at all.

Dead man.

He listened to the wind rattling boards, the rain slashing against eaves and dormers, and thought about death. Not the sudden ceasing to exist, the nearness of whatever lay beyond, if anything did; he couldn't quite deal with any of that yet. Death by murder, himself as the object of a cold-blooded, premeditated "execution." The concept that a stranger, a madman, wanted him dead—wanted it badly enough to plot a bizarre scheme involving Caitlin and Jenna that had lasted for weeks—was as awesome as the specter of death itself. Him, Cameron Gallagher, singled out of millions of other men merely because he happened to bear a resemblance to an unknown felon, a face in a sketch. Going about his normal routine, struggling with all his other problems, not asking for much more than survival and a little peace of mind, while the madman stalked him day and night, schemed and assembled his plan, and put it into action.

The thought plagued him that he could have saved himself by telling the authorities about Hendryx immediately after Jenna vanished. Yet he knew it wasn't true. What could they have done except talk to Hendryx, check into his past? No grounds for a search warrant there, either—and they wouldn't have found anything in the house even if they had gotten a warrant, just as he hadn't found anything last week. Jenna had probably been dead since that Friday night, her body buried far away from here. The county CID wouldn't even have had cause to keep Hendryx under surveillance. He'd have been free to do as he pleased—and what he pleased to do was take Cameron Gallagher's life.

The fear in him had surfaced, but only in the shadows of his mind. Mostly what he felt was a hatred for Nick Hendryx that was as powerful as any Hendryx felt for him. He, too, wanted another human being dead. Would make him dead if he could. Would strangle him, bludgeon him, shoot him, stab him, *kill* him if he could.

For now the hatred was sustaining. He focused on it, nurtured it as if it were a seedling, held it and stroked it and urged it to grow. The more it grew, the greater the barrier to hold fear at bay. But for how long? Until Friday—that long? Another seventy or eighty hours trapped in endless night?

If the fear grew faster and stronger than the hate, if it swarmed over him and began tearing at his soul, he'd be lost. He'd be ten years old again, screaming and pissing on himself. He'd beg for his life when the time came, crawl to his death with all sanity blown away. Somewhere else, anywhere else, the hatred might continue to sustain him, and he could die with rage and dignity. But not in this house where Rose and Paul had died in shame. Not in this attic where part of himself had died along with them.

ick sat in the front room, wrapped up in his coat, no fire because he didn't want the smoke to alert anybody that might be in the area. Eating a bag of M&Ms and drinking coffee he'd made with murky tap water. Still feeling good, thinking about Annalisa.

And somebody came up on the porch.

Thump, thump—he heard it plain. Then the doorknob rattled. Whoever it was trying to get in.

He jumped up, spilling the coffee, and ran out into the hall. Got there just as the door came flying inward, wind and rain and a figure in a hooded raincoat barging right into his house. Intruder leaned back against the door to get it shut, face coming up so he could see under the hood.

Caitlin.

Nick stared at her, she stared at him. "You *are* still here," she said. "I didn't see your car, so I thought—"

"What's the idea, barging in here like that?"

"I thought you were gone."

"Then why'd you come inside?"

Her face was pinched and white, mouth tight set, eyes bright. Stressed out. Damn flood, maybe, and maybe not. Voice sharper when she said, "This is my house, Nick."

"Just caught me by surprise, that's all. How long'll the roads be open?"

"Not much longer. I almost didn't get through."

"Better leave quick, then, before you're stranded."

"What about you?"

"Me, too. Right after you."

"Where's your car?"

"High ground, close by. Why'd you drive all the way up here, anyway?"

"My brother's missing," she said.

Nick put on a surprised face. "Missing?"

"Since last night. He didn't come home, and his wife's frantic. She called me before dawn."

"Maybe he got drunk or went off with a woman. Or both."

Headshake. "Cameron wouldn't do anything like that. His car's still at Paloma Wine Systems. Hallie had an employee go and check."

"So he went off with somebody. He'll turn up, don't worry. Might even be home by now."

"Nick . . . did you see him last night?"

"Me? No. What made you ask that?"

"You weren't over in the Paloma Valley?"

"I came straight here after work. What the hell, Cat? You think I had something to do with him going missing?"

"I don't know. You didn't, did you?"

"No."

Kept looking at him, picking at his face with her eyes. Trying to make up her mind whether or not he was telling her the truth.

"You think he's here, is that it? Well, go ahead, look around, waste the time. Then neither of us'll get out before the roads are closed."

"Maybe I should. Hallie asked me to."

Goddamn woman, making it hard for him and bad for both of them. "Rain's coming down harder," he said.

No answer. Now she had her nose up and was snuffling the air like an animal.

"What's that smell?" she said.

"Smell?"

"Don't you smell it?"

"No. Listen, we don't have much time—"

She moved away before he could do anything about it, walking quick along the hall to the kitchen.

He went after her, not as fast as he should've. *Had* to get her out of here one way or another, before she took it into her head to snoop around upstairs. Gallagher heard her, he'd start yelling. But Nick couldn't catch hold of an idea, and by the time he was in the kitchen, she was already out of it, on her way to the back porch.

His nose twitched. Oh man, she was right about the smell. Why hadn't he—?

He broke into a run to the porch.

Too late. She was at the far wall, standing in front of the fucking thing that squatted there.

"Rotten meat," she said. "Nick, I told you the freezer doesn't work right, doesn't keep things frozen, and with the power off—"

"Cat, don't open it!"

Opened it anyway. Looked inside.

He got to her just as she started to scream.

66

am heard it. There was a momentary lull in the storm, and the cry came up thin and shrill through the old walls and floors, then cut off on a rising note. The wind . . . but it hadn't sounded like the wind. Human cry. The voice of terror.

He sat up on the mattress, still hugging himself with his chilled hands tucked into his armpits, and listened. Beat of the rain, skirl of the wind. Inside—nothing. Imagination, hallucination. A shriek out of the past, out of his nightmares.

Fresh tremors set his teeth chattering. Time to move again. Stand up and walk hunched and shuffling like an old blind man, from one end of his cell to the other. Or crawl along the floor, with a stop to peer once more at the tiny, sodden piece of the outside world that was left to him. Keep moving as often and as long as he was able. Lie huddled too long on the hard mattress, and his joints would seize up, he'd lose all motor response, and eventually the cold would stop his heart. Not that that was such a bad way to die. Sure to be less painful than whatever Hendryx had in store for him. Later, that might be an option. Now he still had the rage, he still had the will to live.

He pushed up onto his knees. Got one foot down on the floor and prepared for the effort it would take to stand.

Noises in the hallway below.

Footsteps, heavy and uneven. And then something thudding onto the floor or against the wall near the attic door.

"Gallagher! You hear me up there?"

Cam dropped to all fours again, crawled sideways to the top of the stairs.

Hendryx's shout was louder this time: "I'm going to open the door. Your sister's down here with me. I see or hear you on the stairs, I'll put a bullet in her head."

Caitlin!

"You hear me, Gallagher? Yell out so I know."

His voice box might have been rusted shut; it took three tries to produce more than a creaky whisper. Then, with his head pushed into the stairwell and his pulse hammering, he managed, "I hear you. Don't hurt her."

"Not if you stay put."

Three, four, five seconds. And Cam heard the scraping and banging of the two-by-four being lifted from the brackets. A key scratched in the lock. He jerked his head back as the door swung outward and light framed the opening below. Thin, filtered daylight that didn't penetrate the shadows within, couldn't possibly reach up to where he was crouched.

Tensely, blinking, he watched Hendryx move across the gray rectangle, out of sight again. Sounds. And Hendryx reappeared, carrying an inert shape in his arms. He stepped through the doorway, laid the shape at the foot of the stairs—slowly, almost gently. When he straightened and retreated, he turned his body, so that the last thing Cam saw was the stubby phallic barrel of the gun.

Another shout from behind the door: "Stay where you are until I'm gone. Then you can come down and get her."

The door slammed shut.

Cam listened again to the key in the lock, the bar dropping into place. Instead of retreating footsteps, Hendryx's voice came once more, thick and muffled.

"She didn't give me any choice. You hear me, Gallagher? I don't want to punish her, but she didn't give me any choice. You tell her that. She's the one to blame, not me."

A little silence. And then the footsteps, going away.

As soon as they faded, Cam was on the stairs, sliding down the risers on his buttocks because he was afraid of falling if he tried to descend standing up. He could hear the uneven rasp of Caitlin's breathing before he reached her. When his hands found the rough cloth of her coat, she made a throat sound, half moan and half retch. He wrapped his arms around her thin body, lifted her, maneuvered both of them until they were sitting huddled on one of the lower steps. Held her, whispering protective words that brought a flash of childhood memory, big brother and little sister on a long-ago stormy night when the power had suddenly failed: "It's all right, Cat, don't be afraid. It's all right."

Terror and confusion had her when she first came to. She struggled in his grasp, crying out. He kept talking to her until the familiar sound of his voice penetrated; she sagged against him for a moment, then pulled away abruptly and scooted over against the wall.

"It's so dark," she said thickly. "Where are we?"

"Attic stairwell."

"Locked in?"

"Yes. Cat, what're you doing here? Did he bring you?"

"No. Drove up myself."

"Why?"

"Hallie called, said you were missing—"

"The police? Do they know you came here?"

"No. I left right away . . . didn't really believe you'd be here, even after what Hallie said, but she was so upset. . . . Roads are flooded, they almost didn't let me through. . . ."

"You sound woozy. What did he do to you?"

"Hit me, my cheekbone—" She broke off and he heard the sudden sharp intake of her breath. "Oh God, Cameron! The back porch, the freezer—"

"What about it?"

"A body; what's left of a woman's body! Jenna Bailey . . . he's the one, he killed her. . . ."

Cam tasted sickness. "Jenna," he said.

"He . . . my God, my God, he's a monster. . . ."

Chills chased along Cam's back. The freezer. Not a grave somewhere, here in the house. The whole time he'd been here last week, she was right there in the freezer. If he'd opened it then . . . if he'd just thought to look inside . . .

"I believed in him, trusted him." Caitlin's voice was a whisper, heavy with loathing. "How could I have been so stupid!"

"Don't blame yourself."

"I should have listened to you, I should have—" A fit of coughing seized her, dry, painful sounds in the cold blackness. When it was over, she asked, "Why does he hate you so much? Why did he bring you here?"

"He thinks I'm the one who ran down his wife." He told her about the sketch. "He's completely delusional. It doesn't even look that much like me."

"First Jenna Bailey and then you and now me. He's going to kill me, too."

"No, I'm the one he—"

"He can't let me go after what I saw. He . . . oh Christ, Cameron, we have to get out of here. One of the attic windows, we can climb out on the roof—"

"He boarded them up."

"Another way, then. There has to be some way . . . we have to get out of here!"

"We will," he said. "We'll find a way."

But it was another lie.

Hendryx intended to kill both of them. And there was no way out.

67

Drive, drive, day ride, night ride. Needed to do that more than anything else right now, the car, the open road, tires whispering engine humming everything rushing past and him inside safe, secure, in control of his destiny, hours and hours hurtling through the daylight and the dark, going home to Annalisa. But he couldn't drive, couldn't go home yet, couldn't even get out of this fucking house with the river rising, water inches deep on the road already, water everywhere he looked, it was like being trapped on an island in a swamp and the rain wouldn't let up, just kept beating down beating down, and in here he could smell her in the freezer even with the windows open, why hadn't he smelled her before, why hadn't he taken her body somewhere and buried it instead of trusting that goddamn freezer, so what if somebody'd found the grave, it wasn't his fault and they couldn't tie her to him, what was he thinking that night, head up his butt, if he'd buried her he wouldn't have the smell, he wouldn't have Caitlin. Why'd she have to come here today, now he'd have to punish her too. What choice did he have, punish her along with Gallagher and he didn't want to do that, poor Caitlin, he liked her, he really did, she wasn't a bitch like the Bailey woman, she reminded him of Annalisa just wanting to be held, but now she was in his way making him change things all around, do things he didn't want to do. And he couldn't sit still, couldn't drive, couldn't do anything but walk walk walk, one room to another, upstairs downstairs, rain and cold blowing in through the open windows it was like an icebox in here, like a freezer no don't think about that, why wouldn't that dead woman smell go away? Walk with the cold in his bones, walk with the stink in his nose, he couldn't stand two more days in here like this no three more days but what else could he do he couldn't change the schedule and even if he could even if he executed Gallagher now Caitlin now he couldn't get out couldn't get the car couldn't drive couldn't go home couldn't see Annalisa until the rain quit flood quit all he could do was walk and it felt like the top of his head was coming off walk cold wet dead smell walk walk walk because he couldn't drive drive drive—

Cam knelt alongside the rear window, one eye close to the gap between the boards, watching the river run wild below. Rain lay like crinkled cellophane wrap on the dirty glass, so that everything outside seemed shimmery, distorted—the low-hanging black clouds, the half-submerged trees along the banks, the drift and wreckage riding the churning brown flood. As much of the property as he could see was underwater; there was probably water in the first-floor rooms by now. He could hear the sound of it out there, a constant thrumming rhythm, even with the rain drumming furious riffs above.

It was late afternoon now; the already fading daylight told him that. And yet his time sense was so fouled by the oppressive darkness that it seemed as though he'd been trapped in the attic much longer than nineteen or twenty hours. Days, endless days. He had difficulty recalling when he'd last seen the sun, or bright warm light of any kind. The rain, the blackness, might have been inside him as well, so that if he looked into a mirror, into his own eyes, what he'd see would be a wet, gray, swampy place, a landscape as desolate as the one he was witness to outside.

Caitlin stirred on the child's mattress. "Cameron? What're you doing?" Her voice was listless, a dissonance in the dark like the rain and flood sounds.

"Watching for rescue boats."

"You might as well be jerking off."

He didn't respond to that.

"What's the use?" she said. "Roads are all closed by now. By the time anyone finds us, it'll be too late. We'll be dead."

"Not if the storms let up soon enough."

"Nick will kill us before he'll let us be rescued. You know he will."

"Don't think that way, Cat. Don't give up."

"Shit," she said, "I already have."

He resisted an impulse to go to her, try to give her a little comfort. The one time he'd attempted that, after she discovered just how escape-proof the attic was, she had pulled violently away from him and huddled up on the mattress, claiming it for herself. She hadn't said much since then. He wondered if she blamed him, at least partly, for what was happening to them, in the same way she'd always blamed him for Rose's death. Probably. We're still not brother and sister, he thought, we're still a pair of old antagonists. The grim, terrifying intimacy of the trap they were in, instead of drawing them close, only intensified the rift and strain that had built up between them. Even the prospect of dying together couldn't bring them close to each other again.

She was right: What was the use in pretending there was hope when there wasn't? Hendryx had removed anything Caitlin might have had in her possession that could be used on the screws, and the boards couldn't be budged by hand; abrasions and splinters and a torn nail were all he'd gotten from that effort. The door below was an impregnable barrier. And the gun and his weakened state made the situation that much more hopeless.

His fear was like the river outside, continuing to rise and slowly, steadily tearing down what was left of his defenses. He could almost smell it in himself, an oozing stench like the brown-slime odor of the flood. He couldn't withstand it much longer. If it weren't for Caitlin being here, he might already have been swept away.

For another minute or so he watched the slanting rain, the turmoil of conflicting currents and weird boils and eddy lines in the main river channel, the soapy yellowish white foam that scudded along the ravaged banks, the debris weaving drunkenly across the range of his vision. Reluctant to exchange even such a scene of devastation for the suffocating blackness and more of Caitlin's bitter silence.

A sudden gust of wind seemed to rattle and shake the entire house. That, and a gathering cramp in his leg, finally drove him away from the gap. He managed to stand, flexed his leg until the cramp eased, then began to make his way around the walls in a humped-over, shuffling stride, his hands sliding over rough wood and through clinging strands of spider silk. When he reached the front dormer window, he made another futile try at loosening one of the boards with his hands. Moved on, kept moving, through two full circuits around the perimeter of their prison.

Muffled sobbing sounds stopped him. He lowered to all fours again, crawled to the mattress. Caitlin was curled up on it tight as a shrimp. When he touched her face—wet, cold-hot—she jerked away as if from something obscene. He sat back on his haunches, helpless, his mind blank.

A long time passed before the sobbing ended and she said, "I'm a baby. A goddamn baby."

"No. It's all right."

"It's not all right. I'm like you were the night Ma died—curled up on a fucking mattress, bawling my head off. Next thing I'll be pissing in my pants."

Words, just words. They didn't hurt him; words couldn't hurt him anymore.

Another long silence. Then, dully, "I'm sorry, I didn't mean that. I don't know why I said that."

"It's all right," he said again.

"I understand what it must've been like for you. Jesus, Cammie, for the first time I really do."

Cammie. She hadn't called him that since she was eight years old, probably didn't even realize she'd used the name. He yearned to touch her, but he didn't. He couldn't stand to have her shrink away from him again.

"I wish I had a cigarette," she said. "I'd kill for a cigarette right now." She coughed, laughed a little wildly, stifled another cough. "I don't know how much more of this I can take," she said.

"You'll be okay, Cat."

"Like hell I will. The dark . . . you know I've always hated the dark."

"I know."

"I think . . . I'm scared I'll lose it. I mean really lose it, Cameron. You understand?"

"Yes. Me, too. But it won't happen."

She snuffled and started to cry again. Still he didn't touch her—and then abruptly he did, a lowering of his hand to her shoulder that was almost like a spasm. This time she neither drew away nor cringed. Just lay there sobbing, her shoulder trembling under his hand.

So thin, so small, not much bigger than either of his daughters. Leah, Shannon . . . images of them crossed his mind. An image of Hallie. He felt wrenching pain. Never see any of them again, die here with Caitlin because of a stupid crazy accidental resemblance to a face in a sketch. . . .

For a long time Hendryx had been on a rampage through the house, back and forth, up and down, running, banging into things, as if he were as out of control as the flood. Then the noises had stopped, and for a while now he'd been quiet. Where was he? What was he doing?

Waiting, Cam thought. Same as we are.

No, not the same. The difference is, Hendryx isn't afraid—and Hendryx is already insane.

Nick woke up in bed. Still dressed, coat, shoes, everything on, buried under a pile of blankets that didn't have any warmth in them. Freezing cold. He didn't remember going to bed. Last thing he remembered was walking and walking because he couldn't drive.

His head still hurt. He felt funny, like some part of him wasn't there anymore. He remembered Caitlin showing up, the freezer, all of that, but it seemed fuzzy and far off, things that'd happened long ago. This morning? Yesterday? Pitch dark outside the bedroom window, and the rain had stopped. He got up, went and looked out. Wind still blowing hard, water rippling and gleaming everywhere. Almost pretty in the night, trees dancing shadowy jigs all around. Magical. One of Annalisa's words. He might've thought so, too, if she were here. But she wasn't here. And Denver was a long way away. And he had to stay here in this house, this flood, until Friday.

How far off was Friday?

He looked at his watch, but it'd stopped. Forgot to wind it. Now he couldn't tell what time it was. Not that it mattered too much. He'd know when it was Friday, all right. Better believe he'd know when it was time.

Hunger pains in his gut as he turned away from the window. Long time since he'd had anything to eat. Checked his pockets, but he was out of M&Ms. Some left in the kitchen? Might be. Crackers and peanut butter, too. Thought of going below with that thing in the freezer bothered him, but he had to do it. You had to eat, you'd get sick if you didn't. He wrapped one of the heavier blankets around himself and went downstairs.

Water down there. Muddy goddamn swamp down there.

Crept into the house while he was asleep. Foot deep now, brown and gleaming. Stank worse than what was in the freezer, smell so thick in the damp air it made him choke. He cringed at the idea of wading through it. Knew what it'd feel like on his skin, wet and cold and stinking like something dead and full of rot, like the bimbo on the back porch. But he had to do it, didn't he? Had to get some food so he wouldn't get sick, didn't he?

He held his breath and stepped down into the brown crap. And it was bad, it swirled around his legs when he moved, clutching like dead hands trying to drag him down into it. He gagged and started to run. Splash, splash, splash into the kitchen, yank open cupboards, yank open the fridge, crackers, peanut butter, carton of milk, last two bags of M&Ms, and splash, splash, splash back to the stairs with the food clutched against his chest and all the while trying not to puke.

Ran upstairs, ran into the bedroom. Dumped everything on the nightstand and stood there shaking, looking down at his legs. Brown shit all over his shoes and pant legs. He ran out to the bathroom, tore off his shoes and socks, shucked free of his pants, kicked it all into a corner. Washed the dead brown off his hands, his feet, washed and washed until his skin was raw and red and clean.

Shaking like a leaf when he went back to the bedroom. Not hungry anymore—thought of food made him gag. Crawled into bed and piled the blankets on, covering his head, and lay there like a block of ice.

Everything felt wrong now. Part of him missing, dead thing downstairs, Annalisa so far away, Friday so far away. Wasn't supposed to be like this. Flood, bimbo, Caitlin, freezer, brown shit, even Gallagher— all of it was wrong. And he didn't know how to make it right again.

Too late to make it right again?

I t's the laughter that wakes him up.

He knows right away what's going on. Her and Fatso, downstairs in the spare bedroom. When did Fatso show up? He's not supposed to be here. Didn't Dad warn her she better not let Fatso come around here anymore?

I hate you. I hate you, Ma.

I'm gonna tell Dad about this, too. You better believe I am. Soon as he comes up tomorrow.

The laughter stops. Now it's quiet again.

I know what they're doing. How can she do it with Fatso, right here in our house? How can she do it with him at all? That time I saw them, her all white and sweaty, him with his belly and hairy ass, and she was . . . I never thought I'd see her do anything like *that*. . . .

Banging sound. Bedboard hitting the wall.

Another laugh that turns into a kind of yell.

He puts his hands over his ears, burrows down deep under the covers.

After a while he pokes his head out and listens. Quiet downstairs, but now it's raining again. Wind howling, rain smacking on the roof and against the window. Is Fatso still here?

He gets up and goes to the window. There's his truck in the yard. Jeez, is he going to spend the whole night here?

I hate you, Ma. You and him both.

He's in bed again when he hears the voices downstairs. Loud at first, Fatso saying, When can I see you again, sweet tits? Her saying, Keep your voice down, you want to wake up the kid? Then he can't hear what they're saying because the door's open and the wind is whistling in. Then the door bumps shut again. Outside, Fatso's truck starts up and he guns the engine the way he likes to do. Damn son of a bitch Fatso. Then the truck backs out and roars off, and it's quiet again except for the storm.

But not for long.

Now there's another car in the driveway. Not Fatso's truck, engine sound's different—Daddy's car! Dad's here!

He jumps out of bed, rushes over to look. Dad's car, all right, Dad getting out and running through the rain. Door slams downstairs. Hard footsteps heading for the kitchen. "Rose? I know you're down here, I saw his truck." Thump, thump. "Right where I knew you'd be, you bitch." And then Dad starts yelling and swearing, real loud. Oh jeez, he's pissed! I never heard him that pissed before.

And she starts yelling back at him, calling him dirty names. She sounds drunk. Sure she is, her and Fatso must've been drinking whiskey. They did that the last time, too.

Her: Do what I please, don't have to answer to you, fucking bastard.

Dad: Whore, slut, right here in our house with the boy upstairs, what kind of mother are you.

Smack. Shriek. Wow, he must've hit her! Serves her right, the dirty whore.

Her: Leave me alone damn you don't you lay a hand on me again or you'll be sorry.

Dad: Had all I can stand can't take any more.

Her: Chrissake what're you doing with that, put that thing away, are you crazy?

Dad: Show you what I'm going to do with it.

Her: You don't have the guts you wimp you pisspoor excuse for a man.

He's over at the door now, opening it, looking out and listening. And then—

Bang!

Oh no, that sounded like a gun—

"Rose!" Dad's voice, different, all moany and wild like the wind. "Rose, God, I didn't mean . . . Rose!"

Little noises.

"No!" Dad again, like he's wailing. "No no!"

Quiet.

And then—

Bang!

Dad, Daddy, what—?

And he's in the hallway, at the top of the stairs. His heart is pounding like it wants to burst through his chest. He leans over the banister and stares down. Dark except for light coming from the kitchen, long pale wedge of light.

"Dad?"

Thud, thud, thud of his heart.

He's afraid, more afraid than he's ever been. He doesn't want to go down there, he's so scared of what he'll find. But he has to go, he has to find out—slow and then fast and then slow again as he reaches the bottom.

"Dad? Daddy?"

Thud. Thud, thud. Thud.

Along the hall into the kitchen. It's empty. Lights are on in the spare bedroom, too, and he keeps going that way, the floor cold under his bare feet. He's shivering as he nears the open bedroom doorway.

Smell comes out at him and makes him stop.

Burned smell. Gunpowder smell.

Don't go in there, don't look!

He goes in, he looks—

Oh God oh shit!

Both of them—

Dad Daddy on the floor—

And her on the bed—

And the gun on the floor—

And bright red all over both of them, her nightgown, his head and face, wet, glistening, dripping—

Daddy's eyes are open, staring, and her eyes—

Shut, they're shut—

And he wants to run, but instead he goes to Daddy, maybe Daddy's not dead, and he bends down and looks close—

Dead dead dead.

And the gun lying there—

Don't touch it don't pick it up!

His hand reaches down, he can't stop himself—

And then he's holding the gun and he hears the bedsprings squeak, somebody groaning, and when he looks—

She's moving on the bed, groaning and sitting up.

She's not dead!

Holding her chest with one hand, looking at Daddy, looking at him, her eyes all funny and big. Saying, He shot me hurts call a doctor call nine-eleven don't just stand there you little shit call somebody!

He can't think, can't move.

And she says, Goddamn you what's the matter with you can't you see I'm hurt?

But he can't make his legs work—

And she says, What're you doing with that gun give it to me damn you give it to me!

She reaches out for him, her hand like a claw, and her fingers are on the gun, pulling on the gun, she's saying, Give it to me! and he lets her have it—

Oh God, he lets her have it but—

His finger is on the trigger and—

The gun roars, he yells, the gun flies away, and she she she—

Mama!

She falls back, another big hole more blood, run to her run away from her but his legs won't work and now she isn't moving anymore and her eyes—

Her eyes, they're—

Wide open, staring at him.

Accusing him.

No! I didn't do it! You did it!

Accusing him with her dead eyes.

"It's not my fault!" Yelling it. Again. Again.

And then at last his legs work and he's running shivering running crying running back up the stairs but not into his bedroom up the attic stairs hide in the attic safe in the attic scared cold shaking all over Daddy Mama hide hide hide!

HE WAS SITTING up on the cold floor, staring stunned into the blackness. Sweat on his chilled body, his face and throat burning, the echo of his own terrified voice in his ears. And the nightmare, the memory, the truth as bright as blood in his mind.

From the mattress Caitlin's voice said groggily, "Cameron, what—?"

And he said in a painful rasp, "Pa didn't kill her, I did. God help me, I'm the one who killed Rose!"

⫷ 71 ⫸

omething woke Nick up. Yell or scream. He uncurled under the
pile of blankets, shaking off sleep and listening.

Wasn't raining and the wind had slacked off, so he could hear one
or both of them moving around in the attic. Floorboards creaking, muffled noises that might've been voices. Still dark outside, must be middle
of the night . . . what were they doing? Wasn't much they could be doing. Not even a rat could get out of there, the way he'd fixed it.

One of them cracking under the strain? Caitlin . . . he didn't want
it to be her. Bad enough, what he was going to have to do to her. She
cracked up, then she'd cry and beg and Christ knew what else, make it
twice as hard for him to go through with it.

Shoot them in the head, that was the way he'd decided to do it. Make
them kneel down, let them pray, then one bullet for each. Just Gallagher,
like it was supposed to've been, he'd have thought of some other way,
not so quick, but now with both of them it had to be a bullet. Humane.
He really didn't want Caitlin to suffer any more than she had to.

Still moving around and talking up there. No more yells or screams,
so maybe she hadn't cracked up. Or him, either. All right. Let them talk
all they wanted, didn't make any difference. It was almost Friday. He'd
know when it was and then he'd use the gun and then he could go home
again. Everything was still all right.

Only it wasn't.

Caitlin, the thing in the freezer, the brown shit getting deeper and deeper—but that wasn't all. Something else wasn't right, something important wasn't right. He didn't know what it was, but maybe he would on Friday. After the executions maybe he'd know.

Right now all he knew was that what should've been right was wrong wrong wrong.

"For God's sake, Cameron, what're you *talking* about?"

He couldn't get any more words out right away. His throat was on fire, the inside of his mouth like hot ashes. Fever. But the nightmare hadn't come out of delirium; it had come from the same place as all the others, only deeper, a sudden eruption from the long-dormant core of him.

Caitlin said, "What did you say about Ma?"

"Pa shot her first." The same painful rasp, as if words were tearing membrane off his larynx. "But only once, not twice."

"What? Cameron, make sense."

"He didn't kill her. Must've thought he did, that's why he shot himself. But he only wounded her."

"That's crazy. . . ."

The wild acceleration of his pulse was easing. He felt sick, awed, guilty—and in spite of the magnitude of his discovery, suddenly very calm again. At another time in another place, he might have been trying to deny it; would surely have struggled to come to terms with it. But not here, now, in the house where it'd happened, the attic where he'd gone to hide. The truth was irrefutable. After twenty-five years of protective self-delusion, he had been shocked into confronting the terrified ten-year-old trapped inside him.

"I thought she was dead when I went in," he said. The words came less painfully now. "Her and Pa both. The gun was there on the floor. I picked it up . . . I don't know why. And she opened her eyes and saw me. Sat up, ordered me to call for help. I couldn't move. Then she saw the gun and grabbed for it, tried to take it out of my hand, and I . . . it went off. That was the shot that killed her."

Caitlin made a moaning sound of protest and disbelief.

"I'm so sorry, Cat."

"My God. My God!" Then, "*That's* why you ran up here and hid afterward."

"Yes."

"And you never told anybody? Twenty-five years you lived with that kind of secret?"

"No, that's not—"

"Why tell me now? Damn you, Cameron, why?"

"I *didn't* know, until just now. Another nightmare, only this one the way it really happened. I repressed that part of it, blanked it out."

"Bullshit . . ."

"I couldn't face it, so I made it go away. Happens in trauma cases, especially in kids. You know it does."

"I don't know anything anymore."

"Being here like this, what's happening to us . . . that's what brought it out. But I think it might've come out anyway, sooner or later. Other nightmares I've had recently—"

"Shut up! I don't want to hear any more of this. You and your fucking nightmares. Crazy, mixed-up nonsense, that's what nightmares *are*."

"No." The traveling soul, he thought, imprinted with images of hell. "That's the way it happened, Cat."

After a few beats, she said with sudden harsh anger, "All right. You killed her, not Pa. Then you did it on purpose. You hated her, you wanted her dead—"

"Christ, no. I hated her, yes, for what she was doing to us. But I'd never have intentionally harmed her. It was an accident. A terrible accident."

"You said *you* killed her."

"Yes, but I didn't want it to happen, I'd give anything to go back and stop it from happening. That's why I couldn't face myself."

Silence. He didn't break it; there was not much else to say.

"Why'd you have to tell me?" Caitlin's voice was dull, lifeless again. "Isn't it hard enough sitting here in the dark waiting to die?"

"I had to let it out. And you have a right to know."

"Yeah. I have a right to live, too, but that isn't how it's going to be. What do you want from me, Cameron? Forgiveness? Poor baby, it wasn't your fault?"

Fault. Blame. That was really what this was all about, he thought, past and present. Everybody blaming everybody else, Nick Hendryx included, and Cam Gallagher smack in the middle blaming himself. And all of it wrong, unnecessary, like so much blame and fault, because the acts that had spawned those feelings were beyond any control of theirs. Victims, all of them, like Rose and Paul and Hendryx's wife.

He said, "Is it too much to ask, the way things are?"

"Damn right it is. I don't forgive you, and I won't."

"Will you at least try not to hate me?"

Nothing from Caitlin.

And nothing more from him. He'd shot his wad. Words, all his emotions, were used up.

After a time he heard her moving on the mattress: She'd lain down again. He lay down, too, on the floor nearby, drawing into himself. He was so cold his skin felt brittle, as if pieces of it might begin to flake off. He could feel the fever working in him. His thoughts were as raw and hot as his throat.

The closeness of death no longer frightened him. Instead he was enraged by it. Knowing the truth about the night of January 4, 1974, dealing with it at last, wasn't half so difficult as living the lie had been. Dr. Beloit had been right after all; his only failing was that he hadn't dug deep enough or in the right place to get at the root cause. Cameron Gallagher *had* had a death wish, *had* been indulging in a pattern of systematic self-destruction for a childhood sin that wasn't a sin at all. The truth was like a rebirth. He'd wanted to die, and now that death was imminent, he had never wanted more intensely to live.

After ten or fifteen or twenty minutes Caitlin's voice came again, small and empty like a child's voice. "Cameron? You asleep?"

"No."

"It's so cold. I can't stop shaking."

He said tentatively, "We could try huddling together, the way we did when we were kids."

He counted a dozen seconds before she answered. "All right," she said.

In laborious movements he crawled onto the mattress, stretched his body out next to hers. The mattress was barely wide enough for the two of them, and so short their legs extended well beyond the one end. He embraced her, gently, as he had so long ago. She was rigid against him at first; then, gradually, some of the tension went away. It took a while, but what heat was left in their bodies began to rub a little of the edge off the chill.

Against his chest she said, "I don't hate you, Cameron. I thought I did, I wanted to, but I can't."

"I'm glad," he said, but he was thinking about something else by then.

He was thinking about life instead of death.

⊰ 73 ⊱

ouldn't sleep, couldn't rest. Up at first light, look out the window. Water everywhere, in the sky, on the ground. Walk fast to the stairs and halfway down. Brown shit higher, over the bottom couple of risers. Like it was climbing up after him, slow but steady, like it wanted to drag him down and smother him in its sewer stink.

Head hurting, belly hurting. Couldn't eat even though he was starting to feel weak. Every time he looked at the milk and crackers and peanut butter, he wanted to puke. Couldn't even suck on the candy, one little M&M'd make him puke, too. Drank some water in the can, but it wouldn't stay down. Heaved it right back up into the sink.

Drive. Oh Lord, how he wanted to drive! 'Fifty-six Chevy Impala with the dumped front end and mag rims and bad shimmy, '82 Ford Taurus, what a piece of shit, '65 Pontiac GTO, candy-apple red, sweet-and-mean driving machine, '85 Olds, '89 Merc, '91 Ford, '90 Plymouth, '94 Mazda sitting up on the hill waiting for him, and it might as well've been ten thousand miles away—all those safe and secure metal-and-leather cocoons where he could exercise control over his life, his destiny. Night riding to unwind, for pleasure, to keep his problems at bay. Longer the drive, the better it was—major highways, two-laners, back-country roads, unpaved mountain tracks—Annalisa beside him, warm hip touching his, soft breast pressing his arm, heat building in him until it gave him a hard-on, wanting her bad and knowing she wanted him the same way, two of them part of a missile like a huge lighted cock splitting the night, holding it apart like two black thighs, penetrating it, taking it for their own—

—but he couldn't drive, couldn't sleep and couldn't eat and couldn't drive, all he could do was prowl the hallway up here, front bedroom to rear bedroom, back and forth, back and forth, back and forth like an animal in a goddamn cage and the brown shit climbing up to drag him down and smother him and the wet outside and the Mazda so close and Annalisa so far away and Friday so close and so far away and upstairs in the attic, upstairs in the dark death cell—

—somebody screamed.

Caitlin screamed, woman's voice thin and high like a siren going off.

He was in the hallway when she cut loose. Turned him toward the attic door, stopped him right there. And she hollered again, and then she was rushing down the stairs, heard her running in there, and when she hit bottom she started beating on the door with her hands and yelling like a crazy woman.

Yelling his name, saying "Nick! Nick, let me out of here, please let me out, he's dead, he's *dead*, I can't stay in here with my brother lying up there dead!"

Dead? Gallagher?

"I know you're there, Nick, I heard you walking." Bang, thump, bang. "Please let me out, please!"

He moved closer to the door. "What're you trying to pull? Gallagher's not dead, he can't be."

"He is, he is!"

"No, it's not Friday yet."

"He must've died during the night. His heart, or the cold . . . I don't know, I touched him just now and he's not breathing, he's *dead*. I can't stay in here with his body, I'll go out of my mind if you don't let me out!"

"You're lying," he said.

"Go up and look, you'll see—Nick, please, for the love of God . . ."

His head hurt so much he couldn't think straight. Trick, some kind of trick. But what could they do? He had the gun and they didn't have anything and Gallagher would have to be half dead by now anyway so he could be all the way dead—

Was he dead up there?

Everything wrong, and now this.

"I'll shoot you right now if this is a trick."

"It's not a trick, Cameron is dead."

Dead before his execution?

"Nick, if you ever cared anything about me let me out of here!"

". . . Go back upstairs first."

"What? I can't—"

"Go upstairs, or I won't open the door. He's really dead, I'll let you out."

"He is, oh Nick—"

"Go on go on go on."

Thump, thump, thump—back up the stairs. He ran to the front bedroom, got his flashlight, and brought it back with him. "Cat? Sing out so I know you're still in the attic."

"Hurry, please hurry."

All right. He lifted the two-by-four free, leaned it against the wall. Gallagher, you son of a bitch, you can't be dead. He took the automatic out, took the key out, used his left hand to slip the key into the lock. Listened. Can't be dead. Turned the key, stepped away from the door as soon as the lock clicked.

It stayed shut, no trick there.

He reached out with his left hand, turned the knob, pulled the door open, creaking on its hinges.

Thick dark, cold air, Gallagher dead in the cold dark? He bent toward the opening, switched on the flashlight.

And something came rushing out at him from the light-splashed blackness.

Something white and big as the door, mattress with hands clutching it on either side, *Gallagher using the mattress as a shield*, and Nick squeezed the trigger, blew a hole in the mattress, and then Gallagher and the thing hit him and drove him backward and smashed him into the wall.

⇜ 74 ⇝

The gun going off was thunderous in the confines of the hallway. Cam felt the bullet's impact high up on the mattress, but it didn't come through. An instant later, his legs already giving out, he collided with Hendryx and they slammed the wall, slanted downward to the floor. The mattress was under him and on top of Hendryx, his weight pinning the other man despite a furious flailing of arms and legs. Over the pulse-roar in his ears, Cam could hear Caitlin running on the attic stairs.

He was too weak to hold Hendryx down. It had taken all his strength and Caitlin's help to quietly maneuver the mattress into the dark stairwell and then to mount his charge. Hendryx bucked and squirmed, freed part of his body. Dimly Cam saw an arm come up, a hand with the gun still in it. He clutched frantically at the weapon; his fingers slid off, but he managed to clamp a grip on the wrist as Hendryx writhed all the way out from under the mattress.

They were sprawled together then, thrashing body to body, face-to-face, bulging eyes staring into his half-blind ones. Hendryx's other hand ripped at his imprisoned wrist, struggling to free it. Cam would have lost the scuffle if Caitlin hadn't been there. She came up cursing shrilly and kicked Hendryx in the head, hard enough to bring a bellow of pain. Cam twisted, got his other hand on the gun. A second kick caused Hendryx's fingers to spasm, slacken their grip, and Cam was able to tear the weapon loose.

He couldn't hold it; it skidded along the hallway. He kicked away from Hendryx, scuttled after the gun on all fours. Didn't see it, didn't see it . . . it was as though he were crawling in slow motion through a thick, viscous liquid. Behind him there was a confusion of sounds, Caitlin still hurling obscenities. Then he saw the automatic, over against the far baseboard. He scrambled that way, and just as his hand closed over the butt, Caitlin shrieked; an instant later, he heard the thud of a body smacking the floor.

Cam came up on his knees, swiping at his eyes to clear them. Caitlin wasn't hurt; Hendryx must have toppled her somehow, and now she was scooting away from him on her back, knees and clawed fingers upraised like a cat in fighting position. Hendryx, bleeding, seemingly dazed, paid no attention to her. He was dragging himself up the wall opposite, leaving blood smears on the paper forget-me-nots.

Cam's hands were shaking; he wrapped both tight around the automatic to hold it steady. Caitlin had flopped over and was getting up. He sent a ragged shout at her: "Stay there, I've got the gun!" Hendryx was on his feet, swinging around against the wall to look in Cam's direction. Another ragged shout held him where he was: "Don't make me shoot you!"

Frozen tableau for a clutch of seconds, the three of them in a triangle, staring and breathing noisily, blood dripping down from a gash in Hendryx's cheek. His mouth hung open; the whites of his eyes showed.

Caitlin moved first, taking a sideways step toward her brother. That acted as a release on Hendryx. He rotated his head and body and went stumbling away along the wall.

"Shoot him, Cameron!"

But he couldn't shoot a man in the back, any man. He struggled to stand, and Caitlin rushed to help him. "Jesus," she said, "what if he has another gun?"

Hendryx had reached the rear bedroom; Cam could see him through the open doorway, heading straight to the window in the far wall. He staggered forward with his left arm around Caitlin's waist, his legs so wobbly he would've fallen without her support. He saw Hendryx tugging at the window sash. It came ratcheting up, letting in a blast of frigid wind and rain, as he and Caitlin piled through the doorway.

"Hendryx!"

The madman bent his body into the opening, throwing one leg over the sill.

"Hendryx! Don't do it, you can't get away!"

Caitlin cried, "Cameron, let him go!"

Hendryx threw a look at her, another at Cam. His face was an anguished crimson mask.

"I didn't hurt your wife," Cam yelled at him. "I'm not the one who hurt your wife!"

Hendryx shook his head. "Wrong," he said clearly, "it's all wrong."

And he swung his other leg over the sill and pushed off.

The splash was audible even with the noise of the cataract. Cam let go of Caitlin, fell to his knees in front of the window. The wind flailed him with rain and surface spume as he thrust his head out. The floodwaters had risen to within a few feet of the window, mostly inundating the downstairs rooms by now; they boiled and frothed, creating little whirlpools clogged with flotsam. Hendryx was caught in one of these thirty yards out, turning this way and that, his arms lifted high as if seeking absolution. All around him other wreckage heaved and churned.

"God," Caitlin whispered.

Cam said nothing. Another few seconds, and the madman wasn't there anymore.

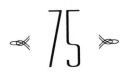

 nnalisa!

≈ 76 ≈

hey were trapped in the house for another twenty-eight hours before rescuers came.

The rains stopped for good late Thursday afternoon, and the river was no longer rising at nightfall. Rescue boats and helicopters were out at dawn Friday morning, as the floodwaters slowly began to recede. Caitlin, wrapped in a blanket and keeping watch at the rear bedroom window, saw the boat coming their way shortly before ten. Three men wearing neoprene wet suits, two of them Paloma County sheriff's deputies, were in the house a few minutes later.

Cam was pretty sick by then. High fever, hot and cold chills, swollen lymph glands. He was in bed in the front bedroom, swaddled in the remaining blankets. Caitlin had made him swallow as much drinkable water as was left in the hot-water pipes and water heater; made him eat most of the food Hendryx had left, to keep up his strength. But he was still dehydrated and too weak to walk by himself. The rescue team wouldn't risk taking him out by boat; they called for a medevac helicopter. Two hours after that, he was in a private room at Santa Rosa General, jabbed full of antibiotics and hooked up to an IV.

VISITORS THAT NIGHT, after he woke up:

Hallie, her eyes moist, holding his hand and saying, "There's no fluid in your lungs, darling, you don't have pneumonia. The doctors say you should be able to come home in a day or two."

The county CID lieutenant, Dudley, asking terse questions and reporting that Hendryx's body hadn't been found yet. They thought it might have washed out to sea, but there was so much cleanup left to be done along the river, it might yet turn up.

"Any chance he survived?" Cam asked.

"I wouldn't worry about it, Mr. Gallagher."

And Caitlin, almost shyly uncomfortable, not making eye contact and not staying long. Their conversation was limited to the flood, the worst in the river's history, with a crest of forty-nine feet, six inches, and enough about the house for Cam to know that it had suffered considerable damage and that she no longer wanted it in her life, either. Both avoided the issue of Rose's death. There would be another time to talk about that.

IN THE MORNING Hallie brought Leah and Shannon to see him. After ten minutes she sent the girls out so she could speak to him alone.

"There're all sorts of media people waiting to see you," she said. "You'll have to talk to them sooner or later."

"I can stand it. Have they bothered you?"

"Not much. I won't let them bother me."

"Am I going to be charged with anything?"

"No, thank God."

"Lucky," he said. "Lucky all around."

"Caitlin told me about your nightmare in the attic, how Rose really died. How do you feel about remembering?"

"Like a weight has been lifted off me."

"Caitlin knows it wasn't your fault. I think she wanted me to tell you that."

"I hope she can forgive me."

"There's nothing for her to forgive," Hallie said. "You're the only one who has to do any forgiving."

"Of a terrified ten-year-old boy."

"Exactly. Then maybe the nightmares will stop."

What Hendryx had done to him was terrible, monstrous, but some good had come out of it. He'd learned more things about himself than he might ever have otherwise. And he'd found out how to be Somebody. He'd found out how to be Cameron Gallagher.

"Yes," he said. "Then the nightmares will stop."

AFTER HALLIE HAD gone, Lieutenant Dudley came again.

"We've tracked down quite a bit of information about Nick Hendryx, Mr. Gallagher," he said. "I figured you should know before we release any of it to the media."

"About his past, you mean?"

"That's right. Came mainly from his wife's family in Denver. The Fosters. He was in contact with them periodically over the past six years. They kept trying to talk him into coming back there so they could get him psychiatric help, the last time a few days before Christmas. But he wouldn't listen, and he'd never tell them exactly where he was."

"Six years?"

"That's how long it's been since the hit-and-run."

"He talked as though it was no more than a year or so."

"He was more disturbed than you could've known. He kept sending the Fosters letters addressed to his wife, for them to hold until she got well enough to read them. Six years of letters, sometimes more than one a week."

"Did they open any?"

"The first few. After that, they let them pile up until about a year ago. It's too bad, but Mr. Foster couldn't take it anymore and burned them all. Burned the ones that came afterward, too."

"Why would he do that? Isn't there any chance his daughter will get well?"

"Annalisa Hendryx died three weeks after the accident, Mr. Gallagher. She's been dead nearly six years."

H e regained his senses at the edge of high ground, caught in a snarl of brush and other junk, humped in the crotch of the tree limb he'd grabbed onto. He crawled out of the flood, up a grassy slope. Buildings nearby, house and barn. He was hurt and half-drowned, but he could walk all right. Made it to the house, nobody there, residents evacuated long ago. Back door wasn't locked. He went in and found a bed and stripped and fell into it.

Stayed in the house all that day and night, sleeping mostly, eating canned stuff from the larder. Morning of the next day, he woke to patches of blue sky and the flood level dropping. Cleaned himself up and left the place wearing somebody's clothes that fit him well enough, carrying what was left of his own. Followed a muddy road back of the barn until he saw the ocean in the distance. Then he threw his old clothes into some weeds in a gully. Only things he kept were his Colorado driver's license and the sketch. Lamination had kept the flood from damaging either one.

After a mile or so he came to a highway that ran along the ocean. Mouth of the river was there, long bridge across it, and on his side of the bridge a skinny old guy was working hard to change a flat on a mud-spattered pickup. Nick offered to help. Old guy looked him over and wanted to know what'd happened to him. He said he'd been working in Guerneville, got caught and hurt in the flood, lost everything he owned. When he finished with the tire, old guy asked him if he'd ever worked on a sheep ranch. Nick said no, but he'd do any kind of work as long as it was honest.

So he went with the old guy up the coast to Mendocino County, a sheep ranch back in the hills, and started work the next day. Hard work and not much money, but all his meals came with the job, and the old guy's wife was a good cook. Pretty soon the rancher let him do some driving around the place, into the nearest town to pick up supplies. Felt good being behind the wheel again, even if it was almost all short rides and daylight mileage.

He stayed on the sheep ranch three months, saving up. Then the old man sold him his other pickup, a dented GMC Nick'd done some engine work on, for five hundred dollars, most of what he'd earned working there. First time he went out night riding, he didn't come back. Just kept on going up Highway 1 into Oregon.

In Eugene he got a job delivering pizzas and then wrote Annalisa a long letter and then started showing the sketch around. Showed it all over Eugene, Salem, Portland, then up in Washington. He landed a driving job with a short-haul gypsy outfit in Tacoma and stayed with it long enough to build up a stake. Then he bought a better set of wheels, 'eighty-nine Toyota that had 97,000 miles on it but ran fine with a little tune-up.

It was late summer when he rolled into Phoenix. Been there once before, so long ago he could barely remember it. Found a soup kitchen, ate and got cleaned up, and went out showing the sketch. More he showed it, more he had a good feeling about this town. Nothing to get excited about, not yet, but a feeling with hope in it.

Went to a mall that night, big covered mall, lots of people. He was showing the sketch in front of a bookstore when the man came out.

Nick had a good look at him, straight on, and it was like being kicked in the groin. He couldn't get his breath. Blood pounding in his ears like the ocean during a storm, a wild roaring that was hate and excitement and thankfulness and a dozen other feelings all wrapped up together.

Him. Man in the sketch, the face he'd lived with every day, that haunted his sleep, that he'd been hunting so long. Son of a bitch bastard who'd hurt Annalisa. No doubt of it, no mistake like he'd made with Gallagher and the five or six others before Gallagher.

It was him!